Beached in Retribution Bay

Aussie Heroes: Retribution Bay

Claire Boston

First published by Bantilly Publishing in 2022

Copyright © Claire Boston 2022
The moral right of the author has been asserted.

All rights reserved. This publication (or any part of it) may not be reproduced or transmitted, copied, stored, distributed or otherwise made available by any person or entity, in any form (electronic, digital, optical, mechanical) or by any means (photocopying, recording, scanning or otherwise) without prior written permission from the publisher.

This is a work of fiction. Names, characters, businesses, places, events and incidents are either the products of the author's imagination or used in a fictitious manner. Any resemblance to actual persons, living or dead, or actual events is purely coincidental.

Beached in Retribution Bay: Aussie Heroes: Retribution Bay

EPUB format: 978-1-922916-00-6
Print: 978-1-922916-01-3
Large Print: 978-1-922916-02-0

Cover design by Mayhem Cover Creations
Edited by Ann Harth
Proofread by Teena Raffa-Mulligan

Dedication

This novel is dedicated to my husband.
For moving halfway across the country with me and then understanding my need to reach the deadlines for this book, even when it meant we didn't see each other much. I appreciate you and love you. I promise no more deadlines until we've settled in to this new city of ours and had a chance to explore.

Chapter 1

Sam took one last look around his temporary office. After three months, it had grown familiar, but today represented an ending. Twelve years in the army led to a lot of memories, many of them good ones. He smiled as he picked up the photo of him and his team mates which they'd taken at the end of his last mission. He'd said goodbye to them in a big celebration just before they'd been deployed again. His gut wrenched as he remembered them flying off without him.

"Are you finished?" Major Hammond demanded.

The final lingering look also had the benefit of irritating the major. Sam rolled his eyes before he tucked the photo into his jacket pocket, turned and nodded. He followed the major from the building. The only thing Sam could think that warranted special attention from the man was that he was moving to Retribution Bay where the major's estranged daughter now lived. Perhaps the major hoped Sam would put a good word in for him. If so, he was dreaming. Not after the way the major had treated Sherlock.

Sam handed over his security pass and then gave one last salute.

The end of an era.

As he drove off the base he slowed as if not wanting to leave. Part of him felt the elation of freedom, the opportunity to do what he wanted, when he wanted, but the other part felt like he'd been switched off life-support and was gasping for air.

The army had been his life since he'd left high school. He'd lived and breathed the rules, the structure, and it had been good for the rebellious eighteen-year-old he'd been. But now he wanted more. Their last mission had been his closest brush with death so far, and it had shaken him. He had other dreams, other goals he'd yet to fulfil, which was why he'd chosen not to sign up for another stint.

Sam drove through Perth towards the rehabilitation hospital where Sherlock currently resided. Arthur 'Sherlock' Hammond had been his teammate since the early days and it had taken Sam a while to come to terms with his methodical, structured personality. Hard to blame him when his father was Major Hammond, the most humourless and structured man in the army. Slowly the team had got Sherlock to open up, occasionally joke with them and go out after work. But it happened infrequently, as Sherlock regularly picked up new missions or extra tasks around base. It was one such mission that had landed him in hospital, and medically discharged from the army.

Sherlock wasn't coping well.

Sam pulled into the parking lot and waved to the receptionist as he walked inside. "G'day, Kylie."

"Sam, good to see you." She smiled at him.

Sam walked along the grey corridor lined with noticeboards until he reached Sherlock's room. Sherlock's brown hair was a centimetre long, having grown out of the buzz cut since the accident. The dark bruises on his face were gone and most of the scratches from the bomb blast had healed. The plain white T-shirt he wore blended with the bed sheet pulled over his right leg, hiding the missing limb, and he stared out the window, not moving when Sam walked in.

"How's it going, Sherlock?" Sam asked.

No response.

Frustration swelled in Sam. It had been over a month and Sherlock had grown more and more despondent. He'd never been the chattiest person, but now he took silence to a whole other level. Sam wanted a response from him, any kind of reaction to make sure he was still in there somewhere. "It was my last day today," he said. "No longer in the army, just like you."

A tiny flinch. Sam ignored the nausea in his stomach at being so mean. The army was the only thing Sherlock had ever known, his one focus, his one passion. It was over now and until Sherlock addressed it, he couldn't move forward. If that meant ranting and raging at Sam, well, Sam was a big boy, he could take it. "Saw your dad. He accompanied me to my car. Probably wanted to make sure I wasn't stealing anything."

Sherlock's fingers curled.

"He asked how you were doing."

Sherlock's head whipped around to stare at him. "Really?" The word was full of incredulity, but underlying it was a glimmer of hope. Sam was an absolute bastard.

"No, not really. I wanted to find out if you were actually listening."

Sherlock's eyes went dull and he turned away. No. They'd done it this way every day since the accident. Fed up, Sam grabbed him by the front of his shirt. "Look at me!"

"Why, so I can see how much better you are than me?" The words were bitter, but at least they were words. "You want me to be grateful to you for visiting every day?" Sherlock demanded. "Taking pity on the cripple?"

"You're not a cripple," Sam argued. "I've seen you walking on the prosthetic. Give it a bit of time and you'll outrun me again."

"Bull shit."

"Don't be such a dumb ass," Sam said. "I'm not saying the situation doesn't suck, but how you deal with it is up to you."

"You've got no idea," Sherlock yelled, colour in his face for the first time in weeks. "I've lost my leg, my career and my father."

"Your father's not worth grieving over," Sam countered. "He's always been an asshole, using you. But you do have your sister and she wants to see you."

Sherlock scowled. "I missed her wedding. She's never gonna want to see me."

"You might be surprised at how forgiving she is. She married Brandon after all."

The tiniest hint of a smile crossed his face before Sherlock's gaze went to the door and his whole expression shut down.

Sam turned. Their shouting had attracted a couple of nurses. At his scowl they scurried away, but it was too late, Sherlock was staring out the window again. Sam huffed, then moved around the other side of the bed so Sherlock had to look at him. His friend was stubborn enough not to turn his head again. "The nurses tell me you're ready to be discharged," he said. "Why don't you come to Retribution Bay? There's plenty of room at my new place."

No answer.

"It's nicer weather, the ocean's gorgeous, and you can get away from all your shit for a while."

Still no response.

Sam sighed. "Think about it. There's more to life

than the army." He'd had enough for the day. He stood. "I'll see you tomorrow." He had to finish packing and maybe he'd pissed off Sherlock enough that he would do more than stare at the wall.

He could always hope.

***

Penelope Fraser wiped over her kitchen table and then thoroughly rinsed the cloth, squeezing it out and hanging it to dry. Her kitchen was spotless, as was the rest of her house. So what was she supposed to do now?

She checked her phone but there were no messages from work calling her in. Damn it.

She wandered through her sparsely furnished rental property. She'd let Gerard keep most of what they'd bought together. She owed him that much. She'd left him and her old inner city apartment far behind. This rental was single storey and built in the seventies, with the tiling to match, but at least that meant it was sturdy after surviving numerous cyclones. She sighed and flopped onto the couch. What was she doing here in Retribution Bay?

After her break-up, it seemed like a good idea to leave everything behind. Gerard had accused her of being a workaholic, obsessing over what needed to be done, and of not caring for him as much as he cared for her. The sad truth was, she now realised he was right on all points. After the accident, work had been her one outlet, her way of proving herself, her penance. She didn't notice she was withdrawing from her relationship.

And before that, her sea snake research had taken her away for weeks or months at a time. Her partner, Emelia had been so passionate about the creatures, Penelope had barely missed Gerard while she'd been away.

That should have told her something if she'd bothered to consider it, but it had been easier not to.

Coward.

She squeezed her eyes closed and pushed away the memory.

Six weeks in Retribution Bay wasn't long enough to give up and run home.

She picked up her e-reader and flicked through the books. "Read it, read it, read it." The only two left unread were ones she'd started and disliked. After reading only five books last year, she'd expected it would take her a whole lot longer to get through her to-be-read pile.

Perhaps she should sign up at the library. Maybe that would connect her with the community. There'd definitely been no welcome basket and friendly neighbours like she'd seen in so many movies.

To be fair, she had arrived in the middle of tourist season where the town's population exploded to over twenty thousand. And she'd had coffee with her colleague, Georgie Stokes, a few times, even going on one of the girls' nights Georgie had organised and meeting the local police officers and some other women around town. It had been nice even if she'd worried about saying the wrong thing. The accident had shattered her confidence in more ways than one.

Penelope sighed. Maybe she should call Georgie and ask if she wanted to go for coffee, but Georgie was in a new relationship and spent a lot of time with Matt. Penelope didn't want to seem needy. She had tried joining the adult horse-riding classes run by Faith on a Saturday, however she didn't like horses or the lack of control she felt being on one. She'd only been to one lesson before giving it up. Perhaps she should have given it more of a chance.

It wasn't as if there weren't things to do. She lived on the shores of the World Heritage-listed Ningaloo Reef, which meant she had plenty of opportunities to snorkel or scuba dive just offshore. Penelope rubbed the goose bumps on her arms. Maybe not scuba dive.

She had an amazing job at Parks and Wildlife Services, but even that wasn't enough to keep her busy, not like the twelve-hour days she'd put in with her research. Besides, she was supposed to be slowing down, getting back on track, rediscovering herself and her confidence.

Penelope stood and walked over to the window to look out at the quiet street. Across the road, kids laughed as they played chasey. They had no problems finding something to do.

With a sigh she picked up her knitting project from the coffee table, and stuck a finger through one of the many holes. What a failure. So much for making her best friend, Ceiveon, a blanket for her newborn baby. At the rate she was going, the child would be at high school before she was finished. She would have to unravel it and try again at some stage, but she had no desire today.

Her phone belted out *Girls just wanna have fun* and she grinned, lunging for it. "I was just thinking about you."

"How's the baby blanket going?" Ceiveon asked.

"Great!"

"Liar. Send me a photo."

Crap. "Ah, the camera on my phone's not working."

"That bad, huh? Why don't you watch some more YouTube videos?"

She grinned at the teasing, happy to hear her friend's voice. "I think I'll need a whole twelve-month course." Penelope sat on the couch, pushing away the pile of knitting, and settled in for a chat. "What are you up to?"

"About to head out to lunch with Alex's parents," she said. "I had two hours' sleep last night, Taris just vomited over her new dress and I feel like the worst mother in the world. Alex told me to call you while he changed Taris."

Penelope smiled. "Glad he's taking care of you."

"He's the best," Ceiveon agreed. "Now tell me I'm a good mother."

"You're the best mother. I bet you drove a hundred laps of Perth to get Taris to sleep."

"Two hundred," Ceiveon replied. "I had to fill up with fuel."

Penelope laughed. "Maybe I should have stayed there instead of moving to Retribution Bay. I could have helped you."

"It's nicer diving up there."

Penelope stiffened. She hadn't done any diving since the incident, Ceiveon knew that.

"How's the job going?" Ceiveon continued.

She exhaled and shook off the tension. "It's good. Different. Not quite so focused." The sea snakes had always been Emelia's passion more than Penelope's.

"Great. Any handsome guys?"

Penelope rolled her eyes. "I'm not looking for handsome men—or any men," she added, knowing how her friend would respond. "If Gerard couldn't handle the way I changed, no one is going to."

"Gerard was an idiot. I always told you he was too self-absorbed. He liked being with the scientist not the woman."

Ceiveon might have been right, not that Penelope wanted to admit it.

Voices in the background. "Taris is ready to go," Ceiveon said.

"You are an amazing mother," Penelope said. "Ignore any comments your in-laws make. You look so put-together, they won't even know you've barely slept."

"You haven't seen me."

"But I know you," Penelope argued. "You've got this. You have a beautiful baby, a husband who adores you, and a best friend who's got your back."

Ceiveon chuckled. "Thanks, Penelope. Gotta go. Love you."

"Love you too." She hung up and stared at the baby blanket. Ceiveon would be amazed if she received a beautiful baby's blanket in the mail. Maybe she could buy one… no, it had to come from her, no matter what it looked like.

With renewed enthusiasm she ran a hand over the soft ball of multi-coloured yarn and then picked up the knitting needles. It took a couple of attempts to hold the needles correctly and then insert her needle into the first stitch. It was tight with almost not enough space for the needle, but she did one stitch, and then another. Just as she was feeling like she was getting somewhere, she dropped a stitch. Crap. She flinched, which only unravelled the knitting further, causing a line through the ten-centimetre blanket.

Penelope closed her eyes, frustration battering her. Perhaps it wasn't as bad as she thought. When she opened them, it appeared even worse. There was no question about it. She would have to start again. But not now. Ceiveon would have to wait. She put the knitting back on the coffee table and scanned the room for something else to do.

This was ridiculous. She was a grown woman in her early thirties. Surely she could amuse herself. She could handle not working every second of the day. She'd moved here for a change of pace. Unfortunately, instead of the second gear she'd hoped for, she was idling in neutral.

Maybe she should go for a jog. It wasn't quite midday yet but it wasn't too hot. While she was out, she could go past the community noticeboard and check whether there were any knitting groups, or she could drop into the library and enquire there. She was clearly not getting this blanket done without a lot of help.

Penelope threaded her curly red ponytail through the back of her baseball cap, grabbed her sunglasses, and headed out. She'd jogged every street in town over the past six weeks. Today she headed for the marina. The development was fairly new, and it was the type of area she'd like to live in. The townhouses were a reasonable size and the water was right outside the back door. She could buy a boat and set out on an adventure any time she wanted to.

If she stayed.

And that was a big if. The quiet of the small town, the fewer drains on her time, the lack of family and friends were all things she had to learn to live with. She could admit to fewer headaches, the constant tension in her shoulders was now gone, and she'd had only one anxiety attack since she'd arrived, so that was something. Her new job as park ranger had her out and being active as well, rather than in an office doing paperwork, which is where she'd been relegated after the incident.

She'd promised Ceiveon she'd give it six months before she'd decide either way.

By the time she reached the marina, she wished she'd brought a bottle of water with her. The sun was hotter than she'd expected and sweat dripped down the back of her shirt. A big removal truck was parked out the front of one townhouse and two large men were hauling a bed frame inside. Someone new was in town. Would they be a permanent resident, or was this a holiday place for some rich city person?

It was then the blue hair of a woman coming out of the house caught her attention. Georgie. She hadn't mentioned she was moving.

Penelope raised her hand in a wave. "Georgie!"

Georgie spotted her and grinned. "Hey, Pen. What brings you here?"

Penelope smiled at the casual nickname. No one had ever shortened Penelope. Her mother wouldn't have stood for it when she was a child, and she'd got into the habit of automatically correcting people.

"I was going to ask you the same thing. You didn't mention you were moving."

Georgie laughed. "Not me. Matt and I can't afford a place like this yet. It's for a friend, Sam. I mentioned he'd bought Rob's tour boat, right?"

"Yeah." She recalled the conversation about Georgie's brother's best friend moving up and taking over Faith's father's whale shark tour business. She was still getting used to the idea that everybody knew or was related to everybody in this town.

"You look hot," Georgie said. "Want a drink?"

Penelope glanced behind Georgie. "I don't want to interrupt."

Georgie grinned. "Please, interrupt. I've been hauling boxes all morning."

Penelope laughed. "Well, as long as no one minds, I could do with a drink."

"Take this." Georgie handed her a box from the truck and then grabbed another one. "This way." The town house was modern and bright, with pale tiles and light walls. From upstairs, the sounds of grunts and curses could be heard. Georgie laughed as she placed her box on the pile against one side of the main living area. "They're dealing with the bed."

Penelope placed her box next to it. "Is Matt with you?"

"No, he had work on the farm. Brandon and Sam are up there and Amy's around here somewhere."

At that moment Brandon's wife, Amy, came in from one of the downstairs rooms. Penelope had met her at the girls' night. "I thought I heard voices. Nice to see you again, Pen."

Penelope smiled. "Likewise. I was walking past and saw Georgie."

"Don't stay long unless you want to get roped in," Amy said.

Penelope glanced around. "I'm happy to help if you need it." It would give her something to do. She'd enjoyed unpacking from her move and making sure everything had its place.

Georgie took a glass from the box on the bench and filled it with water, then handed it to Penelope. "We're almost done, and I'm sure you've got better things to do with your day than helping to unpack."

Penelope took a sip of water so she didn't respond in the negative. How sad was it that she had nothing better to do?

Footsteps thumped down the stairs and two large men entered the room. Penelope hadn't met Brandon, but she'd seen a photo at Georgie's place, so she recognised the dark-haired man immediately. The other man though… Her hand clenched around the glass as she stared at him. He was slightly taller than Brandon and wore a tank top and board shorts, topping the beach look with a pair of thongs. Who wore thongs when moving furniture? The thought was fleeting as her gaze moved up his muscled body to his face. His short strawberry blond hair was mussed as if he'd just run his hand through it, and his eyes were a blue that reminded her of the clear ocean on the reef.

The man glanced at Georgie. "You inviting people to my house already?" The smile followed a beat too long after the words.

Penelope took a step back, mortified. What was she doing here? She placed the glass on the bench, debating whether she should wash it, and decided it would be better just to get out of there. "My apologies. I didn't mean to intrude." She moved towards the door. "Georgie was kind enough to offer me a drink. It's hot today." With her cheeks burning, she rushed out of the town house, ignoring Georgie's call for her to come back. She never would have entered someone's house without an invitation from the owner in Perth. She should have known not everybody was as welcoming as Georgie.

"Pen, wait up." Georgie grabbed her arm as she reached the road.

Penelope slowed, but she didn't stop.

"Sam was joking," Georgie said.

She doubted it, but she forced a smile. "I know. I needed to go anyway, things to do." Yeah right. If only. Then she realised she'd offered to help unpack, so Georgie knew it was a lie. At least she didn't call Penelope on it.

"Do you want to do brunch tomorrow?" Georgie asked.

Penelope frowned. "With you and Matt?"

Georgie shook her head. "No, just the two of us. It's been a while since we caught up outside of work."

That would be a way to kill a couple of hours, and Penelope enjoyed spending time with the younger woman. She relaxed a little. "Yeah, that would be nice."

"How about nine-thirty at Ningaloo Cafe?"

Penelope nodded. "See you then." She waved as Georgie turned to go. Behind her, Sam stood in the doorway of his house. He lifted a hand in a wave.

The mortification flooded back, and Penelope nodded and scurried away.

Chapter 2

Sam woke early on his first work day in Retribution Bay. Had he made the right choice buying the boat? It had been a spur of the moment decision, much like most of the big decisions in his life. Though this one had been expensive. Rob could sell guns to pacifists and he'd made the life sound so appealing. Sam loved the ocean.

He'd make it work. That's what he did.

And he'd have Rob to help him until November.

Sam scanned the living area as he waited for his coffee to brew and his eyes rested on the stack of flat boxes, the only evidence he'd just moved in. He'd put a note on social media to see if anyone wanted them before he recycled them. He still felt kind of bad about Georgie's friend, Penelope. He'd been joking with Georgie and hadn't expected the petite red-head to take offence. He'd have to track her down and apologise. She'd been so proper, stiffening like a new recruit trying to impress a commanding officer. Georgie had mentioned afterwards that Penelope was a little straight-laced.

He grabbed his coffee and gear bag, and walked to

the marina. The sky was an endless blue, and the air was still. Perfect conditions for a day on the boat. Rob was opening the gate to the pens when Sam arrived. Sam shook his weathered hand.

"Good to see you," Rob said.

"Likewise."

Rob showed him onto the *Oceanid*. "We've got a full boat today," he said. "Weather looks to be good. Water should be pretty clear."

Sam took a moment to run his hands over the cool metal railing. This was his now. All twenty-two metres of her. A new life. "What do you do if the water isn't clear?"

Rob shrugged. "Depends. The sharks are usually visible no matter the water clarity and most people are just thrilled to see them." He opened the cabin and went over to the coffee machine in the corner, switching it on. "The whales are a different story. Sometimes we have to cancel and reschedule."

One of the female crew members, lean with short blonde hair, strode in and grabbed the keys hanging on the wall. "Hey, Sam."

Sam racked his brain for a name and Rob helped him out.

"Gretchen's got the bus today."

Sam nodded. "Nice to see you again, Gretchen."

"We'll chat when I get back." She jogged out.

Rob stood and gathered his notes. "We'd better get to it, so we're ready when the customers arrive."

"We leave from here?" Sam asked. Last time he was in Retribution Bay, they'd left from the boat ramp on the western side of the peninsula.

"It's humpback season now," Rob said. "They hang out in the gulf so that's where we go."

Right. Of course. He should have realised. "What do we need to do?"

Over the next hour, Rob took him through the engine room, explaining the maintenance schedule and the paperwork they needed to record for Parks and Wildlife. As more crew members arrived, they readied the snorkelling equipment and prepared morning tea. The business was a well-oiled machine with everyone knowing their role.

Then Gretchen arrived with the customers and Rob did a quick welcome, introduced the crew, and explained the timetable for the day before heading up to the top deck to get them on the way. Sam followed.

"It won't take you long to get used to how the boat handles," Rob said, giving him the wheel as below Gretchen cast off the lines.

The thrum of the engine under Sam's hands warmed him. He'd spent the past few months getting his captain's ticket and steering a number of different boats, but this was different. This one was his.

They were heading to a snorkelling spot first so they could assess how well the customers could swim before heading out into deeper water after the humpback whales.

"Keep to the markers on the way out," Rob said. "There are a few shallow spots over there." He pointed. "This girl will turn on a dime which will get you out of any tight spots."

Sam smiled. He doubted the boat was quite that responsive, but he appreciated Rob's passion. Below Gretchen handed out stinger suits and goggles, snorkel and flippers to half the customers, and one of the crew was chatting with the other half.

Time went quickly as Sam absorbed the information from Rob. When the last customer jumped into the water for their first snorkel, Rob pointed to one person who was splashing more than necessary. "She's not confident," Rob said. "Might need to give her a pool noodle before we get to the whales."

"Do any of them get upset about the offer?"

"Not usually. Not when we say it'll make life easier for them, one less stress when faced with a whale." He chuckled.

Good point. He hadn't swum with a humpback whale yet. "What's it like?"

"When they're as interested in you as you are in them, it's magical," Rob said. "They'll come and check you out. They choose whether they want to swim with you, not the other way around, and there's nothing we can do about it."

Sam nodded. That's how it should be. He didn't want to give any animal anxiety by being there. Especially not a mumma humpback protecting her calf. The radio burst to life and Rob gestured him over. "That'll be our eye in the sky." He grabbed the radio and said, "Morning, Jasmine. You found anything yet?"

A female voice replied, "Got a pod a couple of kilometres north of your location heading your way."

"Roger. Keep us informed."

Sam was yet to meet everyone. "Jasmine sub-contracts to us?"

Rob nodded. "She goes up at nine-thirty, looks around and tells us where we need to be."

"And she's in a glider?"

"Yeah. Between nine-thirty and ten-thirty she's ours and then she takes her own passengers up. But she's always on call if we need her."

The passengers returned and while the crew served morning tea, Sam and Rob motored towards the pod of whales.

It didn't take long to spot them in the distance and Sam heard the excited shouts of the passengers below as they watched the whales frolicking.

"We can't go in yet, right?" Sam asked. "Too

dangerous with them frolicking."

"Right. We'll pull as close as we're allowed and let the passengers watch, and hopefully the whales will settle so we can get in."

Rob had sent him the licence and Sam had studied it, wanting to be clear on the rules. "So we avoid mums and their calves. No going near breeching or tail flipping and the boat is only allowed a hundred metres on the side of the whales."

"Yeah, and three hundred metres in front or behind them."

It was half an hour before the whales settled and the first group of swimmers entered the water. In the distance, on the other side of the pod, another tour boat was similarly letting their swimmers in. Sam monitored his group of seven, making sure they were all right, and no one was in trouble. He moved the boat so he was ahead of where the whale would swim and the second group jumped in while he motored over to pick up the first group.

Even from the top deck he could hear the delighted chatter as the first group of swimmers climbed onto the marlin board. He'd have to try it soon. The whale shark he'd seen when he'd gone out a couple of months ago had been impressive enough, but the whales were far larger.

At the end of the hour Sam headed to pick up the last passengers. Rob swore and pointed. "Orca."

Sam gasped as a single large fin broke the water. The whales scattered and Sam focused on getting to his passengers as fast as possible. Gretchen was in the water with them and she had already started grouping them together so they could get onto the boat quickly. Sam's muscles were tight as he drove, options running through his head.

"It's unusual to see one by itself, so there might be

more around," Rob said. "It's after the calves."

The knowledge didn't make it any less stressful. The last thing Sam needed was to lose a customer on his first day of owning the damn business. Any one of them could be crushed by a panicked whale. He stopped, put the boat into neutral, counting each passenger as they got on board. Gretchen was the last one on and she gave him the thumbs up. He breathed out a sigh of relief. Rob clapped him on the shoulder and laughed. "Bit of excitement for the first day, hey?"

Sam shook his head. "More than I was after." He waited until one of the other crew members confirmed the count and then moved to go.

"Wait." Rob grabbed his arm. "Watch."

The orca was still after the calf. Down below the passengers cheered mum and baby on as the orca closed the distance. The rest of the pod was running interference, but it didn't look as if it was going to work. The baby was falling behind.

Sam gritted his teeth as he urged the calf faster. His hand gripped the throttle. Could he get the boat in between the orca and the calf? Would it endanger his passengers?

He moved forward slowly, judging which way the animals were going.

"Don't do it," Rob warned. "We can't get involved. It's nature."

How could he sit back and watch a baby be slaughtered in front of him? He increased the speed as the mother humpback and her calf turned, heading straight towards them, the orca right behind.

"Turn off the engine!" Rob yelled.

"I can get between them."

"And lose your licence," Rob said. "Turn it off."

Damn it. That was the last thing Sam needed. He slowed and switched off the engine as the whales swam closer.

Then, out of nowhere, the pod turned and charged towards the orca. Defeated, it swam away and the passengers cheered. Sam tapped his chest. "Much more excitement than I was expecting."

"Doesn't matter. You can't get involved. If PAWS were nearby, they'd have your licence. Especially the new woman. The rules are strict."

Shit. He hadn't thought about rules, he'd just reacted. Mumma and baby swam closer, resting underneath the boat. They were far closer than was allowed by the licence. "Should I move?"

Rob shook his head. "Not yet. You don't want to startle or injure them by turning on the engines. We're doing what we're supposed to."

A few people rushed to the top deck to get a better angle on their photos, and still Sam waited. The radio crackled and a voice came over, "That was some show, hey?"

Rob grinned and grabbed the radio. "Sure was, Jimmy. We're waiting for mumma and baby to leave."

"Roger."

Rob hung up the radio. "Jimmy is from the boat over there." He nodded toward the other tour boat which was closer now.

"You ever have problems with the other captains?"

Rob shook his head. "No, we're competitive, but will help each other. We all want our passengers to have the best experience, so if we spot something interesting and there are other boats nearby, we'll let them know."

It was another twenty minutes before mother and calf moved on and Sam could safely shift the boat. His crew prepared lunch and nobody complained it was later than usual. He anchored in a sheltered spot so they could enjoy the food.

"Is it usually this exciting?" he asked Rob.

"First time it's happened in all my time here," Rob said with a grin.

Just his luck, though he had to admit it had been impressive.

What a welcome to his new career.

***

Penelope had spent the day doing spot checks on the tour boats on the west coast of the peninsula. She'd only had to issue a caution when one boat had an extra passenger. The captain said the grandmother hadn't been swimming with the whales, but her hair had been wet. How was Penelope supposed to know if she'd just been snorkelling with the group earlier or if the captain had breached his licence terms? She'd learnt her lesson about not following the rules.

She shuddered as she drove back to the office.

Her boss, Declan, met Penelope in reception, his tall, lean frame tense and a nerve pulsing on his forehead. "We've got a problem." He showed her a social media post with a photo of the *Oceanid* practically on top of a whale and its calf.

She shook her head. "That's Rob's boat." He worked out the eastern side of the peninsula.

"Yeah, you need to sort this out. Fix it. It's already blowing up. I've asked Dot to meet you at the marina."

Penelope raised her eyebrows. "We're getting the police involved?" She'd never seen Declan this uptight before.

"It's a definite breach and we need to be seen to be doing something about it."

It seemed a little strange to call the police in before the investigation, but maybe that was the bane of social media. "Sure, I'll go now."

The boat should be heading back so she could meet them at the marina. Her muscles tightened. This was the worst part about her job. She hated confrontation because no one was ever happy to be told they were doing the wrong thing and they could hardly help it if the whales approached them. Rob was a nice enough guy, and she'd have to make a decision which would affect his livelihood. A wrong decision might have horrible consequences.

Nausea swirled in her stomach as she neared the marina. She took long, slow breaths like her therapist had taught her while walking to where Sergeant Dot Campbell waited. Dot's blue uniform was crinkled with a smear of red dirt on her shirt. Her pixie-cut black hair was further dishevelled as she ran her hand through it.

"Rough day?" Penelope asked.

Dot nodded. "Don't get me started. What do you know about the situation?"

Penelope liked the way she got right to the point. She commanded attention whether she was in an interview room, or a bar, a feat which was particularly impressive because she was only about a hundred and fifty centimetres tall.

"Declan showed me the photo. That's it."

"OK, we'll wait until the passengers disembark and then we'll question Rob."

They didn't have long to wait. The boat motored into the marina and efficiently tied up. The passengers were off and on the way to the bus to take them home within minutes. Dot gestured to one of the crew members and said, "Gretchen, can I have a word?"

Gretchen paled. "Is it Jordan? Has something happened?"

Dot shook her head. "No, as far as I know he's fine. It's a different matter."

The blonde exhaled and placed a hand against her chest. "Good. What do you need?"

So that was Gretchen. Georgie had mentioned

Gretchen hadn't come to the girls' night because she'd been unable to find a babysitter.

"I need to know about the tour today."

Gretchen glanced to the bus. "Can it wait until I've dropped off the passengers?"

Dot nodded. "We'll be here when you get back."

Penelope smiled at Gretchen and followed Dot along the dock to where the boat was tied up. A couple of crew members were already cleaning and two men stood on the deck.

One was Sam.

Damn it. She'd forgotten he'd bought Rob's business. Her face heated as she remembered the weekend. She really didn't want to deal with him. But maybe that's why the incident had occurred. The new guy wanted to flaunt the rules, thought he knew better than everyone else. Anger replaced the nerves. Some people had no idea why the rules were in place and didn't care enough to find out.

"Permission to come aboard," Dot called.

Rob waved them forward, but Sam's eyes narrowed. Perhaps he hadn't suspected his flagrant rule breaking would come back and bite him so quickly.

"Dot, Penelope," Rob greeted them. "How can we help you?"

So casual, so unconcerned. Her anger increased and she shook her head, taking a step forward. "You don't think this is enough to warrant some attention?" She showed him the photo, which had now attracted hundreds of comments.

Rob sighed. "I can explain."

"It was my fault," Sam said, moving next to Rob. "I was behind the wheel."

Penelope was slightly impressed that Sam took responsibility. "On your first day you decided to break one of the most important rules on your licence?" That took some nerve.

"It wasn't like that." He smiled, probably trying to be disarming and damn it, he had a charm about him. Penelope wouldn't be sucked in by it.

Dot raised a hand. "How about we head into the cabin for a chat? It will be more comfortable there."

"Sure," Sam replied, but something in his tone made Penelope feel like he was placating her.

Probably thought they were making a big deal over nothing. She would show him he needed to take the conditions of his licence seriously.

Rob said a few words to one of his crew, and then they followed Dot into the cabin. Sam shut the door. The space was small and Penelope bumped into Sam as she moved to sit next to Dot. She jerked away from his hard shoulder and slid into the chair, refusing to meet his eyes.

Penelope got a notebook out of her backpack and opened a fresh page, writing the date on the top of it. When she was done she looked up and realised everyone was waiting for her. Rob sat on the other side of Dot and Sam lounged against the wall. Dot nodded to Penelope. "Do you want to start?"

Both men were calm, but Rob fidgeted and Penelope couldn't read Sam's expression. She cleared her throat. "Would you like to explain this photo?"

Sam straightened, his voice holding no hint of emotion as he outlined what had happened. "At ten thirty-eight the first batch of swimmers went in with the whale we had identified," he said. "At eleven thirty-five as we were about to pick up the last group, we noticed an orca approaching the pod of whales."

Penelope blinked. An orca. Interesting. There'd been no orca in the photo.

"I may have gone over the eight knot speed limit in order to get to our passengers," Sam continued. "When the passengers were safely on board, I noticed the orca had isolated a mother and its calf and was chasing them towards us.

"I instinctively moved forward to help them, but Rob told me it wasn't allowed, so I stopped just as the mother and calf were on us. Not wanting to give them any further stress, I switched off the engine as per the instructions and waited. The pod of whales chased off the orca, and the mother and baby stopped right next to the boat to rest. I couldn't start the engines without potentially causing the animals further stress and injury. We waited until they swam away before we started the engine again and left the area."

Penelope looked up from her notes. "How long was that?"

"Eighteen minutes," Sam answered.

"So precise?" Penelope asked.

"I spent twelve years in the army," he said. "If you're not precise, you're dead."

Well then. What now? Most of what he'd done was correct, except for moving to intercept the whales. She could understand the instinct, but there was a lot of interest on social media and Declan had told her to fix it. How was she supposed to do that? She glanced back through her notes. "Why didn't you move away as soon as your passengers were on board?"

Rob spoke. "Have you ever seen an orca hunt? It's incredible. We were both mesmerised by it."

"So mesmerised you didn't think about the safety of your passengers or the whales?"

"The whole boat was concerned about the safety of the whales," Rob said. "You should have heard the cheers when the orca was chased off."

She hated this, but she had to follow the guidelines. "You had the opportunity to remove yourself from the area and you did not take it." She tapped her pen on the notepad. "In fact you moved towards them instead."

"It was instinct," Sam argued.

She clenched her teeth. "Rob warned you." She glanced at ·the older man. "Did Sam listen to you immediately?"

A brief hesitation before Rob replied, "Yeah. He stopped the boat."

Liar. "I will need to investigate this further and until I can, I must suspend your licence."

Sam stared at her stony faced, but his tone was calm. "Don't you think that's a little excessive?"

"I only have your side of the story. I need to speak with the person who posted the photo and the captain of the other boat." Penelope gathered her notebook and placed it in her bag.

"It was Jimmy's boat," Rob said. "Call him now."

"I'll call him when I return to the office," she said. "In the meantime, your licence is suspended until further notice."

"Wait a minute," Rob clenched his fist. "We're fully booked for the rest of the season. We need an answer now so we can call our customers."

She hesitated and then remembered what happened the last time she'd not followed the rules. Her gut clenched and she stiffened. "Fine. If you want an answer from the information you've given me, then I am suspending your licence for a minimum of a week for approaching the whales when you should not have. I suggest you start making phone calls."

Not wanting to get involved in further argument, she fled the boat.

Chapter 3

Sam stared after Penelope as she scurried from the room and then glanced at Rob. "She's actually serious, isn't she?"

"It looks like it."

No. This couldn't be happening. He couldn't be suspended on his first day on the job. "I'll talk to her," he said. "We can wait a couple of days while she investigates." Better than a whole week.

There'd been a moment's hesitation when Rob had challenged her decision. He could work with that. He was tired of the woman running away from him. Sam jogged down the dock as she was climbing into a sensible sized white hatchback. "Penelope, wait."

She hesitated, and in three long strides, he'd reached her side. She straightened, keeping her door open, but tilted her chin to look up at him. He'd admire her composure if he wasn't so annoyed.

He kept his distance, not crowding her, and gave her a warm smile. "Rob might have jumped the gun," he said. "We're both concerned about disappointing our customers. We're happy for you to take the time to investigate properly."

She stared at him. "You didn't care about potentially endangering them or the whales when you chose to move forward towards the mother and calf."

"Instinct," he reiterated. "I'm trained to run towards the danger, to help those in trouble." He smiled again and explained. "Ex-army."

"So now my decision isn't what you want, you're asking me to change my mind after forcing me to make a decision on the spot?"

When she put it that way, it did seem unfair. "Rob was upset."

She said nothing.

Crap. Maybe he'd made a bad impression on the weekend. He had to get her to give him the benefit of the doubt. "I apologise about the other day."

She blinked twice, the only sign she was surprised.

"I didn't mean to offend you when you stopped by my house. I'd been joking with Georgie that she was already arranging my life up here, and so my comment was a response to that. I meant nothing by it. You were welcome to stay."

Instead of relaxing her, the mention of the weekend made her stiffen further. "It's fine. I had things to do."

It was a lie. Not only had he heard her offer to help, but she also looked away while she said it. "Well, I'm sorry anyway. Any friend of Georgie's is welcome at my place."

"We're colleagues."

She was a stickler for accuracy. She reminded him a little of Sherlock in that way. At least the way he was before the accident. He smiled again. "OK. I'm glad we've cleared the air."

Penelope nodded and moved to climb back into her car.

"Wait a second. Do you think we could review the suspension?"

"Did you think what happened on the weekend impacted my decision?" she asked, her tone mild, but her eyes flashing.

Shit, he'd irritated her further. She really was prickly. "Not at all, but it's been bugging me since Saturday. I was going to ask Georgie for your number so I could apologise."

She studied him and he continued to smile. "Perhaps instead of an immediate suspension, we could continue operating while you investigate further. It was a rare event. Rob said he'd never seen anything like it in his years up here."

"Rob wanted an immediate decision, so I gave him one. I don't flip flop on my decisions."

Speaking rationally to Sherlock usually worked. "I respect that. We didn't get the chance to suggest alternatives in there. There's scope for compromise."

Penelope tapped her finger on the top of her door frame. "You broke the licence agreements. You're being given the correct punishment. Nowhere in the licence does it mention compromise."

Yep, she was definitely a by-the-book kind of woman. "It also doesn't spell out the exact suspension length for a breach," he pointed out. "Is there something else I can do on top of this to help? Is there some volunteer work at PAWS to reduce the suspension to a few days?"

"It doesn't work like that."

Damn it, she was so straightlaced. "You can't even take pity on the newbie?" he joked, trying to make her crack a smile.

"No." She got in her car, slammed the door and drove away.

Shit.

His charm usually worked. Hopefully he hadn't irritated her enough to increase the suspension.

Gretchen parked in the space Penelope had vacated and got out. "What's going on?"

"Penelope just suspended us for a week for breach of licence."

Gretchen gaped at him. "You're kidding."

"Wish I was. What are you doing here?"

"Dot asked me to come back."

They walked back to the boat. Rob was still chatting with Dot. "How'd you go?"

"No luck."

"I've never known someone so inflexible," Rob said. "She's new, you know."

Sam nodded.

"You wanted to see me, Dot?" Gretchen said.

The sergeant nodded. "Yeah, I thought the interview with these two would go longer than it did, and Penelope would want more statements. Sorry."

"It's fine. I'll call her and offer my version of events. I'm sure she'll see reason."

"Don't bet on it." Sam glanced at Dot. "You don't need anything else from me?"

"No." She smiled and stood. "Welcome to Retribution Bay."

He laughed. He had plenty of time for the short, dark-haired woman who ran a tight ship here. Both times he'd visited Brandon, he'd had to deal with the police and found her capable and likeable. Unlike a certain red-haired park ranger. As they walked out of the cabin, he said, "I'm sorry about your brother."

The smile vanished and she nodded once. "Thanks. I've got to get back to work." She strode away.

Damn it. He shouldn't have brought it up. It was only a couple of weeks since Dot's brother had been killed.

"Let's go," Rob said. "We've got a lot of phone calls to make."

That's right. They had to cancel all their passengers. "Can we get them on another boat?"

"Maybe. I'll call the other captains. Let's go to the shop."

The crew had finished washing all the equipment and cleaning the decks. Sam thanked them as Rob locked the cabin and then they all walked back to their vehicles. This was not how he'd envisioned his first day.

***

An hour later, they had slotted their passengers for tomorrow's tour on different boats. Gretchen had phoned Penelope and given her version of events, but it hadn't made any difference. She'd left them making phone calls as she had to pick up her son from his friend's place.

"That's enough for today," Sam said, stretching. "I'll go chat to the manager of PAWS tomorrow and plead our case. Do you think he'll only suspend us for a couple of days?"

"Maybe. I'm not sure if he can overrule her, but I'll go with you." Rob packed his things and handed Sam a set of keys. "You should have these now. The shop, the bus, the marina, and all the boat keys are on it."

"Thanks."

"Might be a good chance to teach you about the shop tomorrow," Rob suggested. "Paperwork's not fun, but necessary."

"Good idea." Sam waved. "I'll meet you here in the morning."

"Do you want a lift?"

"No, I'm good. I need to walk."

He headed back towards the marina and his house. Perhaps he should have known better than to move to Retribution Bay. Sure, it was a lovely destination, but every time he'd been here there'd been trouble. He pulled out his phone and called Sherlock, wanting to chat to him about Penelope. If anyone could give him advice on how to deal with her, it was him. Unsurprisingly, it went straight to voice mail.

Sam hung up and tried the hospital phone in Sherlock's room, and this time it rang a dozen times before he was disconnected. It wasn't as if Sherlock had spoken to him when he'd been there in person, but damn it, he needed to speak with him. He rang the reception. "Hi, Kylie, it's Sam here. I need to talk to Arthur. Is he in his room?"

"I'll get one of the nurses to check."

He walked past the school and the town oval as he waited. Some teenagers were doing football drills, and they were pretty good. Finally, Kylie came back on the line. "He's in there, but he doesn't feel like talking. Sorry, Sam."

"Can you tell him it's important?"

"Sorry, the nurse has already left. She's got other patients."

"All right, thanks." He hung up and then sent a text message.

Need your advice on a situation. Pick up, damn it.

He waited a minute for the message to go through. Sherlock had never been one to ignore an issue. This time when he rang, Sherlock answered. "What is it?"

Sam huffed out a breath. "Thanks, mate. I've just had my tour licence suspended."

A choked back laugh. "On your first day?"

Sam grinned, thrilled to hear the humour in his friend's voice, even if it was at his own expense. "Yeah." He explained the situation and then said, "The park ranger is by-the-book. I need to understand how she thinks so I can figure out what might convince her to let it slide with a warning."

"Why call me?"

Sam laughed. "Sherlock, you're the most law-abiding person I know. What would make you relax?"

He was silent a long moment, so long Sam wondered if he'd offended his friend. But he also knew Sherlock liked to think about his answers, so he waited.

"Rules are structure," Sherlock said. "You start bending them, shifting and twisting them, and eventually they're going to break. You have no way of knowing whether it will be a hard jerk or a subtle shift that will break them."

Sam stopped walking. What a revelation into the way Sherlock's mind worked. He didn't trust himself enough to know how far he could push it and that was why he stuck by the rules and was so exacting.

Looking back on their years together, he realised Sherlock only broke the rules when somebody else had decided or had ordered him to. Then he couldn't be held accountable. Did Penelope have a similar outlook? Had there been something in her life which made her unwilling to bend?

"Thanks, mate. I get it now. I appreciate your help." He began to walk again. "How's things? Have they given you a discharge date?" Silence. Sam winced and continued, "You should come up here. The weather is beautiful, and I've got plenty of time on my hands for the next few days."

"Friday," Sherlock answered. "They let me out on Friday."

Sam made the calculations. "I can fly down and help you out."

"I'm not an infant." The line went dead.

Sam swore. He couldn't get a thing right when it came to his friend. He called Sherlock's doctor and left her a message to call him back. Sherlock had signed paperwork to say the doctor could discuss his case with Sam and Sam wanted to make sure Sherlock had everything he needed for when he went home. Not that he had much of a home. Sherlock had spent most of his time at the barracks, but he had an apartment and Sam had cleaned and tidied it before he left.

If only he could get Sherlock to come up here for a few weeks. He hated the idea of his friend secluding himself away. The rest of their team wasn't due back until next year and Sherlock didn't have any other friends.

Maybe it was time he told Brandon and Amy about what had happened.

They could help convince Sherlock to come up here.

And it would be one less worry.

***

Penelope drove away from the police station, her mind seething. How dare Sam suggest she'd chosen the punishment based on what happened in her personal life? What a nerve. She could keep business and her personal life separate. She'd wanted to challenge him further and come back with some witty remark that would put him in his place, but she hadn't been able to think of anything.

As she pulled into the office car park, Gretchen called.

"Hi, Penelope. I heard what happened and wanted to ask if you had any more questions."

She didn't, but she couldn't knock back another statement. She got her notepad out of her bag as she said, "Tell me what happened."

Gretchen outlined the same story Sam and Rob had told her.

"Thanks. Tell Sam I'll be in touch after I've spoken with the others."

She walked into the office and went straight to see Declan. He glanced up from his desk, shifting some paperwork into a filing cabinet next to him. "How did it go?"

"I suspended his licence for a week." She clenched her hand, waiting for his response.

He nodded as if satisfied. "That should appease the mob on social media. What happened?"

She explained the situation, making it clear Sam had moved towards the whales when he shouldn't have.

Declan sighed. "Sounds like he's a bit of a cowboy. Good to put a stop to it right at the start."

Penelope relaxed. "Thank you." Her guilt lessened. She hadn't been too harsh. "I'm going to track down the person who posted the photo and speak with the other tour boat operator so I can write my report."

"Good idea. Maybe ask some passengers on Rob's boat too." Declan smiled at her. "You're doing a good job."

"Thank you, sir." She went into her office, pulled up the file of licensees on her computer and found Jimmy's number.

"Hey, Penelope," Jimmy answered. "What can I do for you?"

"I need to discuss the incident that happened on Rob's boat today. I understand one of your passengers took the photo that's on social media."

"What photo? I haven't been online today."

"There's a photo of Rob's boat right on top of a whale and its calf making the rounds on social media," she explained. "It's drawing quite a lot of attention."

Jimmy sighed. "Yeah, it was something to see. We all thought the calf was gonna be caught."

"Can you tell me what happened?"

"Sure. We were on the other side of the pod to Rob," he said. "I reckon we both noticed the orca at about the same time. Our priority was getting the customers out of the water."

Penelope shuddered. If the people had been in the way, it could have been an even more dramatic story.

"After everyone was safely on board, we watched from a distance, but the whales turned towards Rob's boat. Could have gone either way."

"Did Rob's boat approach the whales?"

A pause. "Hard to know for sure from a distance."

How diplomatic.

"Are you able to give me the contact details for the person who posted the picture?"

"I'm not meant to share the info, but I'll call them now to ask if it's all right. I'll call you back in a minute." Jimmy hung up.

Penelope paced her office and flicked through the comments on the post. Some people thought it was amazing and others were outraged the boat was so close to a small baby. Comments like 'this shouldn't be allowed', and 'taking advantage of nature' were common. People wanted to know what was being done about it and Declan had posted a response that they were investigating the matter.

When Jimmy called her back, she wrote down the passenger's number and made the call.

After introducing herself, she asked, "Can you tell me what happened today?"

"It was terrible," the woman announced. "That poor baby whale being chased by the orca and then when it escaped it was preyed upon by the tour boat."

Penelope frowned. "What do you mean by preyed upon?"

"They stayed right on top of it, taking photos, not allowing it to rest peacefully."

"Did the boat move towards it?"

"Well, they didn't move away like they should."

Penelope debated correcting the woman and telling her the boat had abided by the rules, but she didn't want to get into an argument. "Is there anything else you want to add?"

"The government should cancel these tours. It's not right to take advantage of these animals."

Penelope frowned. "Why participate in the tour if you don't agree with it?"

The woman huffed. "Because the opportunity was there. If the government didn't give people the opportunity, they wouldn't take it." The woman launched into a rant about all the things the government had to do to protect nature. Penelope tried to interrupt her, but it was no use. Instead, she took notes and it was half an hour before the woman ran out of steam. "Thank you for your comments," Penelope said quickly. "I'll raise them at our next meeting. I must be going. Thank you for your time." She hung up and placed her head in her hands.

What a day. It was past six o'clock and she'd had enough. She walked to Declan's office, but it was locked. She still believed a suspension was in order. Sam had admitted he moved towards the whales instead of away and as an ex-army soldier, he should have anticipated the whale would take evasive manoeuvres.

But it didn't stop her feeling guilty about it.

Chapter 4

Sam spent the next day in the office at the shop. He met the administration staff who worked for him and went through the paperwork aspects of the business. Aside from booking tours, the shop front sold merchandise, swimming paraphernalia and souvenirs. Rob showed him through the books, explained the booking and ordering processes, and how they coordinated the paperwork, which needed to go to PAWS each day.

The website needed a revamp, and the paperwork was a little unorganised, but it wouldn't take long to sort it out. He imagined Penelope would cringe if she saw the messy filing system and the myriad files scattered all over the computer's desktop.

Around midday, Sam and Rob drove to the PAWS office to speak to Declan. Penelope wasn't there and Sam couldn't decide if that was a good thing. Maybe Georgie could give him some tips as to how best to deal with her.

"Come through," Declan invited, and they entered a meeting room with a large table surrounded by chairs. Declan took the seat at the head of the table.

Immediately putting himself in the position of power. Interesting. Sam hadn't dealt with the man before, but he'd called Georgie the night before and asked her about him. She'd said he was fair and reasonable.

Rob got straight to the point. "Can you overrule Penelope?"

Declan shook his head. "She's quite within her rights to suspend your licence." A slightly officious tone in his voice.

"Absolutely," Sam agreed. "But she suggested she could take other statements before deciding on the length of the suspension."

Declan pursed his lips and nodded. "True, but I've already posted the information on social media. If you'd come to me last night…"

"Come on, Declan," Rob cajoled. "You know me. I'd never do anything to harm an animal."

Declan glanced at Sam before replying. "I'm sorry. Perhaps this will give you time to teach Sam all the land-based aspects of the business." He smiled at Sam. "Give you a chance to get settled in Retribution Bay."

That wasn't helpful. "There's really nothing you can do?"

"Not without undermining my staff. I must admit, Penelope is one of the most fastidious people I've had working for me for a while."

Great. As much as Sam wanted to argue further, it had been Rob's impatience which had caused her to make a decision on the spot. He stood and shook Declan's hand. "Thanks for your time."

Sam and Rob returned to the shop, where they spent the afternoon calling the other passengers booked during the week and rescheduling them. By the time they were done, it was almost four o'clock and Stacey was packing up the shop. "It's time for us all to go home," he said to Rob.

"Are you sure? Got any more questions?"

"Not for the moment."

Rob grabbed his keys. "All right. Don't be scared to change things while I'm still here. Paperwork and technology are not my strong suit. Milly used to deal with that for me in my other businesses."

"I'm not changing anything until I get a better understanding of things," Sam told him. "Say hi to Milly for me." He'd met Rob's wife briefly the last time he was here. Faith's mother was currently planning their first trip around Australia for when the season ended and Rob finally retired.

Sam turned back to the computer. The only thing that bothered him was the website, but he had no idea how hard it was to edit, so he called Brandon's youngest brother, Ed.

"Sam, have you moved yet?"

"On the weekend. Got your brother hauling furniture for me."

Ed laughed. "Good to hear. What can I do for you?"

"I need a new website, but I've got no clue."

"What's the name of the business again?" Ed asked.

Sam told him and heard keys clattering in the background. "Branding is a bit off and it's messy but wouldn't be hard to fix."

"Know of anyone good?"

"Amy's great, but if you want a graphic designer, I'll send you links to a couple I'd recommend."

"Thanks, mate."

"No problem. Say hi to everyone for me. I've got to get back to work." Ed hung up and Sam shut down the computer. Stacey came to the door. "Do you want me to lock up?"

He nodded. "I'm leaving too. Did we have a good sales day?"

"Yeah." Stacey swung her bag over her shoulder. "A few bookings for next week and a bunch of people in to buy new snorkelling gear."

"Great." He waved goodbye as Stacey got into her car and then he glanced towards the ocean. Six more days until he'd be allowed to take people out on it.

The start of his new life had been a complete failure.

Sam huffed out a breath. If he went home, he'd only dwell on it. He wanted company, wanted to moan about his suspension and figure some way around it. Only one person came to mind. He called Retribution Ridge and when Amy answered, he said, "Got room for one more for dinner?"

"Sure. The town getting you down already?" she asked.

"Need some friendly faces."

"That doesn't sound good. Dinner's at six-thirty, but come out whenever you're ready and bring some milk and bread."

"See you soon." Sam grinned as he hung up the phone. Brandon had found himself a gem in Amy. She was so welcoming and friendly, sensible too, not like a certain redhead. Sam didn't bother going back to his house. He stopped by the supermarket to pick up the groceries Amy wanted and continued south out of town towards the sheep station.

An hour later he pulled into the driveway, passing a sign of an angry ram on the gate post. Retribution Ridge. Red dirt, scrubby trees and grasses surrounded him. Nothing like the lush farms he had flown over on his way here. He didn't understand why Brandon loved this place, but perhaps if he'd grown up here, he'd view things a little differently.

The campground was full. It held rooftop campers, twenty-five foot caravans and everything in between. Flotsam and Jetsam, Lara's pet sheep, wandered through the grounds, attracting the delighted attention of children. Sam parked outside the kitchen door of the quirky homestead and got out, breathing deeply and stretching. Maggie, the kangaroo the Stokes had nursed from a joey, lay in the shade thrown by the machinery shed. Across the way, the horse yard contained five horses nibbling on hay.

The tension in his shoulders released and he embraced the peace.

He trotted up the steps and rapped on the fly screen frame as he toed off his shoes.

"Sam! You're here!" Lara's delighted shriek made Sam smile and before he could react, the door flung open and the ten-year-old threw herself in his arms. "Welcome home."

Sam's heart clenched. "Hi, La La. What have you been up to?"

"Just school."

"Competed in any more gymkhanas?"

"There's one coming up next month." She tugged him into the kitchen. "Faith. Amy. Sam's here," she bellowed.

Sam chuckled, rubbing his ear. "Could you yell a bit louder? I don't think your dad heard you out on the station."

Lara laughed and went over to the fridge. "Drink?" She held up a bottle of water.

Always the little hostess. "That would be great, thanks."

Darcy's fiancée, Faith, walked in. "Hi, Sam. You settled in already?"

"Yeah, didn't take long to unpack."

"Good timing," she said. "We're heading out on a night ride. You want to come with us?"

Sam frowned. "I'm too heavy. The horses always groan when I mount them."

Lara laughed. "Dad and Uncle Brandon ride them. You're about their size."

"I'll give it a miss this time. I wanted to catch up with Brandon."

Amy wandered in, her blonde curls damp and hanging down around her face. "Hey, Sam, sorry I didn't hear you arrive. The others shouldn't be long."

Lara handed him a glass of water and he sipped it.

"Need a hand with anything?"

"No, everything is ready. We're just waiting for the boys and Georgie to arrive."

"Georgie is coming out?" Georgie had been a blessing, looking at houses for him while he'd been in Perth. Maybe she could tell him how he should approach Penelope.

"Yeah, she and Matt have been taking it in turns where they sleep now that Matt has a double bed in his room."

A scuffle and thud announced the men returning home from their day out on the station. Darcy came in first, his frame taller and leaner than Brandon's, but he had the same dark hair and eyes. He grinned at Sam as he hung his Akubra on the hook by the door. "G'day, Sam, how's it going?" The family dog, Bennett, trotted over wagging his tail and Sam patted him.

"Could be better."

Brandon came in behind Darcy and, in the same routine, placed his hat on the hook and said, "Are you sick of the town already?"

Sam laughed. "No, but a certain red-headed park ranger has thrown a spanner in the works."

"Penelope?" Faith asked. "What has she done?"

"Suspended my licence for a week."

Everyone stared at him as Matt came through the door and after he hung his hat on the hook, he smiled at Sam and then frowned. "What did I miss?"

"Sam's been suspended already," Brandon said.

Matt's eyes widened. "Seriously? That's gotta be a record."

Sam rolled eyes. "Thanks for the support."

Darcy got glasses out of the cupboard and two bottles of water from the fridge. "So what happened?"

Sam told them the story. "What's your take on Penelope?" he asked Faith.

"She seems kind of shy to me. She didn't say a lot at the girls' night."

Amy shook her head. "Not shy, worried. Worried about saying the wrong thing or doing the wrong thing. I'd say she lacks confidence."

Interesting. He hadn't considered that, but if he reviewed his interactions with her, it fit.

"So, what are you doing for the rest of the week?" Matt asked.

"I'll be learning about the business, but do you guys need any help here?" He glanced at Brandon. Money was too tight and they couldn't afford to hire any help.

"Maybe." Brandon looked at his wife. "I'll tell you about the thing we found later."

Lara clapped her hands together. "Are you going to tell him about the—"

Before Lara could finish her sentence, the fly screen door slammed open and Georgie entered the room making a beeline for Matt. "Hey, everyone."

Matt turned to her and they wrapped their arms around each other and kissed.

Lara made a face. "They do that all the time now."

Sam laughed. Matt had given him the evils during most of his first trip up here because he'd flirted with Georgie. Harmless to Sam, but Matt hadn't seen it that way. Sam was pleased to see the two of them together.

"Dinner's ready," Amy said as the oven timer rang. Lara rushed around setting the table while Amy placed a bowl of salad on it and then took a huge tray of lasagne out of the oven. Sam inhaled. It smelled divine. He wasn't much of a cook, but he did like eating.

Dinner was a noisy affair as Darcy asked Lara about her day and everyone swapped news and gossip. Sam settled in, content to listen. They reminded him of his own family back in the days before his parents had divorced. Although now he thought about it, loud conversations at the dinner table had usually been arguments, not friendly banter. His three sisters had outdone him in voice and noise.

After dinner, he helped with the dishes while the girls got ready for their ride.

"Can't I come?" Lara pleaded, hands together in prayer.

Darcy smiled. "It's a school night, pumpkin. We might not be back until late."

"That's OK. I won't be tired, I promise."

"Not this time, but I'll read you a chapter before we go."

Lara pouted. "You go. I'll get Sam to read to me."

Darcy glanced at Sam. "He might want to spend time with Brandon."

Lara turned to him with her eyes wide. Sam grinned as a warmth spread through him. "I'd rather read to Lara. What are we reading?"

She grinned. "It's this cool fantasy series, with epic heroines who save the world."

"Sounds like just my thing."

Brandon smirked while Darcy kissed Lara goodnight. "I'll be in the lounge when you're done."

Sam followed Lara into her bedroom, taking the book from the bedside table while she climbed into bed. The cover showed a girl wielding a bow and arrow.

Lara patted a spot on her bed. "Sit down."

He did as asked and opened the book at the

bookmarked page.

"Sam, do you have any brothers or sisters?" Lara asked.

"Three sisters."

"Older or younger?"

"Younger."

She pursed her lips. "Did you ever feel left out when they did girl stuff without you?"

Sam almost laughed, but Lara bit her lip, watching him. He sighed. "I didn't really want to do what they wanted to."

"Faith, Amy and Georgie are always doing things together, but they say I'm too young."

Hell. Sam wasn't equipped for this kind of conversation. Why would she even ask him? "Perhaps you have to be an adult for some things they do."

"You don't need to be an adult to go for a full moon ride."

"You've got school tomorrow."

"And they all have to work."

He wasn't winning this conversation. "I tell you what. How about we go for a ride on the next full moon on a weekend?"

Her face lit up. "Really? You'd go riding with me?"

"Absolutely." He didn't have the heart to tell her he was a hopeless rider.

"When's the next full moon?"

He got out his phone and found a website which had the details. "December has a full moon on Saturday."

Her face fell. "That's months away."

"Well, maybe there's one during the school holidays," he said, tucking his phone away. "Now tell me about this book. What's happened so far?"

Lara clapped her hands. "It's about a healer who's trying to find the cure for a contagious disease, and there are dragons in it!" With Lara distracted by the book, he read her a couple of chapters. It was an engrossing read, and he almost kept going at the end of the next chapter, but Brandon came to the door. "You two finished yet?"

"Uncle Brandon!" Lara protested.

Sam inserted the bookmark. "Good timing."

Lara held up her arms and Sam hugged her. The girl killed him with kindness. She reminded him a little of his youngest sister, the one who'd always been excited to see him when he had a break from the army. "Night, La La."

"Don't forget about our ride."

"I won't. You tell your dad about it, and we'll organise something."

Brandon hugged his niece and then turned out the light. "See you in the morning, La La."

Sam followed his friend into the lounge.

"What did you promise her?" Brandon asked.

"A night ride by the full moon in December." He grimaced. "Darcy won't mind, will he?"

"No, he'll think you're sweet for offering, as long as you don't back out of it and disappoint her."

"Wouldn't dream of it." He sat on the brown sofa, noting two old journals on the coffee table. "What were you going to tell me about?"

Brandon nodded at the journals. "Guess what we found in the cellar?"

Sam's eyes widened and he reached for one of the books. "You seriously found something?" He'd been there when they'd uncovered the cellar which had been hidden for decades, but there hadn't been anything more than junk down there. Carefully he opened the cover and read. "This journal belongs to Lilian Stokes." He glanced at Brandon for clarification.

"The very first Stokes at Retribution Ridge. It tells

the story of her journey here from England and reveals the truth of our heritage."

Sam waited for him to explain.

"The real Reginald Stokes, her husband, died in the mutiny when they were shipwrecked on Retribution Island. Lilian was in love with an Irish convict named John and he took over Reginald's identity."

"I always knew you were a scoundrel," Sam joked.

"There's more. Reginald, the real one, had come into possession of a Dutch captain's journal. The Dutch captain also wrecked on the island a century earlier, but he had on board treasure from the Dutch East Indies Company."

Sam shifted as his interest piqued. "Did he find it?"

"Some. It's what sparked the mutiny, but Lilian and John found most of it later when they returned to set up the station. They buried it somewhere on the Ridge."

"You haven't found it?"

Brandon shook his head. "Lilian's clues are cryptic. We've been searching for over a month with no success." Brandon ran a hand through his hair. "We could desperately do with the funds."

"How bad is it?"

"We can't afford shearers for the season. We're almost out of feed and if it wasn't for the camp grounds we wouldn't be able to eat."

Shit. "What can I do to help?"

"Take a copy of both journals and see if you can decipher her clues. A fresh pair of eyes, someone who doesn't know the Ridge like we do, will be good."

"Sure. I'll go through them this week."

Brandon clapped him on the back. "Thanks, mate. Is there anything I can do to help you?"

"If you can sweet talk Penelope that would be great."

He chuckled. "I'll talk to Georgie, ask if she can think of something."

Sam groaned. "There's probably no point. We've already cancelled all the tours and left people very disappointed."

"I'm sorry, mate. I know it's not the start you were hoping for."

"No." But he could roll with it. Reacting to circumstances was what he was good at. "Have you got time to come diving this week?" He shrugged. "I figured I might take the tender out and check out some dive spots."

"Maybe at the end of the week. I'll call you." Brandon sipped his tea. "Have you heard from Sherlock lately?"

Sam flinched at the name. "Why?"

It was the wrong thing to say. Brandon's eyes pinned Sam to the chair. "Amy and I have both tried calling him, and there's been no answer. He should be back from his mission by now."

Sam nodded. "The team left again just before I finished." It wasn't a lie. "You know Sherlock, he lives for the mission."

Brandon scowled. "When he gets back, I'm going to have words with him. He needs to get his priorities straight. Family is important."

"Which is why you stayed away from yours for over a decade?" Sam asked, ignoring the unease in his gut.

"That's different."

"Maybe Sherlock feels as guilty as you did."

Brandon swore. "You could be right. When's the team due back?"

"After Christmas."

"I'll call him then."

Sam pushed down on the guilt. The one thing Sherlock had asked of him was not to tell Brandon and

Amy, and so Sam would keep his promise for as long as he could. He didn't want the guilt Sherlock felt over his sister to compound on his misery of losing a leg and his career. It might just tip him over.

Chapter 5

Penelope had spent most of yesterday tracking down passengers on both Jimmy's and Rob's boats to get a full picture of what actually had happened. One passenger promised to send her a video of the whole thing, but so far it had not arrived. She would chase it up when she got back to the office. Today she wanted to go out to the Muiron Islands. A few spot checks on any boats to ensure they were all doing the right thing and a review of the island were in order. She'd been trying to get out there for more than a week, but Declan had given her other priorities. Today she was getting there, no matter what. Too many people thought they could flaunt the size and catch limits and get away with it.

Not on her watch.

Plus it was nesting season and she had statistics to gather.

She sighed as she parked in the marina car park. Perhaps she wasn't cut out for this kind of job. There were even more rules and every time she stuck to them, she felt inflexible, but the memory of what happened haunted her and she couldn't bring herself to bend.

She'd been too harsh on Sam and Rob. The stress of her first big decision, the knowledge she'd made the wrong call before, all topped with the way Sam put her on edge, had her unable to think straight. Hopefully the video would clarify what had happened and justify the week-long suspension.

Her guilt intensified as she saw Sam's boat, *Oceanid*, still tied in its pen. She scanned the area, but couldn't spot the man. Good.

Moving quickly, she grabbed her backpack and strode over to the PAWS boat. A day on the ocean would clear her head. It always did.

She climbed into the mid-sized, fibreglass boat and dumped her bag on the passenger seat. After putting on her life jacket, she untied the ropes and started the engine, clicking the kill switch to her belt. The last thing she needed was to fall overboard and be stranded in the middle of the ocean.

She radioed the office. "Karen, this is Victor Sierra Foxtrot. I'm heading out towards the Muiron Islands now. I expect to be back by four." It would give her plenty of time to chat with people who might be out on the water.

"Copy that. Have a great day, Penelope."

The communication was reassuring, not that she expected anything to go wrong, but it was better to plan for the worst.

She knew that now.

Penelope eased out of the pen and stuck to the speed limits as she motored between the markers and into the gulf. Light winds rippled the surface of the ocean, but not enough to make it a bumpy ride.

Several boats were already out fishing in the gulf, but not in areas of the marine park. Jimmy's tour boat was ahead of her, motoring towards its first snorkelling spot of the day. As she followed, he spotted her and waved.

A moment later, her radio came to life.

"You after me?" Jimmy asked.

Penelope smiled and picked up the radio. "Not today. Heading for the islands."

"Have fun."

The tour boat operators had been very nice to her. Probably wanted to stay on her good side.

When she reached the point of the peninsula, she slowed and checked her GPS. There were two sanctuary zones here, and between them a recreational zone. Not all people were aware of it or cared to make the distinction, but no fishing was allowed. As part of her role as park ranger, she had honorary fisheries officer status, which allowed her to monitor the fishing as well.

Today no one fished in either sanctuary zone, so she continued towards the islands which lay nine nautical miles from Retribution Bay.

Along the way, she stopped a couple of boats and checked their catch, but all was in order.

She rounded the tip of South Muiron Island and headed for the sanctuary zone off its west coast. One of the dive boats was already moored in place and its divers were getting into the water, so she took a wide berth.

Another two boats were anchored in the area, both with the blue and white flag that declared divers were in the water. One, a rubber tender, was unoccupied, but she spotted a person on the second larger luxury vessel which declared itself *Joy Ridin'* on the side. This vessel had a large back deck, with multiple spaces for fishing rods, though none were out today. It had two huge motors to power it and the marlin board was down. The cabin area was large enough to hold a dining room and several bedrooms, and the upstairs area was undercover to give the captain shade when navigating.

As she motored over, she tried to hail the boat on the radio, but they didn't respond. Maybe everyone was diving. Keeping her speed low and looking for bubbles which would signal a diver surfacing, she approached.

A tall, shirtless man came out on deck, his Lycra bather shorts clinging to his legs, and the tattoo on his upper arm highlighting his muscles. As she moved closer he gave an easy smile and waved, giving her a glimpse of the bulldog tattoo. "Morning."

Penelope moved into neutral and came up alongside. "Good morning. I'm from Parks and Wildlife Services. I'm doing some routine checks of the area. Have you been fishing today?"

"Not here. This is a sanctuary zone." His eyes flicked to the water and then back to her.

"Have you been fishing elsewhere today?"

"No. My mate wanted to go diving, so I'm finishing my book." He gestured towards the cabin.

She couldn't see much of the boat floor from where she was, but the smell of fish wafted towards her. "Mind if I come aboard?"

He shifted towards the cabin. "Ah, I'd really like to get back to my book."

"This won't take long."

"Hey, Grant, give us a hand here." The call came from the back of the boat.

Grant's eyes widened, and he strode to the stern.

Penelope shifted into reverse and spotted a diver floating at the back, a gidgee in one hand and a bag full of crayfish in the other. Illegal fishing in a sanctuary zone. Some people had no respect.

The diver gaped at her and then brought the gidgee around to point at her.

Penelope stared down at the sharp spear, her heart racing. What was he thinking? It had to be a reflexive move. She swallowed. "Lower the gidgee."

"You idiot," Grant said. "Didn't you see the other boat?"

"No one was out here today."

An idiot if he thought no one could turn up while he was underwater. Penelope reached for the radio.

"Don't," the diver said, lifting the spear gun further out of the water.

Grant swore. "What are you doing, Murray?"

"We can't afford to have this reported."

"So what are you going to do, kill her?"

Penelope kept her eyes on Murray, her heart racing. If he shot, could she duck in time from this range? She wasn't certain. In the distance a boat engine hummed, but she didn't dare turn to see where it was.

"We can dump her on the island. Give us enough time to get away."

"She's seen us and the boat. We're screwed." Grant turned to her. "How much will it take for you to pretend you saw nothing?"

Penelope bristled but ignored the comment. She needed Murray to lower his spear. "Murray, are you aware you're fishing in a sanctuary zone?" This was his way out, not that she would give it to him.

He hesitated. "No."

Liar. Still, she could work with it. "You need to release the crayfish."

"But they're dead." He shoved the bag of crayfish up on the marlin board.

From what she could see, he'd speared them all. Idiot. Penelope grabbed her radio. "Base, this is Victor Sierra Foxtrot. Do you copy?"

"Yes, Penelope. What have you got?"

"Put that down!" Murray cried, facing her again and lifting the gidgee from the water. His hand shook, his finger over the trigger.

She gasped. Grant was pulling the crayfish on board

as if to hide it, not paying any attention to Murray. "If I don't respond to the office, they're going to know something is wrong."

As if proving her point, the radio sounded. "Penelope, are you there?"

She reached for it.

"Don't do it." Murray swam closer.

Penelope looked at Grant. "Can you talk some sense into him?"

Grant sighed and then reached behind his back and pulled out a gun. "No. Do as he says."

Penelope froze.

***

Sam surfaced from his dive and inflated his BCD, taking the regulator from his mouth. Bliss. A perfect dive. The coral and marine life was magnificent around the Muiron Islands. He'd have to thank Rob for the recommendation. It was just what he'd needed this morning. Sam checked the time and then hauled himself aboard the rubber tender.

He placed his goggles and fins in a tub and then unbuckled the BCD, placing it to the side. He had another tank with him, but he'd explore the island before he went down again to give him enough time between dives.

The sun's rays warmed him, so he didn't bother with a towel, just unzipped his wetsuit and pulled it down around his waist. As he started the engine, he noticed the luxury launch was still moored on the other side of the sanctuary zone, about a hundred metres away, but another boat had joined it. One with Parks and Wildlife Services emblazoned on the side.

What were the chances it was Penelope?

He motored closer, unsure whether he wanted to see her. She'd probably tell him he wasn't allowed to dive here, even though he'd double-checked the location and the rules before he'd gone down.

Sam headed towards the shore when a glint of something on the deck of the luxury boat caught his eye. His body tensed, the instinct too ingrained after years in the military, and he slowed to take a closer look. One guy stood on the deck and another man was in the water. Both were facing the red-headed woman on the other boat and pointing weapons at her.

Penelope.

He reached for his hand-held radio, saying a silent thanks to Brandon who had recommended he get one and take it everywhere with him. He flicked to the marine rescue station. "I've got a situation here."

"What are your coordinates and the problem?"

"I'm in the western sanctuary zone off South Muiron Island," Sam said. "Parks and Wildlife has stopped a luxury boat called *Joy Ridin'*. Both men appear to be holding weapons on Penelope. Can you notify the police?"

"Roger that. Do not approach."

Like hell he wouldn't.

He replaced the radio as he pointed his boat towards Penelope, being sure to rev the engine so the men had plenty of time to hide their weapons. Sure enough, when he looked back towards the boat, the weapons were gone.

Good.

He analysed how to play this. He needed to get between Penelope and the man in the water so he couldn't attack her. Then he'd have to deal with the person on deck. He had a dive knife, but his knife throwing skills weren't the best.

As he neared, he waved to Penelope. "Hi, Penelope!" He slowed the tender, bumping into the marlin board of the boat and forcing the diver to backpedal.

"Watch it," the diver called.

Sam glanced at him. "Oh, sorry, mate. Didn't see you there. Have you been down today? Isn't it glorious?" The bumbling fool never failed to make guys like this relax. "Can I give you a hand up?" He reached a hand towards the man.

Through the clear water the spear gun was visible, though the diver had shifted it to his outside hand.

The diver glanced at him, then up to his mate on the boat and back.

"Sam, go," Penelope said, her voice trembling. "I'm working."

Fury filled him at her fear and he ignored her, not even looking her way. "Did you see the tiger shark?" he continued. "It was a beauty, gliding through the water. Had to be a good three or four metres long. Scared the shit out of me. I thought I was going to be lunch."

The diver scanned the water below him and then swore and shoved the spear gun on the marlin board and clambered onto the boat. While the diver awkwardly peeled off his fins and climbed into the main area of the boat, Sam shifted his tender so it nudged the Parks and Wildlife boat away from the edge.

"Sam, what are you doing?"

"Sorry, still getting used to the steering on this thing," he called to Penelope over the engine, keeping his eyes on the man standing on the deck, whose hand had moved behind his back. "I wanted to ask you a couple of questions about the island if you've got time. You guys don't mind the interruption, do you?"

The man with the gun smiled. "We were just going," he called. "Knock yourself out." About six feet, well-muscled, brown hair, bulldog tattoo. Sam could take him if it came to hand-to-hand combat.

The diver had discarded his equipment next to a

second set of scuba gear and moved to the front of the boat to pull the anchor. Black hair, skinnier, maybe five-ten and any distinguishing features were covered by the wetsuit.

"Sam, stop it," Penelope hissed. "They need—"

The boat's engine roared to life, drowning out her words. The man with the gun waved as they motored away, heading out to sea. Sam kept his eyes on them until they were far enough not to be a threat and then turned to Penelope. Her face was pale and her hand shook as she reached for the radio.

"I've reported it," Sam said as he moved his boat alongside and cut the engine, throwing a rope to her and jumping over to her boat.

"What?" She blinked at him, expression a little dazed, vulnerable.

Sam's protective instinct kicked in and he pulled her into his arms. "It's all right."

She stiffened, then softened towards him for only a second before she pushed him away. "What the hell is going on? What are you doing here? What do you know about this? Those men were illegally fishing in a sanctuary zone." Her eyes flashed.

"And they both had weapons pointed at you," Sam retorted. "I defused the situation."

"You let them get away."

"I've reported the boat to the police. They won't get far."

She took a deep breath, letting it out. She closed her eyes. "Thank you."

Sam relaxed. "You're welcome. You want to tell me what happened?"

"I need to call the office back." She radioed PAWS, reporting the boat and describing the two men on board. He was impressed with her level of detail.

"We'll report it to the police," the woman

responded.

Penelope clipped the radio back into position and then sank into her seat and placed her head in her hands.

"You all right?" Sam kept his distance, not wanting to set her off again.

"I thought you were clueless," she said. "I thought you were going to get shot."

Sam grinned. "Glad to know my acting skills aren't all bad."

She choked out a laugh. "How did you know? Where did you come from?"

He pointed to where he'd been diving. "When I surfaced, I noticed your boat. My plan was to check out the island until enough time had passed between dives. Then I saw both men were pointing at you and the sun reflected off the gun metal. My instincts kicked in."

She frowned.

"Military," he reminded her. "I called marine rescue with the details before I approached."

"I appreciate your help, but you could have been shot."

"So could you, but I'm used to the risk." No way he could have left her to face the men on her own.

They were drifting towards the island now and Penelope still looked pale. "How about we anchor on the shore for a few minutes? Have a drink, take a breath?"

She nodded and started the engine as if pleased for something to do. Sam ensured the rope to his tender wasn't in the way and tied it to the back cleat as she motored slowly towards the beach. With her gaze on where they were going, he exhaled and tapped his chest. He hadn't considered he might come in contact with guns when he got out of the army. He'd managed less than a week, and he'd had no bullet-proof vest. If the gunman had wanted to kill him, he'd be dead right now.

Not a comforting thought.

He shook off the fear and focused on the woman behind the wheel. She was still pale, though her skin was fair anyway. She stared straight ahead, her fingers clenched around the steering wheel as she manoeuvred around the reef to a gap that would get them to the shore.

When they reached the sand, Sam jumped off and grabbed the anchor from the PAWS boat, anchoring them into position, and then waded out to his tender and did the same. While he was there, he grabbed his esky and carried it to where Penelope waited on the shore, her arms crossed, hugging herself.

"You OK?" He walked past her a few metres away from the water's edge and placed the esky on the ground, getting two bottles of water out. He handed her one.

"I've been better. It's not what I was expecting to face while at work." Penelope ran a shaky hand through her neatly tied back hair. She glanced at him. "Why did they even have a gun in the first place?"

She had a point. Gun laws were strict in Australia and very few people carried them as a matter of course. "What were they doing?"

"Poaching," she answered. "They weren't allowed to be fishing in the area and the diver had an illegal spearfishing gun."

"I'm surprised they didn't run when they saw you," Sam said.

"The diver was still underwater," Penelope said.

Loyalty. That was surprising. Most criminals he'd come into contact with would choose to take off and save themselves. Though it wasn't far from the island so the diver could have easily swum there and waited to be picked up. So maybe the guy was just stupid.

Penelope's hand shook as she sipped the water Sam had handed her. Still shaken. "Why don't we walk it off?" he asked. "I'm feeling a little shaky myself." She raised her eyebrows, clearly not believing him, and he smiled. "First time I've been around a gun without full Kevlar." He walked away, gesturing with his head for her to follow and she fell into step with him.

"Did I thank you?" She shook her head. "Thank you. I didn't know what to do. I froze." She sounded annoyed with herself.

"You're not trained to deal with that stuff. You don't expect to be facing off with a gun as part of your work day in this country."

She nodded and lowered her arms by her side, relaxing the grip she had around her body.

"Do you come out here much?" Sam asked.

"The minimum is a couple of times a month, but maybe more depending on what's happening."

So her timing sucked. "You must love days like this," he said and gestured to the smooth, sparkling ocean. "It's so beautiful out here."

She glanced at him, surprise on her face. "I do."

He smiled, hoping she would open up to him. If he could show her he wasn't a bad guy, maybe she'd give him the benefit of the doubt next time.

Or reduce his suspension.

Chapter 6

Penelope appreciated the change in subject. Though her heart rate had slowed, all her muscles were tight, as if expecting another attack. She exhaled and focused on the man next to her. She'd expected with his cowboy tendencies, he wouldn't take the time to appreciate his surroundings. Maybe she'd been unfair to judge him so harshly. He smiled at her, relaxed and unconcerned. Not the least bit bothered about their near brush with death. "Why are you being so nice? You'd be out on your boat if not for me."

"Seems it's lucky for you I'm not," he answered.

A good point, but not an answer. When she continued to look at him, he sighed.

"No use holding a grudge over something I can't change," he said. "That way leads to misery. Sure, I'd like you to reverse your decision, but you did what you thought was right. Let's forget about it."

Some things you couldn't simply forget about.

Breathing deeply to control the nausea in her stomach, she studied him. Arms relaxed by his side, shoulders down, a partial smile on his face—he seemed genuine.

In the past, she'd been abused by people she'd only given a warning to and she'd stopped him working for a week. Not everyone would have come over when they'd seen her in trouble. She was so glad he had. She blew out a breath and shivered, the fear still very close to the surface even if she was safe now. The radio on her belt squawked.

"Penelope, are you there?" Declan. He'd want a full rundown. She grabbed the radio from her belt and answered. "Yes, I'm here."

"Are you all right?"

"I'm uninjured." She wouldn't get the image of the gun pointing at her out of her mind any time soon.

"What were you doing out there? I thought you were working in the southern gulf."

She bristled. "I'm catching up. I was supposed to be out here a couple of days ago."

"Come back in. You can chat to the police and then take the day off."

She shook her head, even though Declan couldn't see her. "I'm fine. I'll finish what I'm doing here and then return."

"You should come straight back and give the police your statement. What if the men return?"

She shuddered and glanced at Sam. He shook his head, and she breathed a little easier. "I don't think so. Sam did a good job of convincing them to leave."

"Sam still with you?"

"Yeah. We're taking a breather on the island."

"The police want to talk to Sam when he gets back too. Can you pass the message on?"

Sam nodded. "Sure thing."

So easy-going. It was strange. Could his calm reaction be due to his military training? If so, they built them hard. "Roger that. I'll let you know when I'm heading in." She clipped the radio back to her belt.

They resumed walking in silence, and Penelope scrambled for something to discuss. What was she supposed to say to a man whose livelihood her decision had affected?

Maybe she should have been more lenient. He'd saved her life. She rubbed at the goosebumps on her arm and flinched when he spoke.

"Georgie tells me you're new in town too," he said. "How are you settling in?"

"Fine," she lied. "The people I work with are nice, and the work is varied." She cringed inwardly. Such a banal thing to say. She glanced at him. "What made you move here?"

Sam shrugged. "I was trying to figure out what to do when I left the military," he said. "My plan was to move back east and help my youngest sister with her new baby. But a month after I handed in my resignation, she fell in love with a guy who's going to take care of her and her child, and she doesn't need me."

He seemed kind of sad. "Has she had the baby?"

"Yeah, a girl – Josie." He grinned. "She's so sweet. I can't wait to meet her."

"You haven't been?"

"Timing hasn't been right. I'll go in summer after the tour season has finished."

"So why Retribution Bay?" Penelope asked.

"When I visited for Brandon's wedding, I discovered Rob was selling his boat. I didn't want an office job, and I liked it here. Being close to my best friend was also a draw card. Seemed like a no brainer."

He made it sound easy. Not for her. She'd agonised over applying for the job. She'd never even been to Retribution Bay. Ceiveon's dare had pushed her to submit the application. She'd had plenty of time to rue the decision.

Penelope shook her head. It wasn't like her to be so

dour, though having a gun pointed at her head was a decent excuse. She didn't dare ask if Sam thought he'd made the right decision about coming to Retribution Bay, knowing the answer was probably no, and it was her fault. Instead she stuck to easier topics of conversation. "Georgie said you and Brandon started in the military together."

"Yeah, we were paired up on the first day. Brandon was so serious and I was irresponsible. We didn't like each other much at first, but it didn't take us long to bond."

She knew almost nothing about the military. "Did you enjoy it?"

He was silent for a long moment. "Yeah, there's a camaraderie in your team which will never die. You rely on each other to stay alive."

She couldn't imagine it. "Did you see much action?"

"My fair share."

"Do you miss it?"

He chuckled. "What with an orca the other day and the gun today, I'm getting my fair share of action right here."

She smiled. He had a point.

"You should smile more often," he said. "It makes you much more approachable."

Heat rushed to her cheeks. "I'm serious when my job requires it."

He sighed. "It was a compliment," he said. "I can't seem to say the right thing to you."

She held up a hand in apology. "It's a touchy subject. Men don't generally get accused of not smiling enough."

"Fair point. Sorry."

She nodded, and stopped walking. "I should get back." The nausea was gone and though she was enjoying his company, it would be wrong to make the police wait for their answers.

"How are you feeling?"

"Better." She forced a smile. "Thank you."

"You're welcome. I've enjoyed chatting with you."

His wide smile was like a sunbeam, bright and joyous. A woman could be blinded by such a smile. "I'll see you around."

"I'll walk you back."

It would be childish to refuse, though there was no one else on the shore and she hardly needed protection. Not anymore. She walked back the way they'd come.

"You must have visited all the good spots since you've been here," Sam said. "Got any recommendations?"

"For diving?" He still had his wetsuit pulled around his waist, giving her a lovely view of his chest, but her own chest tightened.

"Yeah, or snorkelling."

"Georgie hasn't given you a full list yet?" If he discovered she hadn't been diving, he'd want to know why.

"Haven't asked her."

"The tourists are taken to the Cod Spot." She pointed towards it. "And there's supposed to be a great drift dive between the two islands."

"You haven't been?"

She tensed, her skin prickling. "No."

"You can come out with me if you like," Sam said. "I'm planning a night dive soon."

"We'll see." Her heart twinged. She used to love diving, spending time under the water and exploring. But she hadn't been out since... Images flashed through her mind; Emelia's panicked face, bubbles of air, emptiness.

"Are you heading off?"

She started, shaking away the memory. They'd

reached the boats and Sam pulled in his anchor and placed it in the tender's bow.

"Yeah." She pulled in her anchor as well. The idea of being out here alone wasn't comforting. She'd return to town, give her statement, and come out another day to finish her monitoring work. "Thanks again for your help." She climbed aboard and started the engine. "I'll see you around."

He smiled again. "I'll look forward to it."

Penelope put her boat into reverse, ignoring the warmth his comment brought.

***

Sam stared at the ceiling of his dark room, lying in his comfortable bed, but sleep eluded him. He'd been running the Penelope scenario over and over in his head for hours. His brain was stuck on what would have happened if he hadn't been there.

Stupid.

He hadn't obsessed over an event since the early years in the army. It had been pointless to then, just as it was pointless now. What was done was done, and neither of them had been hurt.

He'd called Brandon to get his take and his first word had been, "Stonefish". It made the most sense. The gun had been the tell. Most rich men who thought they could flout the rules didn't carry handguns, they bought their way out of things.

The men had been tracked to international waters but not caught. They'd had too much of a head start. Dot hadn't been pleased to see Sam twice in three days. "You're attracted to trouble, aren't you?"

He wasn't upset that he'd been there for Penelope. He'd seen her softer side. Faith and Amy had thought her worried, or lacking confidence, but he suspected it was more than that. Something had made her so prickly, so rigid. She'd stiffened when they'd discussed diving.

He wanted to know why. She intrigued him.

She'd worried about him being injured in the confrontation, not just concerned about herself.

Sam had considered getting her number from Georgie and calling her, but decided against it in case she thought he was trying to bribe her.

He'd settled with following her boat to ensure she got safely back to town.

Sam threw back the sheet, wandering downstairs to the kitchen for a glass of water. The light as he opened the fridge illuminated the room and his gaze caught on the copies of the journals Brandon had given him. He hadn't read them yet. There'd been some final unpacking to do, and the writing was small and scratchy, so it would take a concerted effort to read it. He hadn't had the energy.

After pouring a glass of water, he picked up Lilian's journal and held it up to the light of the fridge.

Nope. He might not be able to sleep, but trying to decipher her words would be more than his brain could handle tonight.

He replaced it on the bench and went over to the sliding glass door, which led out to his patio and overlooked the canal. The house across from him was dark and next to it were empty blocks. The moon lit up the land, but the only movement was the ripple of the water.

Peaceful. A balm after the busy days in the army.

Sherlock would be discharged from the rehabilitation centre in two days. Sam would call again tomorrow and invite him to Retribution Bay. He would feel better having Sherlock nearby, where he could monitor him and make sure he was taking care of himself, not sinking further into despair. Plus, the lure of searching for treasure would intrigue him. Sherlock always loved a good puzzle.

They'd kept him longer because of his depression, but the doctor couldn't do anything else. They needed his bed.

Maybe he should fly down and drag Sherlock's sorry arse up here. Brandon would help him if Sam told him about it.

But should he break his promise to Sherlock?

The question did nothing to calm his mind. What he needed to do was go for a walk. He'd yet to explore the town properly.

Sam returned to his bedroom, dressed in shorts and a T-shirt, and laced up his sneakers. Grabbing his keys from by the door, he was out of the house in minutes. He stood on the road for a second and then headed left, towards town.

Only a few streetlights lit the way, but it didn't matter because the moon was bright enough. He inhaled deeply. The night was cooler than he'd expected with a light wind, but it just made him walk faster.

He reached the main street and took the first road which led off it, heading further into town.

This was ridiculous. He should be in bed, not walking the streets at midnight like a creepy person. He walked past the PAWS office where only a security light shone at the entrance. All the other houses along the street were dark, their residents in bed long ago.

Just like he should be.

Still he walked, houses on one side of the street, scrub on the other marking the end of town. Rob had mentioned dingoes occasionally ventured into town looking for food.

Sam cast a wary eye over the bush, searching for movement, and saw none. Hopefully he was big enough to scare away any animal that might be out there.

With that slightly uneasy thought nestled in his mind, he turned right down the next street. Houses lined both sides now, cars and bikes in the driveways. Up ahead, a porch light flicked on and a woman stepped out, the light picking up the rich red of her hair.

Sam slowed. Could it be Penelope? He had no idea where she lived, but there couldn't be too many people in town with hair that colour.

As he watched, she strode down the path towards the street and headed in his direction. Sam moved forward under a streetlight, not wanting to startle her, and her steps slowed as she spotted him.

"What are you doing here?" she called.

"Couldn't sleep." He moved out of the glare of the light and approached her.

"Me neither."

"It was a pretty intense day," Sam said, turning around to walk with her back the way he'd come.

"It's not just that."

He waited for her to explain and when she didn't, he said, "I'm a good listener." Suddenly, he wanted to hear her thoughts and concerns. He wanted to understand what made her tick.

"I can't. You're someone I deal with at work."

"So it's work stuff?"

"Partially."

Interesting. She could have lied and said that's all it was. "Want to talk about the non-work stuff?"

"No."

He chuckled. "Right. OK."

She sighed, the sound loud in the quiet of the night. "I didn't mean it as a slight. I barely know you, and I've only spoken to my best friend about it."

He was doubly intrigued now, but all he said was, "Tell me about your best friend."

A pause and when she spoke, her voice held warmth and affection. "Ceiveon has been my bestie since university. We had rooms opposite each other and connected immediately. She got me into jogging."

"You must miss her."

Penelope nodded. "We call each other regularly. She's been pretty busy with a newborn. She was the one who encouraged me to take this job."

"Does she live nearby?"

"Perth. She believed I'd like the work up here."

They were close to the marina now and Sam let Penelope choose which roads to go down. She knew the town better than he did.

"What were your impressions of those guys today?" she asked.

Sam glanced at her. It wasn't a question he'd been expecting. "In what way?"

"How would you categorise them? Why would they do what they did?"

Her tone was cautious, as if she was fishing for information. "Expensive boat suggests wealth," he said. "Perhaps used to getting their own way and don't think normal rules apply to them."

"And the gun?"

He was impressed by her intuition. "Could be a show of power, a status symbol." But the man on the boat had been comfortable with it, knew how to hide it away at a moment's notice. He wanted to be honest with her about it. "But probably not."

"Why not?"

"What did he do when you first approached?"

"He didn't answer my radio call. He came out only when I came closer."

Assuming Grant had the radio on, he knew who was approaching and he'd come out with a gun in his shorts. That was one hell of a red flag.

She glanced at him and in the glow of the overhead streetlight he saw her hesitation.

"What do you want to ask me?"

"Do you know what happened to Matt a couple of weeks ago?"

Georgie had mentioned Penelope had been there when she'd received the kidnapper's call. "He was abducted."

"Do you know why?"

He nodded. "Do you?"

"No. Georgie said they'd been having issues with someone, and Dot wouldn't tell me a damn thing. It had something to do with animal smuggling." She looked at him for confirmation.

It was a lot more, but it wasn't his place to tell her. "Something like that."

She growled. "You won't tell me either?"

"It's not my story to tell."

That seemed to satisfy her. "Could the men who were arrested today be involved with the animal smuggling operation?"

Definitely intelligent to make the connection. Stonefish Enterprises had their fingers in a lot of pies up here, not that killing a few crayfish really counted as organised crime.

"Sam?"

"Anything's possible. Did you suggest it to Dot?"

"It only occurred to me tonight," she said. "I'll call her tomorrow." She paused and then said, "You know Dot well considering you just moved here."

"I spoke to her at Brandon's wedding." Penelope didn't need to know all the issues that had surrounded Brandon's family in relation to Stonefish Enterprises. His footsteps slowed. Or maybe she already knew. What if she was a Stonefish plant, fishing for information about what they knew. It was possible.

He'd have to be careful what he said.

"Is that when you met?"

Sam had to give her credit, she was smart to read between the lines. There was no reason to lie to her. "I met her the first time I came up, for Brandon's parents' funeral."

"Oh, I'm sorry. Georgie never mentioned that. How long ago was it?"

"In May. It was a car crash."

"Oh, the poor family. Georgie's got three brothers, hasn't she?"

"Four. One died when he was a child."

"She's dealt with a lot. I'm surprised she's still so optimistic."

Sam smiled. "That's Georgie. She's pretty special." They reached the marina and walked to the edge of the rocks to stare out at the dark ocean.

"She's been very welcoming," Penelope said.

The wind had picked up, carrying with it a definite chill. Penelope shivered, wrapping her arms around herself.

"Why don't we go to my place?" Sam suggested. "I can put the kettle on and after we have a drink, I'll drive you home." Perhaps he could find out more about her background.

"I can walk."

"I know, but being the gentleman I am, I'd have to walk you home, and I'd get cold again."

She stiffened, which was a shame. He had enjoyed her opening up to him.

"I can go by myself. The streets are safe, and I've been walking most nights."

He turned to return home. "You want to talk about what else is on your mind?"

Penelope pursed her lips. "What makes you think anything is?"

"Because you mentioned it wasn't just work stuff, and most people are asleep at this time of night, not walking the streets."

She fell into step with him, but he suspected it was because she was cold and keen to get home, rather than actually wanting to walk with him.

"The country is quieter than I'm used to."

Sure it was, but that wasn't the real reason. Could Stonefish have its spines into her? He let it slide and when they reached his place, he got his keys out. "Would you like a cuppa?"

"I should get home."

"Let me drive you."

She placed a hand on his arm. "Thank you for the offer, but I'd like to walk."

With the heat of her hand still warming his arm, she strode down the street. He bit his cheek to stop from calling her back, surprised by the disappointment swirling in his stomach.

Sam had enjoyed talking to her.

He couldn't wait to do so again.

He just hoped she was genuine.

Chapter 7

Penelope should have spent hours staring at the ceiling when she got home last night. Her conversation with Sam should have kept her mind whirring with thoughts, but it hadn't. Instead, she'd arrived home and fallen asleep only moments after her head hit the pillow.

She didn't want to consider the reasons why.

It had been nice to have some company on her midnight sojourn, though she did have a moment of fear when she noticed the dark figure on the street, until she'd recognised Sam.

Then she'd been comforted in a strange way. She'd not been afraid of walking at night while she'd been up here, but he'd been like a bodyguard. It had been far too tempting to accept his offer of a cup of tea and a drive home, but it was a little too intimate, too fast.

Besides, she had more than enough to worry about with the gun-wielding poachers.

Sam had more or less confirmed something more was going on in Retribution Bay and today she wanted to call Dot to discuss it. She needed to know about it so she could be prepared.

Penelope dressed in her uniform of polo shirt and

shorts, and made some toast for breakfast before heading to the office to check in. Declan entered her office before she even sat.

"How are you today?" he asked.

"I'm well, thank you."

He scowled. "Do you need to talk to a therapist? We've got a number you can call." He shoved a card at her and she took it.

"I'm fine, Declan, but thank you for your concern. I'll take the boat out again today because I didn't finish the monitoring yesterday."

"You don't need to go out so soon, if you're not ready."

"Truly, I'm fine. I want to go out. I doubt the men will be back."

"Of course, but if you do see them again, call it in." He didn't seem happy as he walked out.

Definitely something else going on. Georgie walked in. "I heard what happened yesterday. Are you all right?"

Penelope could appreciate people's concern, but the question was becoming repetitive. "Fine." She slipped past Georgie and shut the door. "But I want to ask you about something."

"Go for it."

"What really happened last month with Matt?"

Georgie stepped back. "What do you mean?"

"I know he was kidnapped, which had something to do with animal smugglers, but everything else is rumours."

Georgie twirled her fringe around her finger. "I don't know how much I can tell you."

"Could the men yesterday be involved?" Penelope asked, getting to the crux of her question.

Georgie's eyes widened. "Maybe. Did Dot say anything?"

Penelope scowled. "Everyone is being silent about it, other than asking me how I am."

Georgie smiled and squeezed her arm. "That's because we're concerned about you."

She huffed out a breath. "Then someone needs to tell me what's going on before I stumble upon something that will get me hurt."

Georgie stiffened, her expression suddenly serious. "You're right. You should come out to the Ridge tonight for dinner. It affects my whole family, so you should hear it from them."

Penelope blinked. "Your whole family?"

"Yeah, but don't worry, we're not the mafia or anything. Go ask Dot about the men yesterday and then go to work. I'll pick you up from your place at five thirty." Georgie waited only long enough for Penelope to nod her agreement and then rushed out of the room.

Concern tightened Penelope's muscles. This *was* a lot more than she suspected.

Did she really want to get involved?

***

By the end of the day, Penelope was ready for a shower. She'd received little in the way of extra information from Dot, only advice to call if she saw anything suspicious. The ocean was choppy, which made the journey to the island rough and unpleasant. She was damp, salty and had had enough sun to last her a while.

She drove back to her place to find Georgie waiting for her. Damn, she'd forgotten about dinner. Quickly, she got out of her car. "Sorry, I'm late."

"Don't stress, there's no rush. Go have a shower."

Penelope unlocked the door and led Georgie inside, conscious of how sparsely her house was furnished. "Can I get you a drink?"

"I'm fine." Georgie grinned. "Go have a soak. You

look as if you need it."

Penelope pulled a face. "I look that bad, do I?"

"The ocean was rough today. I've been there." Georgie made shooing motions and Penelope took her advice, spending time under the shower to wash away the salt and fatigue. When Penelope returned, Georgie was examining Penelope's crocheting attempt.

"What is it?"

Penelope laughed. "It's supposed to be a baby's blanket."

Georgie's raised eyebrows spoke volumes. "Amy knits. Maybe you should bring it out and ask for advice."

Though her cheeks warmed, she didn't mind the gentle teasing from Georgie. "I'll show her a photo if the topic comes up." She snapped a photo with her phone and followed Georgie out of the house.

An hour later Georgie pulled into a dirt driveway which had an aggressive looking ram on it, that was also kind of cute. "Nice painting."

"My brother Charlie painted it before he died."

Penelope cringed. "I'm sorry."

"It always makes me smile, and Charlie would get a kick out of knowing it was still here, announcing the entrance to the station."

"How big is the station?"

"About a quarter of a million acres," Georgie said. "We farm sheep, but we've also just started a campground." She gestured to the myriad caravans and tents set up behind a horse yard and sheds.

To Penelope it was all red dirt and straggly bushes. How could anything survive out here, particularly something like sheep? "How long has your family owned the land?"

"Since 1871," Georgie answered, and she pulled up outside a farmhouse, which looked as if it had been added to over the years.

"Wow." It must have been one of the first settlements in the area.

A blue heeler barked and trotted down the back steps to stand next to the driver's side door. "Hey, Bennett." Georgie patted the dog and Penelope followed her up the steps to the porch.

"Did your parents like Jane Austen?" Penelope asked.

Georgie turned to her, smile wide. "Mum was obsessed by her books. Not many people make the connection though."

Penelope smiled. "It's easy to pick when you're a fellow Janeite."

"Mum would have loved you." Georgie's smile faded, and she pulled open the door and called, "We're here!"

A young girl dressed in her yellow and brown school uniform came bounding through the door on the other side of the kitchen, her brown ponytail swinging behind her. "Hey, Georgie!" She hugged Georgie and then turned to Penelope. "You must be Penelope. It's nice to meet you." She held out her hand.

Thoroughly charmed, Penelope shook her hand. "You must be Lara. I've heard a lot about you."

"All good, I'm sure. Faith said you were at her horse-riding class. You can come and ride on the weekend. I can take you to the beach."

She was delightful. "I'm not sure I'm good enough to go riding so far yet, but thank you for the offer."

Faith entered the room. "Nice to see you again, Pen. We're just waiting for the guys to arrive. Would you like a drink?"

"Water's fine." She sat at the kitchen table next to Lara. "I hope I'm not intruding." She wasn't sure what Georgie had told them.

The kitchen door swung open and a tall, lanky man with dark brown hair walked in and hung his hat on a hook by the door. Lara jumped up and hugged him.

"Dad, have you met Penelope yet?" Lara asked.

"I've just walked in, pumpkin," the man answered. He smiled at Penelope. "I'm Darcy. Nice to meet you."

Penelope stood and held out her hand. "Thank you for having me."

"Any time." He shook her hand. Behind him, two other men had entered; Brandon she recognised from the removal day, and Matt she'd met after the incident when he'd been kidnapped.

"Go wash up," Lara told them. "I'm hungry."

"You tell them, La La," Georgie agreed before kissing Matt.

"Sam's not here yet," Brandon said as he walked over to greet Amy, who had entered the kitchen.

Penelope jolted at the name. She hadn't known he'd be here. She wasn't certain she wanted to see him.

"Why's Sam coming?" Georgie asked.

Brandon glanced at Lara, who was telling Matt about a project she'd done at school that day with a girl named Natasha. Brandon lowered his voice. "If we're talking to Penelope about things, we should include him. He could be an asset."

Penelope's skin prickled. What had she got herself involved in?

"We'll wait until Lara goes to bed," Georgie murmured.

"What are you talking about?" Lara asked, turning to stare at them.

"Ears like an elephant," Brandon teased. "Nothing you need to be worried about."

"Can I come in?" Sam's call at the door captured Lara's attention, and though she scowled at Brandon, she turned and flung it open for Sam.

"You'll tell me what the others are talking about after I go to bed, won't you, Sam?" She hugged him and he looked slightly confused as he hugged her back.

"I'm a little lost, La La," he said.

"They're going to talk when I go to bed." She lowered her voice, but Penelope still heard her say, "I think it's about Stonefish."

Sam gave her his full attention. "If you need to know, I'll tell you."

She narrowed her eyes and pursed her lips before nodding. "Deal."

It was nice he was taking the younger girl seriously.

Sam lifted his gaze and scanned the room, looking straight at Penelope. "Hey, good to see you again."

Her cheeks heated, and she nodded. "Sam."

"Let's eat," Amy said, and she gave Sam a hug before dishing up an amazing smelling curry.

They took their seats and conversation revolved around the station work and Lara's school day.

"Natasha and I did our project today," Lara announced. "Matt's idea to do horse-riding was genius," she continued. "We had so many photos and it was a hit."

"So, are you two friends now?" Darcy asked.

Lara screwed up her nose. "She's all right, but I wouldn't invite her for a sleepover."

Penelope swallowed her smile. She remembered primary school hierarchies.

"What did Jordan do his project on?" Georgie asked.

Lara went bright red and glared at Georgie. "Football," she answered and then stuffed curry in her mouth to stop further questions.

"I was thinking of inviting the pony club kids out for a ride and camp out during the school holidays," Faith said.

Lara grinned. "That would be epic!"

Darcy gathered the dirty dishes and Sam asked Lara, "Are you still reading the same book?"

Lara nodded. "You want to read it to me?"

"Absolutely. You need to fill me in on what I missed."

Darcy chuckled. "Why don't you two do that while we clean up?"

"Thanks, Dad," Lara said and grabbed Sam's hand, dragging him out of the room.

"He always got out of cleaning," Brandon grumbled. "It's a gift."

Penelope smiled at the easy banter. It wasn't something she was used to. She'd rarely made it home in time to have dinner with Gerard.

Foolish to regret it now.

Amy placed mugs on the table and filled a teapot with boiling water. "Coffee or tea, Penelope?"

"Coffee, please." It was the one habit she'd yet to kick. Coffee had been her lifeline through many a late night's work and never disturbed her sleep.

By the time drinks were ready and the kitchen was clean, Sam hadn't returned. "He got sucked into the story last time," Brandon said. "If I don't get him, he'll read the entire book to Lara."

"No wonder she wanted him to read to her," Darcy said. "We have a one chapter rule most nights."

Brandon went to fetch his friend and Penelope settled next to Georgie. When Georgie had told her two couples were living in the homestead, she'd thought it would be crowded and uncomfortable, but this house was built to be filled with people. The large wooden kitchen table had to seat at least ten comfortably and everyone did their bit to help.

Sam walked back in. "I have to get a copy of the book," he said. "It's riveting."

"Is it a kid's book?" Penelope asked.

"Fantasy. Lara's big into reading."

"She's a far better reader than I am," Matt said.

Faith poured the drinks and Georgie said, "Let's talk about why we're here." She squeezed Matt's hand. "Penelope needs to know about Stonefish."

Sam didn't seem surprised by the name.

"She caught some poachers on the reef yesterday and they held a gun on her," Georgie continued. "Could be another one of Stonefish's operations."

"Where should we start?" Darcy asked.

"Stonefish Enterprises tried to buy Retribution Ridge," Brandon said, his voice flat. "When Dad refused, they arranged for the car crash which killed our parents."

What? Penelope looked at Georgie to confirm. Georgie nodded, expression sombre. Penelope blinked, trying to figure out what to say. "Why did they want the station?"

"We didn't know at first," Darcy replied. "They tried sabotage and kidnapping to force us to sign."

"Is that why Matt was kidnapped?" Penelope asked.

"No. That was for revenge," Georgie said. "They kidnapped Lara. They have a habit of finding people's weakness, using their love for family to force people to do their dirty work."

"We got our first real insight when Ed gave Tess a lift here from Perth," Faith said. "She witnessed the man we thought was in charge murder someone."

"Ed?" Penelope asked.

"Youngest brother," Amy explained. "You'll get used to everyone soon enough. He lives in Perth and was coming up for our wedding."

"Anyway," Brandon continued, "Tess discovered the secret cellar, and then last month Georgie found the journal of our original ancestor, the one who first settled the area."

Secret cellar. OK, now they had to be making fun of her. She scanned their faces, and no one had the glimmer of a smile. "Are you serious?"

"It's a lot to take in," Georgie agreed. "We've had time to process it, and Sam was here for a lot, so he's up to speed."

"Last month, Georgie and I ran across some animal smugglers who were part of Stonefish's operations," Matt said. "The police got involved, and I was kidnapped as revenge for ruining the operation."

"I shot the kidnapper in self-defence," Georgie said. She traced a scratch on the table. "That's why the PAWS rifle was taken."

Penelope gasped. "Did you kill him?"

Georgie nodded and Matt wrapped his arm around her and pulled her close, neither of them looking at the others.

Brandon narrowed his eyes, but said nothing.

"Lilian's journal revealed there's treasure buried somewhere on the Ridge and we believe that's why Stonefish wants the Ridge," Faith said.

Penelope shook her head. "You can't be serious— kidnapping, buried treasure, murder, and secret cellars?"

"We're sick of it, to be honest," Amy said.

"Stonefish has more than the animal smuggling operation up here," Brandon added.

"Brandon and I are going diving tomorrow to see if we can find anything out at the Muiron Islands," Sam said.

Penelope glanced at him. He'd been silent throughout. "Like what?"

Sam shrugged.

Her brain worked furiously. "You think those poachers are part of the bigger operation?"

"We've learnt not to underestimate them," Darcy said.

"They might have been diving for another reason and taken advantage of the crayfish," Sam added.

"Shouldn't the police be handling this?"

"They're understaffed," Brandon said.

Sam smiled. "Besides, we might find nothing."

"Have you told Dot?" Penelope couldn't claim to know Dot well, but she was fairly certain the sergeant wouldn't appreciate them investigating—military training or not.

"We'll tell her if we find something," Brandon said.

It wasn't illegal to go diving, but they were skirting the line between right and wrong, and Penelope didn't cope well so close to the line. What if she said nothing, and they were injured?

Her stomach swirled and her skin tightened. "You should tell her now." She cringed at the prim, uptight sound to her voice.

"Better to ask for forgiveness than permission," Brandon joked.

She shook her head. "That implies you know what you're doing is wrong."

"It's just a dive, like I did yesterday." Sam's placating tone did nothing to make her feel better.

"I don't like it."

"I told you we should have waited until tomorrow to tell her," Sam said to Georgie.

"She has a right to know," Georgie retorted. "It could be dangerous out there if she's clueless."

Penelope gritted her teeth. When had she become someone who needed to be soothed and handled? She'd once been the one who would have suggested the adventure in the first place. They were going no matter what she said, so she had two choices; tell Dot herself, therefore losing Georgie's trust, or go with them to ensure they stayed out of trouble. But that meant diving again.

She closed her eyes and breathed deeply. Only one option would allow her to respect herself. She forced herself to speak. "If it's just a dive, then you won't mind if I come along."

Both men scowled. "Don't you have work?" Sam asked.

"The reef is my work. If this is bigger than two poachers, it's my duty to investigate and inform the Department of Fisheries and Parks and Wildlife."

"We don't know what we might find," Brandon said.

"All the more reason I go with you so I can document it." She kept eye contact with Sam, not allowing her fear to show. Gerard had called it her ice princess look. If she could change their mind, she wouldn't have to go through with this.

"She's got a point," Georgie said. "Having her along may temper your boof-head tendencies."

Brandon and Sam both turned to her with identical protestation on their faces. "What boof-head tendencies?" Brandon asked.

"The ones that make you think you're invincible and lead you into danger," Georgie said. "Pen will keep you honest."

Brandon looked as if he wanted to protest some more, but Sam said, "Sure, Penny can come."

Shock sliced through her at his acceptance, and she wasn't sure whether it was because of his agreement or the fact he'd called her Penny. It was such an unfamiliar name, but she liked the way he said it.

"Great," she said, though she felt anything but happy about the prospect. "What time do we head out?"

Chapter 8

Sam would eat his hat if Penelope was happy with what she'd just agreed to. She was good at hiding her true emotions, but he'd been with her after the poaching incident and the brief lowering of her guard had given him an insight on how she was feeling.

But he couldn't tell whether her unhappiness was because they weren't telling the police, or because of something else.

Would Stonefish appear when they went diving tomorrow?

He'd raised his suspicions with Brandon and they'd decided to use this as a test. If Stonefish wanted to stop them, out at Muiron was the perfect opportunity.

They agreed to meet the next morning and then talk turned to the buried treasure. He had cringed when the topic had come up. Obviously Brandon hadn't shared his concerns about Penelope with the rest of the family, otherwise they never would have mentioned the treasure.

The Stokes had made little progress since finding the journal, but since Lara was convinced the treasure was out there somewhere, and they were so desperate for money, everyone was still trying to solve the riddle.

"On the weekend, we're going to the gulf to search for Clarke's grave," Faith said. "You're welcome to join us."

Penelope smiled, her face lighting up. "I can search for the treasure too?"

Amy handed her a photocopy of the journal. "We need all the help we can get."

The redhead had a luminescence about her when she smiled. It was a pity it happened so rarely. Though, if she hadn't been the type to get excited over the hint of buried treasure, then she wasn't Sam's type of woman.

Funny how it hadn't taken long to go from irritation to admiration with her. He hoped she wasn't involved with Stonefish, but he'd be foolish not to check.

Penelope stifled a yawn. "Thank you." She started reading from page one.

So methodical. Sam smiled. While the others made plans for the weekend excursion, he watched Penelope read. She covered another yawn and Sam checked his watch. After nine, so not too late, but it was an hour's drive back to town and the Ridge started work at sunrise.

"It's time I made a move," he said.

Brandon nodded. "I'll meet you at the marina in the morning."

Penelope gave another yawn and Georgie nudged him, nodding to her. She must have brought Penelope out because he'd only seen Georgie's car when he'd arrived. Georgie waggled her eyebrows at him and he chuckled. He knew when he was being set up. Georgie had no intentions of driving back to town tonight, not when she could stay here with Matt.

"Hey, Penelope. Can I give you a lift back to town?"

Penelope looked up and blinked. "Oh, I got a lift with Georgie." She glanced at Georgie, who had slid her arm around Matt and was resting her head on his shoulder.

Subtle, not.

Penelope grimaced as she reached the same conclusion he had. "A lift would be great. I don't want to interrupt the lovebirds."

Georgie smiled. "Thanks, Pen. I'll see you at work tomorrow."

As they made their way outside, Brandon pulled Sam aside. "See if you can talk her out of coming with us tomorrow."

Sam nodded. "I'm pretty sure it won't be an option, but I'll try."

He hugged Amy and Faith, and then murmured to Georgie, "You've got some explaining to do."

She grinned, wide-eyed and innocent. "I don't know what you're talking about."

He got into his white Ford Ranger and waited for Penelope to get settled before heading towards the main road.

Penelope sighed, long and heartfelt. "They're a lovely family."

"The best," Sam agreed. "It was one of the reasons I decided to move here."

"You're not close to your own family?"

He thought about it. "It's a different dynamic. The Stokes are just... easy."

Despite everything they'd been through, they were still supportive and welcoming. To their detriment at times—trusting the wrong people.

He glanced at Penelope. She had seemed surprised by everything they'd told her, but it could be an act, or maybe Stonefish hadn't told her much. He should investigate her background before he went down the path of trust. He could ask Sherlock to do that, if only to give him a mission. There had to be a good reason she would move all the way up here for work.

"Georgie was welcoming immediately," Penelope said. "I was worried because Mitchell mentioned she'd applied for my job."

"Georgie's a fish," Sam said. "She loves the water, but it sounds as if she's enjoying being a park ranger."

"I hope so. I feel like the interloper."

"No need. Georgie doesn't hold a grudge. She instantly forgave Brandon for staying away for over a decade."

"What happened?"

"Long story and another one that's not mine to tell," Sam said. "How was your day today?"

"I wasn't held at gunpoint, so that was a plus," Penelope answered.

He was pleased she could joke about it.

"I called Dot today to ask her about the connection between the poachers and the animal smugglers."

His fingers tightened on the steering wheel. "What did she say?"

"Not much," Penelope replied. "What should I say if she calls me tomorrow?"

He remembered what Sherlock said about needing boundaries. "Tell her whatever makes you comfortable."

"You're not going to swear me to silence?"

"What we're doing isn't illegal," he said. "Dot won't like it, but she can't stop us." He slowed as he spotted glowing eyes on the side of the road. The kangaroo stayed where it was as they passed. "And I understand you need to follow the rules."

She was silent and he glanced at her.

"You're not who I expected," she said. "I thought you were some military cowboy who played by his own rules."

He chuckled. "I've been accused of that a time or

two," he admitted.

"But you didn't demand I rescind the suspension."

"It's done now. We've reallocated all the passengers to other vessels or refunded money. There's nothing to do except wait it out. And with this poacher stuff happening, it gives me an opportunity to investigate." He wanted Stonefish stopped as much as the Stokes did. Too many lives had been lost or threatened. "Why did you move up here?"

If she was surprised by the change of topic, she didn't show it. She pressed her lips together. "My best friend told me I was a coward if I didn't."

Sam choked out a laugh. "You don't look like someone who would bow under peer pressure."

"There were reasons she called me a coward. She said it was time I took a risk again." A soft sigh. "And then she said I could go live with her if it all went pear shaped."

"A dare and a backup," Sam said. "I like the sound of your friend."

"Ceiveon would like you."

"Does she like a dashingly handsome man, with a wicked sense of humour and who can handle a gun?"

Penelope laughed, a burst loud like a trumpet which cut off too soon and then she giggled. "Modesty is one of her highest traits."

Sam grinned. That laugh was something else. He wanted to hear it again. "Then she's going to love me," Sam said. "Modest, chivalrous, and I call my mother once a week when I can."

She chuckled. "Pity she's already married."

Sam snapped his fingers. "Damn it. The good ones are always taken."

"You don't know anything about her."

"She's got great taste, and she challenges and supports her friends. That's a pretty good start."

"Yeah, she's pretty special."

"Tell me when you invite her up and I'll get her on board the boat," Sam said.

"Thanks. She'd like that."

This easy banter was nice, but a question was burning on his tongue. Should he ask it and risk ruining the mood? They were still a way from town. "You want to talk about the reasons she dared you?"

"Not right now." She shifted in her seat, turning to him. "It's your turn to answer a question."

"Fire away."

"Were you scared when facing the gun?"

"Terrified." He tapped the steering wheel. "But my choices were to ignore it and let you face it on your own, or do something. I couldn't look the other way."

"They teach you that in the military?"

"Some," he admitted. "If you can't run into danger, you're not much use." He shrugged off the tension brought back by memories of his time overseas. "I took a calculated risk. The dive boat would have heard a gunshot and chances were someone would have looked to see what was going on. I figured the poachers would run rather than fight if given the chance, so I gave them an out."

"How long have you been diving?"

The change in topic surprised him. "About ten years. I get out as often as I can. What about you?"

"Same. I haven't been out since… in a while."

Definitely a story there. "Do you want to stay on board tomorrow?"

Out of the corner of his eye he saw her bob her head, but she said, "No. I'll be fine."

"You can change your mind at any time." He'd get to the bottom of it, eventually.

"I'll be fine," she reiterated, sounding more like she was trying to convince herself than him.

Instead of pushing, he asked, "Will Ceiveon visit while you're here?"

"She said she would, but it will soon be too hot to be pleasant."

"At least you'll be on the ocean every day. It'll be cooler than on land."

"What will you do when the tour season is over?"

It was a good question and one he didn't have an answer for. "I don't know. People sometimes need a charter boat, and mine can convert to sleep people on the deck. Otherwise I might help Brandon on the Ridge."

He slowed again as wild goats bounded across the road. Penelope clutched the door handle.

"Why do they do that?"

"They don't know any better." He kept his speed low and switched on the spotlights. His high beams lit a decent stretch of road, but the spotlights were like driving during the day.

"I vowed to avoid driving after dusk and before dawn up here."

"Good idea if you can, though you have to watch out for emus in town sometimes."

"Crazy," she said, shaking her head but with a smile in her voice.

Underneath the prim exterior was a warmth waiting to come out. Could he break through it? "We were doing exercises out of the Northern Territory once and we had to land on a remote runway except there was a buffalo in the middle of it that wouldn't move. When we were finally able to land, it charged the plane."

Penelope turned to him, disbelief on her face. "Now you're making things up."

"Cross my heart and hope to die," Sam swore. She laughed, that trumpeting laugh of hers, and he grinned, his heart light. "What's the strangest thing you've seen?”

"I saw a crocodile that had caught a small shark once,” Penelope said. "I was in the Kimberley doing some work experience while I was at university and the crocodile dragged it to shore to eat.”

He raised his eyebrows, impressed. "That must have been a sight.”

"I'll have to show you my photos sometime.”

"Sounds great. How about dinner tomorrow night?”

Silence.

He glanced at her and wasn't sure whether to be amused or offended by the complete surprise on her face. "The brewery does a good pizza,” he continued, hoping the casualness of the offer would relax her.

"I don't know,” Penelope said. "We work together.”

"Not really,” he said.

"Others might think I'm favouring you.”

He laughed. "What, by suspending my licence?”

"Or that you're trying to make me change my mind.” She ducked her head.

Sam shrugged. "I don't think you will. You've made your decision and I respect that. It's just two people sharing a meal and photos of interesting things they've seen. I can bring some photos of my own if you like.”

She hesitated. "Can I wait until after the dive tomorrow to decide?”

He wanted a yes. He didn't want to wait. "What would Ceiveon say?”

She sighed. "I'm going to regret telling you that, aren't I?”

"I'll only use it when I really want something.”

"Why do you really want to go to dinner with me?”

"Because I find you fascinating, and I want to spend more time with you.”

She screwed up her nose. "You like the stickler for the rules who won't bend?”

He took a moment to decide how to word his reply. "I like the woman with the loud laugh and sense of humour," he said. "I have an army buddy who was very much a by-the-book kind of guy, and it took a while to get him to open up."

"And now he's the life of the party?"

"Not so much. He lost part of his leg during his last mission and is still recovering."

"I'm sorry."

All at once, he wanted to talk to someone about Sherlock. "I'm doing my best to get through to him, but he doesn't want to talk. The army was his life."

"Does he blame himself for the accident?"

That had never occurred to him. "I don't know."

"It's always harder to recover from something when it's your fault." The words were whispered.

"Are you speaking from experience?" he asked, making a mental note to ask Dobby for the report on Sherlock's accident.

"Yes."

"Do you want to talk about it?"

"No."

"Have you spoken to Ceiveon about it?"

She sighed. "Yes."

Good. "Well, if you ever need another sounding board, I'm available."

"Thank you, Sam."

He liked his name on her lips. The quiet murmur, the heartfelt words. "So are we on for dinner tomorrow night?"

A slight chuckle. "All right, but I reserve the right to cancel."

"All right." He'd make sure she wouldn't want to.

Chapter 9

Before Sam left to go diving the next morning, he called Sherlock. When Sherlock didn't answer, he called Kylie.

"He goes home today," Kylie said. "You won't have anyone who can ask him to answer."

Yeah, that was one of his concerns. "He'll have some home visits for a while, won't he?"

"As long as he doesn't decline them."

Maybe he could tell Ed about Sherlock. Ed wouldn't have an issue checking on him while the team was away. The only problem would be getting Ed to promise not to tell Amy and Brandon about it. "I'll sort something out."

"You're a good friend, Sam," Kylie responded. "Try him again and I'll send a nurse to his room."

Sam rang his friend and this time Sherlock answered. "What do you want now?" Again with the angry growl, but at least he was talking.

Sam went with mock innocence. "Hey, I can call you just to chat. What makes you think I want something?"

A pause. "So you don't want something?"

Sam laughed. "OK, you've got me. I need you to investigate someone for me."

"I'm not a private investigator."

So literal. "No, but you know people, and can find out anything."

Sherlock snorted. "Who am I investigating?"

"Her name's Penelope Fraser." Sam ignored the twinge of guilt. He was fairly sure she wouldn't be involved with Stonefish, but they'd been fooled before.

"Where does she work?"

"Parks and Wildlife Services."

"You want me to investigate the woman who suspended your licence?" Sherlock sounded incredulous.

"Not for that reason," he said. "I need to make sure Stonefish Enterprises hasn't got to her."

"Didn't the two main guys get killed?"

"We don't know who the head guys are," Sam said. "Stonefish have a habit of blackmailing people into doing their bidding. Penelope blames herself for something that happened in her past."

"What is it?" Curiosity tinged Sherlock's voice.

"She won't say."

"Then how do you know?"

"Because she's hinted at it." This was his chance to lure Sherlock here. "A couple of days ago she caught some poachers on the reef, and they pulled a gun on her. Georgie decided Penelope needed to know about Stonefish, and Amy gave her a copy of the journal with the details of the treasure."

"Amy trusts her?"

"Yeah, but I've got to be certain."

"Is Amy in danger?"

Finally some genuine concern for someone else. It had been missing for a long time. "I don't know. It's possible."

"What's your gut telling you about Penelope?"

Sam swore under his breath. "I like her, Sherlock.

My gut might be ignoring signs."

"You always pick the difficult ones." A quiet laugh.

"Then you'll help?"

Another pause, this one longer. "Email me her details, but I won't promise anything."

Relief filled him. "That's great. Thanks. You need any help to get settled down there?" Sam hoped the question wouldn't shut him down.

"I'm fine. I'll contact you if I find something." Sherlock hung up.

Sam sighed. It was the most he'd got from Sherlock in weeks. Hopefully it meant he was improving. Perhaps visiting him every day hadn't been the right thing to do. Maybe it had just reminded his friend of all he'd lost. He should have thought of that.

But he wouldn't regret it.

He would never abandon his friend.

***

This was absolutely the worst idea Penelope had had in her life. It beat her decision to move to Retribution Bay hands down. Why she'd thought she could do this was beyond her.

The sick swirling in her gut had started last night when she'd woken from a nightmare about that terrible day. Then she'd tossed and turned, unable to get back to sleep. When she'd admitted defeat and got up, making herself a very strong cup of coffee, her eyes were grainy and her head thumped.

Going into the room where she'd stored her scuba gear had increased the uneasiness to storm-like proportions.

Penelope placed a hand on her stomach and focused on her breath like her psychologist had taught her.

She could do this.

Scuba diving had once been one of her greatest joys.

Until…. Her breath quickened and her gut clenched as she pushed the thought away, trying to clear her mind and focus on her breathing.

Long, slow in-breath, long slow out-breath.

When she could breathe without gasping, she methodically reviewed what she might need, placing the items into her backpack in case they fell out of her BCD jacket in transit: waterproof pad and pen to take notes, dive torch, waterproof camera, safety marker buoy. She made sure her dive watch was working correctly and cycled through the functions, placed her weights in the BCD, and examined the regulator hoses for signs of wear. All looked good. All she had to do was fill up her tank on the way to the marina.

She should tell Declan what she had planned. He would tell her to leave things alone. With the thought giving her hope, she packed her equipment into the back of the car and drove to work.

By the time she arrived, she'd convinced herself Declan would tell her not to get involved, and her steps were confident as she walked into the building.

"Morning, Karen. Is Declan in?"

The receptionist nodded. "Check his office."

Declan sat behind his computer, staring at the screen, his expression one of displeasure. Penelope rapped on the door frame. When Declan glanced up, she asked, "Is this a bad time?"

Declan sighed and pushed back from his chair. "Just reading the latest from senior management. They really don't understand how things work up here."

"Maybe they should come up and spend a week shadowing one of us."

Declan laughed. "Like we'd get them to leave their cushy offices. What can I help you with?"

Penelope smiled. "I'm planning to head back to Muiron today. I wanted to check the poachers hadn't left any pots or nets behind."

"Good idea, but you can't dive alone. Mitchell can go with you tomorrow."

Penelope stared at him, her gut clenching again. She'd been certain he would refuse. "You're fine with it?"

He nodded. "Between you and me, something strange is going on in town—first with Matt being kidnapped by animal smugglers and now the poachers. I haven't seen this much illegal activity in a while."

Damn it. "Georgie invited me out to the Ridge for dinner last night, and when I mentioned I was planning to dive the area, both Sam Hackett and Brandon Stokes offered to come with me." A slight lie wouldn't hurt, but maybe Declan wouldn't want her going down with civilians.

A brief hesitation. "Great. Check their dive cards before you go. Make sure they have licences."

Penelope smiled. "Of course." She'd almost guarantee they wouldn't bring them and she wouldn't have to go down. "I'll call you if I find anything."

The horrible nauseous feeling built again as she read her emails and tidied her desk, delaying the inevitable until she was in danger of being late. She couldn't put it off any longer.

She waved goodbye to Karen as she left the building, her heart racing.

Breathe.

Her hand shook as she inserted the key.

First step, start the car.

Her wrist twisted of its own volition. Great what muscle memory could do. The engine purred to life and she had the vehicle in reverse before she could think about it.

Keep going.

Still breathing long slow breaths, she drove to the

local dive shop to get her tank filled. "Brilliant morning for a dive," the guy who filled it said. "Visibility should be at least ten metres, maybe even fifteen."

Penelope managed a weak smile. "Yeah, should be great."

At the marina she parked close to where the PAWS boat was penned and carried her equipment down. By the time she'd finished, Sam and Brandon had arrived.

Licences.

She let out a shaky breath as they approached her, each carrying a bag of equipment and an oxygen tank as if they weighed next to nothing. Sam smiled that easy grin of his and the fluttering in her stomach clashed with the nausea. She forced her own smile. "Morning. Before we start, I need to see your dive licences."

Sam set his things on the jetty and pulled out his wallet, handing her his licence. She took it, annoyed at the way her fingers trembled. It was valid.

She handed it back and glanced at Brandon. "Your card."

He shook his head. "I didn't bring it. Sam will vouch for me. We got it together."

Penelope stiffened her spine. "No. I'm sorry, but I can't let you dive without seeing a licence."

Brandon's incredulity was clear. "It was our idea to dive. You wanted to come with us."

Inwardly she cringed, but she kept her tone no-nonsense. "It's a PAWS requirement."

"Shall we take your boat?" Brandon asked Sam.

Sam studied her and she met his gaze, determined to keep the fear out of her eyes.

"You don't have to come with us," he said.

She had to do her job, had to move past this fear. Her therapist had told her she should dive as soon as possible after the incident, but she hadn't been able to. It was now or never. She gave a curt nod. "Yes, I do."

Sam turned to Brandon. "You can be our watch," he said. "Stay on deck."

"All right."

This was such a bad idea. Sam should have been annoyed, Brandon should have insisted, and they should have gone off on their own. Then she couldn't have dived without a buddy. Why couldn't either of them get uptight and angry about being told what to do?

"Fine," she managed. "Stow your gear on board and we'll head off." She busied herself with doing her pre-start checks and by the time she was done, the men were perched on the edge of the boat waiting patiently for her to finish.

She'd never felt so pedantic.

As she handed out the life vests, Sam focused on her, his eyes probing as if trying to figure out what she was hiding. She looked away and cast off the lines before motoring out of the harbour.

Penelope ignored the men behind her except for the occasional glance to make sure they hadn't fallen overboard without her hearing. The engine was noisy and Sam and Brandon had their heads close together talking.

Probably planning what to do when they got out there.

She almost hoped they came up with a legitimate excuse why none of them could go under.

No. It was time to be brave.

Ceiveon would tell her she could do this.

But the horror of the memory chilled her.

She slowed the boat as she approached the area where she'd stopped the poachers. Circling, she stopped above a sandy patch. Brandon climbed onto the bow and threw out the anchor, the splash making Penelope flinch. She turned to find Sam had already slipped on his wetsuit and had attached his tank and regulator to the BCD.

So organised.

"Ready when you are."

The powerful urge to throw up had her place a hand on her stomach as she unzipped her bag and withdrew her wetsuit.

One step at a time. She'd worn bathers underneath her clothes, so she changed into the wetsuit, using the long strap to zip it at the back. Meanwhile, Sam had attached her tank to the BCD and the regulator to the tank. Her BCD already had the correct weights in it.

She double checked his work, both on her own gear and his. When she finished, he smiled at her. "Happy?"

Not even close.

Her throat closed over as he slid on his fins and clipped up the jacket. There had to be some way she could stop this madness.

Her fingers shook as she clipped the safety marker buoy to her BCD and filled her pockets with the gear in her backpack. Then she struggled to get her fins on, before Brandon helped her with the tank.

The click of the BCD vest was like a gunshot in the air, and she flinched as she did each one. Finally she put her goggles on.

"Ready?" Sam asked.

"No!" She stepped forward, almost tripping on her fins. His eyes widened, and she swallowed her panic. "We haven't done our buddy checks."

"You've already checked the equipment," Brandon pointed out.

"The recommendation is doing buddy checks," she stated, and ran through the acronym in her head. "BCD." She checked Sam's was fastened correctly. "Weight belt." He had one separate to his jacket, so she made sure it was sitting where it should and was done up correctly. "Regulator." Air came out when she pressed the release, and just to make certain she checked where it attached to the tank as well. "Air." The tank was on and the air flowed. Final check. "Do you feel ready to go down?" She lifted her gaze to his eyes only to see his concern and compassion.

"Yes, I do. Do you?"

Penelope glanced down and nodded while he completed the same checks with her equipment. She would do this. She was protecting the reef and the animals who lived there.

"Penny, if you don't want to dive, you don't have to," Sam murmured as he checked the air. "No one is going to judge you."

She wasn't doing a good job of hiding her fear. It wouldn't make him feel confident about going down with her. She blinked the moisture from her eyes before she looked at him. "I need to."

"We'll take it slow."

She nodded again and retrieved her waterproof camera from the bag, attaching the strap to her wrist. When she looked up, it was in time to see Brandon nod at something Sam had said and then glance at her.

Great, now they were talking about her. With far more confidence than she felt, she said, "Shall we go?"

At Sam's nod, she leaned backwards and fell into the water.

The shock of the cold made her suck in a deep breath and then another one as she inflated her BCD and waited for Sam. He splashed in only moments later and swam over to her.

"We'll go down and then explore the area?" he suggested.

"Yes."

He placed the regulator into his mouth and lifted the air valve up. As he sank below the water, fear gripped

Penelope. She lunged for him, dragging him up. "Wait!"

"What's wrong?"

Her brain fumbled for something to say. "Checks," she blurted. "I don't know I did the checks correctly."

"You did them more thoroughly than I've ever seen them done." Sam paused and then asked, "What happened the last time you dived, Penny?"

She pushed away from him, every nerve in her body primed to flee. She shook her head. "I'm fine."

"Clearly you're not."

Frustration and fear collided like a frontal assault of two charging armies. "I need to be."

"Then what can I do to help?"

Tears sprang to her eyes, unwanted, but unstoppable. "Humour me. Let me check. Go slow."

He swam closer and spun so she had access to the tank to check it was turned on. She ran through her checks again and when she was finished, Sam slipped his hand into hers.

"Slowly?" It was more a question whether she wanted to go down, and she nodded.

His firm, warm grip grounded her. Here was a man who'd been in the military, who had faced many life-threatening situations. He wouldn't panic if something went wrong. She was sure of it. Penelope lifted her air valve and together they sank beneath the surface. She kept her eyes locked on Sam's for any sign something was wrong, but his clear blue gaze was soft like a baby's blanket, calm and comforting.

Emelia had been calm until she'd run out of air.

Then no amount of tugging on her arm had got through to her. Suddenly Penelope was transported back to that horrific day.

Emelia stopping in front of her, slicing her hand across her throat in the no air signal, her eyes bugging out of her head. Penelope fumbling for her spare regulator, then looking up to see Emelia was already ascending.

Penelope had grabbed her fin, pulled her down and Emelia had fought, kicking and punching, not processing the spare regulator Penelope had held out to her so they could share the air as they ascended. She'd slipped from Penelope's grasp and Penelope had watched helplessly as her friend had surfaced alone.

They'd been diving all week, to various depths, and they'd followed a rare sea snake to almost thirty metres on this day. It required both a decompression stop and a safety stop. By the time Penelope had safely surfaced, Emelia was complaining of shortness of breath, pins and needles and dizziness. She hadn't even got on to the boat by herself. It had taken Penelope precious time to get her on board and then radio for help.

Too long.

They'd been at Ashmore Reef, far from civilisation and emergency services. Penelope had comforted Emelia the best she could while they waited for medical evacuation. By the time it arrived, it was too late.

It wasn't until Emelia's body had been taken away that Penelope examined the equipment. Emelia's tank had been empty.

She'd gone back through the day, trying to remember the level it had been during the morning checks, and that's when she remembered they hadn't done the checks. Emelia had spotted the rare sea snake in the water and had gone in before they could do them.

Penelope should have done them.

Had she checked Sam's tank level?

Panic gripped Penelope, and she grabbed Sam's tank gauge, the numbers blurry as she tried to read it. No, this couldn't happen again. She wouldn't let it.

Sam waved his hand in front of her face and she

blinked, glancing at him. He gave her the 'OK' signal, and she shook her head. She couldn't do this. All she wanted to do was run through the checks over and over and over again to ensure she hadn't missed anything. She gestured up and together they headed to the surface.

Penelope dumped her regulator and gasped for air as her head popped out of the water. "I'm sorry," she said to Sam. "I'm sorry. I'm sorry."

Sam inflated her BCD for her and then squeezed her hand. "Slow breaths, Penny. It's all right. We're both safe." He gestured the OK signal to Brandon on the boat. Keeping his head while she lost hers.

"I thought I could do it," she said. "But I keep seeing her face."

"Whose face?"

"Emelia's." She had to tell him. He deserved to know. "She ran out of air. Panicked."

His eyes showed his compassion as he held out his tank gauge. "We've both got full tanks, Penny."

"I know." But she couldn't do this. Not today. "Take Brandon down."

"Even though you haven't seen his licence?"

She flinched. "Do you swear to me he's qualified?" She didn't blink as she stared at him.

"I swear."

"Fine. Get me back on the boat. I'll do his checks." They'd come all this way and someone needed to ensure the poachers weren't doing more harm to the animals and the reef. She'd be failing in her duty if someone didn't go down.

Sam circled his hand in the air, some sort of signal which had Brandon reaching for his wetsuit. By the time Penelope was on the boat, and had removed her equipment, he was suited up ready to go. She passed him the camera and then ran through the checks twice.

"Promise me you're licensed to dive?"

His lips twitched at her choice of words, but then he was solemn as he nodded. "I promise. We'll be fine down there. Sam and I buddy all the time."

She checked his equipment one last time before she forced herself to step back. "You're good to go."

Sam was still in the water, and Brandon joined him with a splash. She watched as they sank beneath the surface, her hands gripping the edge of the boat. They would be fine, both of them.

They were trained to be calm in an emergency.

She, on the other hand, was a complete mess.

She sat on one chair and placed her head in her hands. Why couldn't she go down again? She'd checked everything numerous times, she knew they wouldn't run out of air, and they weren't diving to the depths she and Emelia had been diving.

Ceiveon had tried to get her to go diving again, but Penelope had always had an excuse not to go. She hadn't fooled Ceiveon, who had insisted she pack her dive gear when she moved and had said she expected to be taken to all the good dive spots when she visited.

Well, Penelope had tried.

She scanned the water for the men, but couldn't see them. Her chest squeezed and she breathed through the panic again.

She was a hypocrite. All her talk about doing things by the book and she'd let Brandon go down without checking his licence. What if they'd both lied? What if they had an accident?

Penelope grabbed her phone and, seeing she had reception, she dialled Amy's number. She should have considered this earlier. When Amy answered, Penelope took a deep breath. "Hey, it's Penelope."

"Hi. Is everything all right? I thought you would all be diving by now."

Penelope swallowed to clear the lump in her throat. "Sam and Brandon are, and I have some things to do on the island," she lied. "But I need to write a report of the dive and Brandon left his dive licence at home. Are you able to send me a photo of it?"

"Oh, sure. He keeps a bunch of cards in a drawer. Let me see if it's there."

There were the sounds of rummaging from the other end and Penelope stared at the water, her heart racing as she waited.

"Here it is. Give me a second and I'll message you the photo."

Penelope exhaled. "Thank you. I'll see you on the weekend."

She hung up and then examined the photo when it came through. Definitely qualified. A little of the tension in her muscles relaxed.

Needing something to do, she unpacked her BCD, drying everything and replacing her gear in her backpack. Then she reviewed the other items in there, checking the first aid kit was up to date, and her survival kit had everything it needed.

They still weren't back yet.

Her skin tight, she kept her gaze on the water, scanning the area in case they surfaced away from the boat. It was almost an hour before they did. Definitely experienced divers.

She moved to the back of the boat to take their fins from them. "What did you find?"

Sam hauled himself aboard, tank and all. "Nothing."

Brandon joined them and he handed over the camera. "Got some good shots of the marine life. It's thriving."

Penelope flicked through the photos while the men dealt with their dive gear. Relief swept through her. This wasn't something to do with Stonefish, it was simply some rich arseholes who thought they could flout the rules.

She exhaled and turned the boat for home.

Chapter 10

It was six-thirty before Sam allowed himself to knock on Penelope's door. He wanted answers, wanted to make sure she was OK after today's freak out. He hadn't liked to leave her after the dive trip, but she'd insisted she had more work to do after she'd dropped them at the marina. The tension hadn't left her until they'd arrived back and unloaded the boat. She'd smiled and waved as if she was fine and left them to put their gear in the car.

He didn't believe her. He wanted to find out what happened to Emelia. Plus, she had agreed to go to dinner with him, not that they'd confirmed a time after the dive incident.

The door opened and Penelope stood there, still wearing her PAWS uniform. Her shoulders slumped in resignation. "Sam."

He'd had cooler welcomes, but not by much. "We had a dinner date, and I wanted to see how you are."

She opened the door further and gestured him in. "I'm fine."

The house was cool, the air conditioner on low,

though it wasn't overly hot outside. A single couch with a jumbled-up piece of knitting on it—maybe the beginnings of a scarf or blanket. It was hard to tell whether the random holes in it were intended, but they were big enough to be noticeable even with the multi-coloured yarn she was using.

A modest-sized television, sitting on a wooden cabinet, and a single coffee table. Not much for someone who had to be in her early thirties.

No photos lined the walls or were displayed in photo frames and only an e-reader on the table, which meant he couldn't tell what books she was into.

"I'm sorry. I forgot about dinner." She gestured to the kitchen bench where vegetables were laid out ready for chopping and a packet of corn chips was open. Without asking, she poured him a glass of cold water and handed it to him.

"You've had an emotional day."

She looked at him. "What do you want to know?"

Straight to the point. He could appreciate that. "How's Emelia now?"

Penelope closed her eyes and he knew the answer before she spoke. "She's dead. She died before we could get back to shore."

Fuck. He reached out and brushed her arm. "I'm sorry."

She swayed towards him and then stepped away, getting another glass for herself. "I tried to save her."

"What happened?" Two stools were next to the kitchen bench, and he perched on one, while Penelope stood on the other side and chopped cucumber for the salad she was making.

"We'd been diving for almost a week. We were researching sea snakes out at Ashmore Reef and getting some fantastic data. Our last morning while we were preparing to dive, we saw a rare species, and we didn't want to miss the opportunity to track it, so we jumped in after it without doing our checks." She transferred the cucumber to a bowl and chopped a tomato. "Emelia was always more disorganised, slower to start in the mornings, so I'd prepared my gear, but hadn't done hers."

Sam could see where this was going. "She didn't have a full tank of air?"

Penelope shook her head. "It was the same tank as she'd gone down with the day before. Might have had forty bars if she was lucky." She sighed. "I didn't realise, didn't even think of it until she panicked. We were both so enthralled by the snake."

"Why didn't she take your extra reg?"

Penelope glanced up, misery in her eyes. "I don't know. I thrust it at her, but either she didn't register it, or she thought I was low too... she pushed me away and swam for the surface." She stared at him. "We'd been diving deep for days. We'd been down for a while. I had to do the safety stop."

Her eyes begged him to understand, and he did. "If you'd followed her, you might be dead too."

"I had a full tank. We could have shared all the way to the surface."

He walked around the bench, unable to ignore the pain in her voice. "People panic all the time. It's not rational, it's instinctive. You did your best." He stroked her arm and she turned to him.

"I should have done better."

"You couldn't have. She was past reason." He slipped his arms around her and though she stiffened for a split second, she then relaxed and softened, melting into him. A couple of red curls tickled his nose and he shifted, running a hand over her hair to brush it away. She smelled like salt and ocean, but underneath that was a hint of something else, a citrus, lemony scent which probably came from body soap or shampoo. It suited her—sweet yet sharp.

Penelope trembled in his arms and her breath hitched. Was she crying? He snagged a tissue from the box on the counter and handed it to her.

She took it, stepping back and dabbing at her eyes. "Thank you. I'm sorry, I thought I'd cried all I could."

This woman was too hard on herself. "You're allowed to cry. It's cathartic. Besides, it's hardly a sniffle. You should see my sisters when they're upset. They could flood the room."

She smiled, which was what he was aiming for. "How many do you have?"

"Three." He gave a fake shudder. "As a teenager I learnt very early to avoid the house one week out of every month. They were very emotional teens."

Penelope chuckled. "And now?"

"Not quite as likely to cry if you look at them the wrong way," he said. "Though most weeks I just call them."

"You call your sisters every week?"

He shrugged, uncomfortable with the incredulity on her face. "Mostly. When I was away I couldn't, so I made up for it when I was back."

"You must have a good relationship with them, particularly if you were going to move in with the one who was pregnant." She continued chopping her tomato.

"We get along all right. Izzy is the baby and she's always had a special place in my heart. I was about ten when she was born and I remember holding her in my arms and she smiled at me and farted." He grinned. "Made me laugh so hard I almost wet myself."

Penelope snorted and he moved back around the bench to give her space and sat on the stool. "What are you making?"

"Vegetarian nachos."

"Are you vegetarian?"

"No, but I try to have a couple of vegetarian meals each week, and this one is easy to prepare."

He completely understood the desire for easy. In the city, he'd lived off take-away because it seemed too much of a hassle to cook for one.

"Do you want to stay for dinner?" Penelope glanced at him. "I always end up chopping more than I need or having half a tomato which goes off in the fridge, and we had arranged to go out."

"Sure. I'd love to. What can I chop?"

She pushed over the red onion. "It's your turn to cry. I'll rinse the beans."

He chuckled. "I hope you have plenty of tissues." As he chopped the onion, he asked, "Did you speak to Dot today?"

"Yes. I also told her about the dive, which she wasn't happy about. She told me to report anything strange to the police immediately, but wouldn't talk about Stonefish."

"How did she react to the name?"

She glanced at him, expression wry. "If looks could kill."

He laughed. "Yeah, I figured she wouldn't be impressed. The fewer people who know, the better as far as she's concerned."

"Are you going out to the Ridge tomorrow for the treasure hunt?"

"Wouldn't miss it. Do you want a lift out?"

She hesitated, not for long, but he noted it. "Yes, please."

"No problem." He added the onion to the bowl, and she stirred in the beans and the rest of the ingredients. Then she divided the corn chips into two bowls, stacked the salsa on top and added cheese and sour cream. She handed him a bowl and a fork.

"Thanks."

"I'm sorry I don't have a lot of furniture yet." She sat next to him at the bench.

"Are you shipping stuff up?"

She shook her head. "I gave most of the furniture to my ex. Figured I'd start from scratch."

He raised his eyebrows. "You were married?"

She shook her head. "No. We lived together for a few years." She cleared her throat. "I, ah, changed after Emelia's accident and it didn't work out."

"Changed how?" He kept his question light.

"I used to be fun," she said. "Not so strict about the rules." She stared at her bowl and shrugged. "I obsessed about work, wanting to finish Emelia's research for her, and Gerard grew tired of it."

"Then it's his loss," Sam said.

"You make no sense to me," Penelope said. "I suspended your licence, treated you terribly, and yet you keep coming back."

He smiled. "It's because you fascinate me," he replied. "Underneath the rule-abiding surface is a woman with a killer laugh, and when you drop your guard, you're lovely."

She blushed. "Gerard always compared my laugh to a goose honking."

"No, it's much more a blazing trumpet of joy."

She laughed, highlighting his argument. "That's the nicest and most ridiculous comparison I've ever heard."

"It's true. You should laugh more often." When they were finished, he collected both their empty bowls and took them to the sink to wash. "What did the police officer say to his belly button?"

She frowned at him. "I don't know."

"You're under a vest."

Her laugh burst out even as she rolled her eyes.

"That wasn't funny."

"You laughed." He went through the list of bad dad jokes Dobby always told. "Two guys walked into a bar. The third guy ducked."

She chuckled. "Where did you get these from?"

"My commanding officer knew every single dad joke and made up a few of his own. He'd subject us to them every time we shipped out together."

"Is that a new form of military torture?"

He grinned. "Should be, though I'm not sure they would translate well." He dried the dishes while Penelope cleared the bench. "What's brown and sticky?"

"I know that one. A stick." She smiled, turning from putting things in the fridge just as he turned to place the bowls on the bench. They bumped into each other, and Sam used his free hand to steady her. She stared up at him, her smile wide, their bodies only inches apart. Her eyes widened, and her gaze darted to his lips.

Yes, please.

He shifted closer and she didn't move away. Then, because he didn't want her to feel a conflict of interest, he said, "I really want to kiss you." He slid his hand down her back, drawing her closer. "It has nothing to do with our jobs, and everything to do with me finding you incredibly attractive and sweet."

A moment of uncertainty flashed across her face at the mention of work.

"What would Ceiveon say?" he murmured.

A flash of a smile before her lips were on his. Soft, warm, passionate, there was no holding back. She kissed him as if she had no doubts and he hardened. He teased her tongue with his and she pulled him closer, though they weren't far apart.

His body ached he wanted her so much. He tugged at her shirt, which was still tucked in, and finally it released to give him access to her smooth skin beneath.

She moaned softly, a sexy exhale of breath. Where was her bedroom?

Suddenly a shrill voice sang, *Girls just wanna have fun.* Penelope leapt away as if caught by her mother and spun, hand to her chest.

The culprit lay vibrating on the bench.

Penelope exhaled and laughed. "Ceiveon."

He chuckled, stepping back, still hard. "You should get that. I don't want her to think I'm taking up all your time."

"She would love it," Penelope said, and answered the phone, turning away from him as she did so. He adjusted himself as she said, "Hi, Five."

Penelope moved over to the couch and said, "Just finished dinner." She grimaced at something her friend said and glanced at Sam. "Actually, Sam came over." Her full laugh followed, and it made him smile and move closer. Something about her drew him in. "Sam owns the tour boat whose licence I suspended on Monday." She placed the phone against her chest and said, "She wants to know if you're trying to seduce me."

He grinned and held out his hand. "Can I talk to her?"

"Sure." She passed the phone over.

"Ceiveon, you interrupted my seduction attempt with your phone call." He winked at Penelope.

Ceiveon gasped. "I don't know whether to be impressed or worried you're taking advantage of Penelope."

He chuckled. "Be impressed. I made it clear the reason I wanted to kiss her was nothing to do with our work."

"And what was the reason?" Ceiveon sounded intrigued and a little amused. He liked her vibe.

"It's because underneath her prickly exterior she's

incredibly sweet, and she has a laugh that trumpets joy."

Penelope blushed and tried to take the phone from him. He wagged his finger at her and moved away.

"What did you do before you were a tour boat operator, Sam?"

He recognised the beginnings of an inquisition. "I was in the army for twelve years. Decided my last brush with death was too close and got out a week ago."

"And already you've bought a tour boat and been suspended?"

"The suspension was a misunderstanding." Penelope hovered next to him and kept reaching for the phone, so he kept moving around the room. "And the decision to buy the tour boat was made a couple of months ago when I came up here for a friend's wedding."

"Are you married?"

"No, and never have been. No children either. I own my house, have a very nice four-wheel drive and a penchant for camping."

"Family?" There was laughter in her tone.

"Three sisters, all living over east, but who I call each week. Parents are over there too, and I speak to both every Sunday." He flicked to the camera, took a selfie and sent it to her. "Photo on its way."

"Any police record?"

"All misunderstandings with the law are sealed behind a juvenile record, or I talked my way out of them."

Her phone dinged as the photo arrived. "Nice photo. I think I like you," Ceiveon said.

"I know I like you," Sam replied. "If you hadn't dared Penelope to come up here, I never would have met her."

"She told you that?"

"Yeah."

"Did she tell you the reason?" Her tone sobered.

"Not immediately, but we went diving today."

A gasp. "Was she all right?"

"She is now, but I took care of her. She told me about Emelia."

"I need to speak to her."

Sam respected the worry in her voice. He handed the phone back to Penelope. She scowled at him. "Tell tale." Then she put the phone to her ear. "I'm fine, Five."

He went into the kitchen and put the kettle on while Penelope spoke with her best friend, her voice lowered, but he still caught some words. "I'm fine, but I couldn't get past the buddy checks. I didn't get far under water before I couldn't get further. Sam understood. He took me back to the boat, and he dived with a friend.

"I will. I'll go out again when there's no rush," she said. "Yes, I'll take someone with me."

"I'll go with you," Sam said.

She smiled her thanks. "Sam said he'll go with me." She sighed. "Yes, hang on." She held out the phone to him. "She wants to speak with you."

He took the phone and said, "I won't push her, but I'll take excellent care of her."

"You'd better, otherwise I'll have to come up there. I don't care if you're military trained, I'll get the drop on you."

He loved that Penelope had someone so protective of her. "I hope you'll come and visit anyway. Penelope would love to have you."

"Travelling with a newborn who has decided she doesn't need to sleep is not my idea of fun, but I'm trying to get there." In the background a baby started crying. Ceiveon sighed. "Just so you know, my husband is in the police force and I'm going to get him to do a background check on you." A male voice said something Sam couldn't quite catch. "Tell Penelope I'll call her later." She hung up.

Sam gave the phone to Penelope. "Is her husband really a police officer?"

Penelope groaned. "Yes, but he doesn't do background checks on her order."

He laughed. "It's her go-to threat, isn't it?"

She nodded.

"I like her style."

"Her third degree didn't bother you?"

"No, it was sweet. I'm glad you've got someone looking out for you."

She smiled. "You're an interesting man, Sam."

He stepped closer. "Interesting tends to be a synonym for unusual and not in a good way."

"Is intriguing better?" She tilted her head as he approached.

"Much." He brushed her cheek with his thumb and kissed her briefly. As much as he wanted to go back to kissing her senseless, the moment was gone and he didn't want to rush her. "Thanks for dinner. I'll pick you up just before seven tomorrow?"

"You don't want to stay longer?"

"I'd love to stay longer, but I suspect Ceiveon will call back the moment her baby settles and she's going to want all the gossip about me." He kissed her again, because he had to. "You'll want to tell her how wonderful I am without me in earshot." He winked again and moved towards the door.

She laughed. "There's that modesty again." She walked him to his car. "Thanks for everything today, Sam."

"Any time. Tell me when you want to try again, and I'll make time for you."

One last kiss, this time lingering a little longer. Her taste was becoming addictive. "Sweet dreams, Penny."

He backed out of the driveway and waited until she

waved and went back inside before he drove away.

He'd be dreaming of her.

Chapter 11

After Sam had left the night before, Penelope was at a loss at what to do. Dinner had been lovely, and the kiss had been amazing. Then Sam had proved he had good instincts when Ceiveon had called back demanding all the details, and calling Sam, "hot, hot, hot".

Penelope smiled. She was definitely right.

The pile of yarn on the coffee table had mocked her and so she'd unravelled the mess, cast on the required stitches, knitted a row, and then placed the yarn and needles into a bag. She'd take it out to the Ridge today and ask Amy to help her.

Now she was waiting for Sam to arrive. She'd made herself a coffee and was going to make Sam one too, except she didn't have his phone number, and didn't know what kind of coffee he liked. She considered calling Georgie, but it was early and she was probably still asleep.

The growl of an engine came down the street, and she grabbed her coffee and backpack, locked up and was on the front step as Sam pulled in. She jogged over to the car.

"Did you want a coffee?" she asked.

Sam tapped the mug in the drink holder next to him. "I'm sorted. Did you sleep well?"

She'd fallen asleep thinking of him. "Yes, thank you." She threw her backpack in the back and climbed in next to Sam. He had used some kind of body wash or aftershave which smelled spicy and manly. Nice.

Pulling out her phone, she asked, "What's your number?"

He told her and she plugged it in. "Send yours to me," he said. "I was going to call and ask if you wanted coffee, but I didn't have it."

She smiled. "Same."

Penelope put down her phone and realised they hadn't gone anywhere. "Are we waiting for something?"

Sam leaned closer. "I was hoping for a good morning kiss."

Her pulse accelerated as she shifted closer to him. "All right."

Their lips touched. A slow, thorough kiss, which woke every inch of her body.

"Good morning," Sam said when they separated and then he backed out of the driveway.

"Isn't it," Penelope agreed. She settled in and studied him. The sun was glowing in the east and there was enough light to see him. He really was a sexy man. Two-day-old stubble covered his face, and it gave him a rugged look. Today he wore a loose long-sleeved shirt, the type fishermen often wore and a pair of board shorts. Looked like he planned to go swimming. She wore her own bathers underneath her clothes.

"Did Ceiveon call you back?" He glanced at her with a smile.

"Of course."

"Does she approve?"

Penelope smiled. "Of you? I'm not telling."

"I take that as a yes."

She laughed. "Maybe I'm trying to protect your feelings."

"We both know you'd tell me the truth if you weren't interested as well." His cocky grin should have been a turn off, but on him it was charming. There was enough teasing in his tone to not take him too seriously.

"There's that ego again," she said.

"Just part of my charm."

It was true, so she changed the subject. "Have you read Lilian's journal?"

"Yeah, last night. I couldn't see many clues. What about you?"

"She respected Clarke and the indigenous people but had little respect for her first husband."

"He was pretty awful to her."

"It doesn't come across in the journal, but I'll bet she was pleased to find the treasure when he couldn't. It serves him right for not involving her."

"Things could have turned out differently for her if he had."

Penelope was glad Lilian had ended up with the man she loved. "Would Clarke's wife have arranged for his body to be retrieved?"

"I hadn't considered that. There wasn't a lot of infrastructure here back then, but she might have arranged a ship to transfer his body to Fremantle to be buried."

"So we might find nothing," Penelope said. "If he's still there, he'll only be bones. Dingoes might have dug him up when he was first buried." Not a nice thought, but a possibility they should consider.

They chatted about other possibilities on the drive and when they arrived at the Ridge, Brandon was loading an esky into the back of a ute.

"Are we late?" Sam asked as they got out.

"No, just getting things organised. The others decided it was a nice morning for a ride, so they've taken the horses. It's us and Amy driving down."

Penelope followed them inside and Amy sat at the kitchen table knitting what looked to be a bear. "Hey!" She put down her knitting and hugged Penelope. "Glad you could make it."

"Me too. That looks so much better than my attempts at knitting."

Amy's eyes lit up. "You knit too? What are you making?"

Penelope laughed. "I'm attempting a baby's blanket for my best friend's newborn, but she'll be in high school by the time I finish."

"The first few attempts were hard for me. You should bring it out. I'll give you a hand."

Penelope smiled. "Georgie mentioned you knitted, so it's in my bag. I unravelled everything last night because it had a lot of holes."

"I can vouch for that," Sam said. "I wasn't sure what she was trying to make." He kissed her cheek to soften the tease and Amy's eyes widened, and then she grinned.

Penelope blushed and reached into her backpack. "I've cast on the required stitches and done the first row."

"Wow, your stitches are tight," Amy said. "My first recommendation would be to not tighten the yarn so much. You'll find it easier. I'll sit with you when we get back and we can go through the pattern together."

"Thank you."

"Let's go," Brandon said. "The others should be there soon and Lara won't wait for anyone."

Penelope left her knitting on the table and followed them outside. Sam took her hand as they walked and opened the door for her.

She wasn't sure what to make of the old-fashioned gallantry. They'd gone from a kiss to this overnight. He'd declared his intentions to Ceiveon and Penelope had yet to decide how she felt. The whole point of moving to Retribution Bay was to figure herself out, stop working so hard, stop blaming herself for what happened to Emelia, and relax. Should she add a relationship, or whatever this was, to her list of wants?

She had to admit Sam had an easy-natured charm that Gerard never had. And his kisses set her alight, but she conceded it might simply be the excitement which came along with a new relationship. He was good-looking and a protector, and those characteristics spoke to her instinctual needs. And to top it all off, he was so very nice.

She'd be foolish to ignore this opportunity because it didn't fit with her timing, and she was tired of being foolish.

The drive to the gulf was through Ridge land and the track was bumpy. It took half an hour before Penelope spotted five people on horseback ahead of them. Brandon slowed as he drove past and Penelope waved at Lara, who waved frantically back. The car drove over a small hill and the ocean spread out before them. Mangroves to the left and a large island directly in front.

"That's Retribution Island," Sam said. "It's where the Retribution and the Dutch ship wrecked."

It didn't look too far away, but it would take time to ferry things back and forth if you only had a makeshift raft like the survivors had.

She got out. Nearby, the riders were dismounting and tying the horses to a hitching post. Lara unsaddled hers in record time and threw the saddle over the post before dashing towards Sam. "Hey, Sam!"

Sam opened his arms and picked her up, swinging her around. "Hey, La La."

She squealed in delight.

Seems as if Sam had a way with all women.

"Where are we searching first?" he asked her.

"It can't be far from the shore," Lara said. "They would have buried him above the high tide mark and the Retribution was wrecked on this side of the island, so I reckon between the track and the mangroves."

Penelope was impressed with her reasoning. It made perfect sense.

Sam held Penelope's hand, and they followed Lara over to the mangroves. A metal plaque was nearby. "What's that?"

"It lists all the passengers on the Retribution when it crashed," Lara said. "We don't know who put it there though."

Maybe it was more than a marker. "Could it have replaced a gravestone?"

"The journal says they buried him behind the small sand dunes," Lara replied.

"The sand might have moved since then," Penelope replied.

Lara's eyes almost bugged out of her head. "Really?" She raced over and dropped to her knees, and started digging.

Penelope moved closer to the plaque. A lot of names were listed on it, more than the people Lilian had mentioned in her journal. She took a photo. She'd compare it to the journal later.

"Hey, La La, not so fast," Sam said. "If it is a grave, you need to be careful. The body could be a mess."

She screwed up her nose. "Won't it be bones?"

He shrugged. "I don't know. We should clear the sand away carefully. Brandon brought some shovels."

While the others watched Lara dig, Penelope examined the coastline. Her knowledge of sand movement was limited, but she knew about sea levels.

The sea had risen about twenty centimetres since the body was buried and so it was possible the dunes had shifted at least that much, pushed back or eroded by the waves.

If she was burying a body in this area, she'd do so at least a metre away from the back of the dunes, but any wooden cross would have blown away decades ago.

Georgie joined her. "What are you looking for?"

She explained her theory. "If the plaque didn't replace the gravestone, there's still a lot of ground to dig."

Georgie lowered her voice. "This is an exercise to humour Lara. Darcy's already told her she can't dig up the entire area, not without a reason, so today all we're searching for are any traces of what could be a gravestone."

Penelope glanced back at the plaque where Lara was struggling with the length of the shovel, but scraping at the sand with fierce determination. "You realise she'll see anything as a trace?"

"Yeah, but eventually it will get too hot and she'll want to go swimming." Georgie grinned. "So… you and Sam, huh?"

Penelope smiled. "Very observant."

"Getting a lift home with him worked out for you?"

She knew Georgie had set her up. "I'm not sure Sam got the best out of it."

"Why not?"

She hadn't told anyone but Sam about Emelia, or her life before she'd come up here. "I have issues, Georgie. Sam shouldn't be lumped with them."

"Does he know about them?"

"Yeah."

"He doesn't seem to mind." She nodded towards the others where Sam was watching them. He gave Penelope the OK signal.

She returned the gesture with a smile.

"Sam is the best," Georgie continued. "You two will make a great couple."

"I found something!" Lara's yell put an end to the conversation, and they hurried back to the plaque.

Lara brushed sand off what appeared to be a long, black plastic-wrapped package.

Georgie got out her phone and started filming. "Ed and Tess will never forgive me if I don't capture this."

"Get back!" Sam yelled.

Before Penelope could process the words, Sam leapt between the grave and the rest of them, arms outstretched. He hauled Lara into his arms and grabbed Penelope's hand, dragging her away. He didn't stop until they were at the car.

Penelope's heart raced as she took a moment to get her breath back. "What's wrong?"

Brandon was right behind them, herding everyone else away.

Sam's chest heaved, his eyes wide, scanning the area for threats.

"What is it, Sam?" Penelope asked.

He ignored her, glanced at Brandon. "Cache?"

Brandon nodded, expression flat.

Penelope placed a hand on Sam's arm and he slipped it around her, placing himself between her and the beach.

"Brandon, you're scaring us," Amy said. "What's going on?"

The men exchanged a look. "Weapons cache," Sam finally said. "Saw things like this overseas."

Lara slipped her hand into Darcy's. "Is it dangerous?"

"Nah," Sam replied. "But we don't want to mess up any evidence."

He was lying. Penelope wasn't sure what it was, a

hunch in his shoulder, a glance away, but something convinced her the package was far more dangerous than they let on.

"We need to call Dot," Brandon added. "Amy, you and Penelope take the car and drive to the house. Tell her what we've found. The rest of you take the horses back."

"You should leave it here and come with us," Georgie said.

"We'll monitor it in case a tourist happens past." Brandon handed Amy the keys to the ute and glanced back as if measuring the distance.

What tourists? This was Ridge land.

"Faith, you and Lara go with Amy," Darcy said. "I'll lead the horses."

"Georgie, you go with them too," Matt added.

Georgie raised her eyebrows. "We've discussed this." But she pocketed her camera and went to saddle her horse. They worked quickly, the urgency making it hard for Penelope to breathe. She looked around for Sam.

"Get in the car, Penny." Sam's voice was low, urgent.

"What is it?"

"Probably nothing." He opened the door for her.

"And if it's something?"

Faith and Lara carried their saddles to the ute and placed them in the tray. Then they got into the back seat.

"Caches like this are often booby-trapped, so they don't fall in the wrong hands. Sometimes they have a delayed trigger..."

Penelope felt dizzy. Lara had been digging there moments ago. They had all been standing on the edge, ready to help. She shuddered and Sam stroked her back. "You need to come with us," she said.

"No, we need to keep an eye on it. Brandon's getting the rifle out of the ute."

Sure enough, he and Amy were talking quietly as he got the gun out of a locked box on the back of the ute.

"I'm staying with you." The thought of not knowing what was happening to him while she waited in safety was like reliving Emelia all over again.

"No, you're not."

"Yes, I am. I can't not know." Her voice cracked.

Sam swore. "We have a radio. We'll check in every fifteen minutes."

She shook her head. Not good enough.

"Penelope, get in the car," Amy called.

"I'm staying."

"Like hell you are," Brandon responded. He strode over. "You'll get in our way. We need to be focused."

Sam nodded and Amy waved for her to get inside.

She didn't want to go, but didn't want to risk her staying distracting Sam. "Every five minutes." She met his blue gaze.

"Ten," he responded. "Promise."

It would have to be good enough. She kissed him and thrust her backpack at him. "I've got food and water in there." She jumped in the car.

Amy turned them around and drove back towards the Ridge, passing the others who were already on their way on horseback.

"Was it a bomb?" Lara asked, her voice quiet and full of fear.

Penelope exchanged a glance with Amy, but it was Faith who answered.

"We don't know, pumpkin. Brandon and Sam are being overly cautious. They saw a lot of things when they were in the army."

"Will they be all right?"

"Yeah, they're sensible. They won't go near it until

the police arrive, and the police will have the right equipment."

A small-town police station wouldn't have the equipment or knowledge to defuse an explosive booby trap. There were only a few people who would have those skills.

Sam and Brandon could.

Penelope sucked in a breath at the realisation. Horror filled her. Lara was still asking Faith questions in the back, so she murmured to Amy. "Would they try to defuse it themselves?"

The blood draining out of Amy's face was all the answer she needed. Amy slowed, but as Lara asked her next question, she clenched her jaw and kept driving.

They had to keep the others safe.

Chapter 12

Sam smiled at the backpack Penelope had shoved at him. It was sweet that she was worried enough about him to provide him with food and water. He set his watch to alarm every ten minutes and took the radio from Brandon, clipping it onto his shorts.

"She's got issues," Brandon said as he swung the rifle onto his back and opened the esky.

Sam didn't bother glaring. "You mean like Amy has?"

Brandon grunted. "Amy's got me now, and Sherlock, if he ever gets back from his mission."

Sam ignored the gut clench.

"Why'd she want to stay?" Brandon continued. "You two slept together yet?"

Sam shoved his friend harder than was necessary. "It's none of your business. Penelope deserves your respect."

Brandon glanced at him. "You serious?"

He wasn't asking regarding the respect comment. "I think I might be." When he'd recognised what the plastic package could be, his first instinct was to step between it and Penelope. The thought of her being injured had chilled him.

"OK. Enough said. You heard back from your investigator?"

"Not yet." He hated the suspicion still lurking in his mind that she could be a Stonefish plant.

"All right. I'll tell the others to avoid talking to her about this until you're done."

It didn't sit well with Sam, but he needed to be sure. Sam crouched next to him to see what they had to work with. Lots of food, drink and ice in the esky, but nothing particularly useful. He opened Penelope's backpack and laughed. "Jackpot." First aid kit, survival kit containing a multi-tool, wire, rope, fishing hooks, water filtration tablets, and a couple of energy bars.

"She's a prepper," Brandon said.

Sam sobered. This was probably in response to not having what she needed to save Emelia. "More of a Girl Scout prepared for any emergency." And right now he was thankful for it. "It'll take Dot at least an hour and a half to get here."

"If she takes the western track, she might cut it to an hour." Brandon grimaced. "She's good at getting here fast."

All since Stonefish had showed their hand. "How do you want to play it?"

"Let's examine it again. We'll work out the best course of action and then when we hear the car, we can move."

Sam nodded. That's what he'd figured, too. That way if something went boom, there would be someone who could help them. His watch beeped, and he took the radio from his belt. "You ladies made the right choice," he said. "Air conditioned comfort. It's getting hot out here."

Penelope's voice was a stiff hiss. "Do not do what you're planning."

Brandon raised his eyebrows. "I wondered how long it would take for it to sink in."

"You listen to Penelope, Brandon." Amy's voice was low. They probably didn't want Lara to hear. "I will divorce you if you don't."

Brandon winced and ran a hand through his hair. "Shit."

"Surely you don't mind if we eat all the cake you packed, Ames," Sam replied. "It's hot out here. You can make another one when you get back."

"Eat everything in the esky, as long as that's all you do."

Sam reset his watch.

"Do you think she's serious?" Brandon asked.

"I'll do it." He'd been planning to anyway. "You can drag me to safety if it goes bang."

"Amy will be mad either way," he said.

"What are our choices? Dot doesn't have the skills or expertise to deal with this."

Brandon swore again. "Yeah, you're right."

Sam took his phone from his pocket and they approached the uncovered plastic. Lara hadn't uncovered much. "How long do you think it's been buried?"

"Not long. Anything this shallow would have been dug up by dingoes if it was organic, and the plastic isn't faded."

"The plaque's a good marker." He took some photos.

"The only reason to booby-trap it is to hurt us," Brandon said. "We're the only ones who would dig it up accidentally."

Sam wouldn't put it past Stonefish. They would be getting frustrated as the branches of their business were being revealed. "So, what do you want to do? Dot will have to call the bomb squad in, and that will take hours."

They both studied the piece of plastic. They needed to uncover the package to see how big it was but shifting the sand might trigger the trap if there was one. Sam took stock of their equipment again. The rope and esky would give them enough distance. He got to work, explaining his theory to Brandon as he emptied the esky and tied the rope to its handle. Then, using the multi-tool, he cut the lid of the cake tin, straightening it out to create a shovel and stuck it to one edge of the esky.

"Best we can do," Brandon agreed. "Use the esky lid as a shield."

Sam tested his knot and then placed the esky on one side of the plastic, being careful not to apply too much pressure. Then he let out the rope to give him a safe distance before he dragged the esky over the plastic, which picked up the sand as it went.

A makeshift scoop.

He did several passes, each pass clearing more of the sand from on top of the package. His watch beeped. Sam sighed, wishing he hadn't promised Penelope he'd call. "You back at the house yet?"

"Not far," Penelope answered. "You enjoying the cake?"

"It's delicious," Sam lied. "Washing it down with an ice-cold bottle of water. Incredible how these insulated bottles hold in the cold."

"I'll radio when we've called Dot."

Brandon laughed. "She didn't believe you. We're both going to be in the doghouse tonight."

He was happy Penelope cared enough to be worried. The esky had uncovered the plastic to give the dimensions of the package, over a metre long and at least half a metre wide. He kept his distance from the hole, but took several photos, zooming in to examine the package for any wires or triggers.

Brandon stood behind him while they studied the photos. "It looks clear."

Perhaps he'd overreacted. He could hook the plastic and drag it open to see what was inside. "Let's eat the cake now while I rig up a fishing rod." Penelope's survival kit had a few different sized fishing hooks.

"Sounds good." Brandon spread out the picnic blanket and Sam dug out the hook and line.

"What's the latest with Georgie's court case?"

"Could be a year before she goes to court," Brandon answered. "There was a preliminary hearing where the court heard about the kidnapping and that she shot the guy in self-defence. The judge seems to think Lee will be caught and be able to provide evidence."

"Any word on him?"

"Nothing. Dot was trying to get some tracker dogs up here, but she had no luck." Brandon growled. "I don't know why Georgie's protecting him."

"He probably saved them," Sam said. "Do you think those guys out at Muiron were just poachers?"

"I'm not discounting anything."

"Stonefish are tenacious," Sam said. Stonefish had been beaten at every turn and had lost some people who were high in the organisation.

"I was worried they'd come after Georgie, but it's been quiet. It's making me nervous."

Sam understood how he felt. He finished the fishing line and bit into the banana cake. He groaned. "Wow, this is good."

"Ames has got talent," Brandon agreed, biting into his slice.

The radio came to life with Amy's voice. "Dot and Nhiari are on their way. They were at the airport, so they shouldn't take long to get there. Dot said not to touch anything."

Sam handed the radio to Brandon so he could

answer and got to his feet. Time to get to work.

The sound of an engine reached him and he exchanged a glance with Brandon. Far too early to be Dot and Nhiari, unless Amy and Penelope had got hold of them on the journey back and not told them.

He wouldn't put it past them.

He and Brandon worked together to gather their things and move off the beach, down amongst the red dirt and scrubby trees.

Brandon settled low on the dunes, rifle pointed towards the sound.

"How far?"

"Could be another ten minutes. Hard to tell when it's this still. Noise carries."

"Should I check the package?"

Brandon nodded. "If the car is Stonefish, and that's a weapons cache, they'll have the advantage."

Sam grabbed the esky lid and moved fast, taking the hook he'd fashioned over to the bundle. His heart slowed, and he regulated his breathing, focusing on the task at hand. Brandon had his back. He didn't have to worry about the approaching car. All he had to do was hook the canvas and pull it back. The esky lid would provide a little protection if shrapnel was involved. Not a lot, but it was better than nothing.

He crouched low, holding the lid in front of him, and then hooked the canvas, pulling it slowly away, inch by inch, ready for anything.

No click to signal he'd triggered anything, no explosion, nothing.

He counted to twenty, standing still holding the lid as a shield before he shifted, and moved forward to peer into the hole.

Holy shit.

He whistled low and moved around the other side of the hole. A glance at Brandon showed he was still monitoring the approaching vehicle, binoculars to his eyes. He lifted his hand in a gesture which said it was safe and stood.

Must be the police.

Sam turned his attention back to the package and peeled back the other side, careful to keep the esky lid lifted.

No bang.

Again, he counted to twenty before he stood and checked the hole. This was no dead body, nor was it anything that had been buried during the wreck of the Retribution. This was pure twenty-first century weaponry.

Hand guns, semi-automatics, a sniper rifle and a bag Sam would bet had cash or drugs in it. Maybe both.

He radioed the homestead. "Dot and Nhiari are just about here. Will contact you when we need a pick up."

"Everything OK?" Amy answered.

"All good, Ames. Talk soon."

Brandon peered in and whistled. "Gotta be Stonefish."

"Why bury it here? They know you come down here regularly."

"Easy to hide the fact a hole has been dug in beach sand," Brandon said. "The plaque is a good marker as well. Maybe they didn't think their guys could find it in the bush."

It made no sense. If Stonefish could afford weaponry like this, they could afford a couple of GPSs to mark the drop spot. He took a couple of photos, focusing on the bag which sat on top of the weapons. It was nestled in there comfortably. Too comfortably. "I wouldn't lift the bag."

Brandon glanced at him and then crouched to get a better look. "You could be right. It's too easy."

"Trap?"

"Might be." A good way to get rid of the Stokes or the police.

Speaking of which… Dot pulled to a stop a short distance away, a look of disgust on her face. "You ignored my instructions, didn't you?" She stalked over, her senior constable, Nhiari Roe, right behind her wearing an equally annoyed expression.

Sam smiled. "Got the message too late."

"Bullshit," Nhiari said. "We saw you with the esky lid."

They both peered into the hole and Dot swore. "Maybe this will be enough to get major crimes up here," she muttered.

Nhiari took photos while Dot opened her notebook. "You know the drill by now."

Sam let Brandon tell the story, though he omitted all references to the journal and looking for Clarke's body. Instead, he simply said Lara had been digging in the sand and had uncovered it.

Sam's stomach curdled at the thought of what could have happened if she had discovered it and unwrapped it without warning.

"What else?" Dot asked.

Brandon raised his eyebrows as if he didn't understand.

"You must have thought it was suspicious if you called us and got the rest of your family to evacuate."

"My fault," Sam said. "It looked a lot like some weapons caches we uncovered on duty. They were usually booby-trapped."

"Hence the esky shield?" Nhiari asked.

"Was all we had to hand," Sam said. "But I think there might be a trigger under the bag."

Nhiari's eyes widened. "Why?"

He pointed. "It's too snug. The rest of the weapons are stacked almost haphazardly, but not around the bag.

They make a square for it to rest in."

"How big an explosion?" Dot asked.

"Depends on what they've used. There's danger of the ammunition exploding as well and that could hit anyone."

Dot ran a hand over her face. "This is beyond what we can deal with. I'm making the call."

She went back to the police car and got on the radio.

"Everyone was out here?" Nhiari asked.

Brandon nodded. "Georgie and Matt had ridden out with Darcy, Faith and Lara. Sam and I drove with Amy and Penelope."

Matt was Nhiari's younger brother. "Tell Georgie and Matt I want to speak with them again," Nhiari said. "As soon as they're back in town."

"Why?" Brandon asked.

Nhiari pressed her lips together. "Need to check some information."

Brandon frowned.

It was more than that. Had to be something to do with Matt's kidnapping.

Dot eventually returned. "They're catching the midday flight," she said. "Colin will bring them out. We'll stay here to guard."

"Want us to keep you company?" Brandon asked.

"No," Dot responded.

Sam smiled and radioed Amy. "We're ready to be picked up."

"We'll be there soon. I'll bring refreshments."

The food they'd dumped in the tray of the ute would still be good. He offered the officers a couple of pieces of cake and some fruit.

"Is this Amy's cake?" Dot asked.

"Yep," Brandon answered. "She'll bring more when she comes."

Sam didn't like the idea of leaving the women here

alone, though he knew they were both extremely competent. It was a good six hours or more before backup would arrive from Perth, and if Stonefish had access to this kind of weaponry, they could be in real danger.

He scanned the bush looking for a glint or a colour which shouldn't be there, then he checked the island and the mangroves. Nothing.

Would Stonefish have responded by now if they were going to respond? Or perhaps they had hoped the booby-trap would have done the work for them.

If Lara had found it on her own…

He shuddered. "What can we do to protect the others?"

Dot sighed. "We don't know who else is involved, where they are, or what other activities they're involved in."

Stonefish were back to being a faceless entity.

"There's Lee," Nhiari pointed out.

The last Sam had heard, Lee had been seen camping in the ranges. He could be anywhere by now, and finding him in the warren of caves under the ranges would be impossible.

Brandon made a noise in his throat.

"Do you know where Lee is?" Dot asked.

Brandon shook his head.

"Would you like to share your thoughts?" Nhiari said.

"Are you going to share with us?"

Dot gave him a withering stare. Sam appreciated how the look gave her authority and shouted cut the crap, especially since she was almost a head shorter than both of them.

"You want to talk to Georgie and Matt again," Brandon said. "Nhiari mentions Lee. You must suspect Georgie didn't really kill the guy who kidnapped Matt."

"What makes you suggest that?" Dot asked.

"Georgie wears her heart on her sleeve. She once cried for days when she couldn't save an abandoned lamb. If she'd killed someone, no matter whom he'd threatened, she would be devastated. She hasn't shed a tear."

"Have you run your theory past her?" Dot asked.

"She denies it, but she can't lie for shit."

Dot nodded in agreement. "She's protecting someone."

"Going to gaol for manslaughter is a big step for anyone, let alone someone who has done bad things to your family," Sam said.

"Lee saved Tess," Brandon pointed out. "That might be enough for Georgie."

"He must have saved Matt as well," Sam said. Then Georgie would take the fall.

"Why not just say so?" Nhiari asked.

"Because he's still working for Stonefish," Brandon said. "You report Lee killed the kidnapper, and he'll have Stonefish after him."

It made complete sense. The only question was, why? Why had Lee turned against his organisation?

"You're implying Stonefish have people in the police." Dot turned away and brushed back her hair.

"Tess already suggested it," Brandon said. "Everything is digital these days. The guy wouldn't have to be in Retribution Bay to get access to your report."

But it would be something to look into. They didn't know how long Stonefish had been operating out of the area, but if they had someone on the police force, it would make sense why they hadn't been noticed until recently.

"Can you get Georgie to tell the truth?" Nhiari asked.

"Can you get Matt to?" Brandon countered.

"You'd have a better chance," Nhiari said. "Matt knows I have to report anything he tells me."

"I'll work on Georgie. She'll crack eventually."

"And then you'll tell us," Dot put in.

"Only if you don't record it."

Another glacial stare, but Dot nodded.

Maybe they could make some progress.

Chapter 13

When Penelope and the others arrived back at the homestead, Faith took charge. "I'll hitch the horse float and go pick up our horses."

"Is there enough space to turn around?" Amy asked.

"I'll find it." The determination in her voice concerned Penelope. They'd already called the police the moment they had reception, but Faith's actions suggested there was still a threat out there.

"I'll help," Lara said.

Amy unlocked the kitchen door, threw Faith the car keys, and then led Penelope inside.

"Are Georgie and the others in danger?" Penelope asked.

Amy shrugged. "Probably not, but whatever is buried is enough to freak Brandon out, so I want everyone back at the house where I know it's safe."

Understandable. "Is there anything I can do?"

Amy shook her head. "Not unless you know how to stop Stonefish." She filled the kettle with water and turned it on, and then began filling a backpack with cake and bottles of water. "Dot and Nhiari might be out there a while. I can take them some refreshments when we pick up Brandon and Sam." She glanced at the radio. It had been more than ten minutes since they'd heard from them.

Lara stormed in. "Faith won't let me go with her." Outside, the car started and Lara glanced over her shoulder, and stamped her feet.

She was worried as well.

"Don't worry, be happy," Amy sang, then smiled. "It's what Mum used to sing to us when my father was away." She put an arm around Lara. "You can keep us company. I was going to examine Penelope's knitting and see if I can help her." She gestured to where Penelope had left it on the table. "Want to help me teach her?"

Lara pouted. "All right."

Penelope grimaced. "It's fine. I don't need to learn."

"Do you have a photo of what your first attempt looked like?" Amy asked.

She handed Amy her phone with the picture. Amy winced and showed Lara. Lara laughed, then slapped her hand over her mouth and said, "We can help you."

Great, even a ten-year-old could knit better than her. Still, if it kept all of them distracted for a while, it was worth it. She didn't want to think about what Sam was doing.

They sat at the table. "Show me your technique," Amy said as she poured them all tea.

Penelope picked up the needles and knitted a few stitches, finding it difficult to get the needle through each stitch.

"Definitely too tight," Amy said.

"She's holding the yarn funny too," Lara said.

"It's a different style," Amy explained. "There's continental and English knitting. Let me get mine." She left the room and a few minutes later returned with her work. She demonstrated her method, which had her holding the yarn more like Penelope had seen crocheters hold it.

Penelope watched and then mimicked her, finding the other method a little easier. She made a couple of false starts, but she didn't have to worry about her stitches falling off the needles because she never let go of the needles. "This is so much better."

The radio crackled and Sam's voice came over it. "Dot and Nhiari are just about here. Will call when we need a pick up."

Penelope exhaled while Amy answered. Her relief was mirrored in Amy's expression. Both men were safe. They hadn't done anything foolish.

"We should take Dot and Nhiari the shade shelter when we pick the guys up," Amy said.

By the time they'd finished loading Darcy's ute, Faith had returned with the first load of horses. Lara went to help her unload and then joined her on the second trip. It must be safer now.

Sam radioed to tell them they were ready for a pickup. He sounded his usual friendly self, as if he hadn't been standing guard over a potentially deadly situation for the past hour or more.

He was incredible.

The trip to the gulf this time around seemed to take forever. "Has this been going on since May?" Penelope asked.

"Yeah," Amy responded. "Too long. Almost every month it's some new drama."

Penelope couldn't imagine what they'd been going through. "Maybe there's a clue in whatever is buried."

"Maybe," Amy agreed, but didn't sound hopeful.

When they reached the beach again, Penelope's heart leapt seeing Sam standing near the police car chatting to Dot, Nhiari and Brandon. He was in one piece, no injury, no concern.

She exhaled and got out, striding across to them with Amy by her side. Her footsteps faltered as she glanced towards the hole and the cache of weapons.

Shit.

They'd been right. She'd never seen so many guns up close before and the reality was frightening.

Amy kept moving, making a beeline to Brandon, but Penelope stopped, leaned closer for a better look, fascinated by the equipment before her.

Suddenly she was jerked back, and Sam was there, pushing her away from the hole, keeping his body between her and the weapons. She tripped, and he picked her up and kept moving her away.

"Sam. What are you doing?"

"It's not safe," he said. "The bomb squad is on the way. We think it might still be rigged to blow."

Her breath caught. "Seriously?" Who did that?

"Yeah." He stopped and squeezed her tightly. "You scared the shit out of me."

"*I* scared *you?*" She shoved him away. "I'm not the one who opened a booby-trapped weapons cache with absolutely no protection."

He was unapologetic. "I have the skills to do it," he said. "You looked as if you were going to reach in and grab something."

Though his words were sharp, the tone harsh, his hand shook as he ran it through his hair.

Unable to resist, she stepped closer and pulled him into her arms. "We're both OK," she soothed. "We're safe." She rubbed his back, and he relaxed against her, almost crushing her as he hugged her.

Penelope peered up at him and his lips crashed against hers, stealing her breath and kissing her with a passion brought about by fear and relief.

She kissed him back, equally relieved.

Perhaps it was the circumstances—first her panic

attack, then this bomb threat, which brought them closer together, but she wanted this man in a way she'd never wanted anyone.

A piercing whistle cut through her haze. She stepped back in time to see Sam give Brandon the finger. Heat flooded her cheeks as she realised she'd been making out in front of everyone. She'd forgotten they were even there.

Sam slipped his hand into hers. "Let's go."

They walked to the police car where the others smirked at them. Awkward.

"Ready to go?" Amy asked.

Penelope nodded.

"We'll be in touch," Dot said.

"We can swap notes," Brandon answered. The look which passed between them all was telling.

"What have you planned?" Amy asked.

Brandon smiled. "I'll tell you later."

Both Dot and Nhiari scowled but said nothing as they walked them back to the car. Amy got the backpack and sunshade out of the tray. "I figured you could use some refreshments and shade while you wait."

Dot smiled for the first time. "Thanks, Ames. We appreciate it."

Brandon and Sam set up the shade and seats and then joined the others in the car.

By the time they got home, Darcy was brushing his horse in the horse yard and the other horses were already nibbling on hay. They gathered inside for a debrief and Sam explained about the bag on top of the weapons.

"You think it was a trap for us?" Darcy asked.

"We won't know until the bomb squad confirms whether a trigger is sitting under the bag," Brandon replied.

"How long will that take?" Matt pulled Georgie closer, as if he couldn't bear for her to be so far away.

"Perhaps by the end of the day," Sam answered.

It was a terrifying thought.

"It can't have been meant for us," Faith protested. "How would they know we'd dig there?"

"We've been searching for the treasure for a month. If they have the other journal, as we suspect they do, they'd know we're searching for treasure." Georgie tugged on her fringe.

Not knowing when something could happen would be incredibly stressful. Penelope felt for the whole family.

Darcy sighed. "Looks like it's time to go through everything again."

Sam shifted next to her. "I might take Penelope home."

She glanced at him, surprised. She'd been certain he would want to help his friends.

Brandon smirked. "Good idea. No point us all going through this again."

His words made no sense, but the smirk did. He figured she and Sam would pick up where they left the kiss. Heat flooded her cheeks. "We can stay and help."

"They've got this," Sam said, and held out his hand to help her up.

Penelope waited until they were on the road before she asked, "What are you and Brandon planning?"

He glanced at her, a picture of innocence. "What do you mean?"

"You two and Dot and Nhiari have something planned."

He pressed his lips together.

He didn't trust her. She shouldn't be surprised since they'd only just met, but it hurt. "Never mind."

"It's not that I don't want to tell you," he said. "I

promised I wouldn't."

"All right." She respected that. "Did you see a lot of weapons caches when you were in the army?"

"More than I would have liked. We got used to expecting the worst with everything."

What an awful way to live. "Could Georgie's parents have been involved in something the children don't know about?"

Sam jolted. "I hadn't considered that."

"Would there be any way of proving it?"

He shrugged. "I'll discuss it with Brandon."

Penelope's stomach rumbled. She hadn't eaten since her very early breakfast and it was already mid morning. "Do you want to get a bite to eat when we get back to town?"

He smiled. "Sure. Where do you want to go?"

"How about Ningaloo Cafe?" They might time it right to miss the breakfast rush and the lunch crowd.

"All right."

She stared out at the passing bush. Today had not gone as she'd expected. She'd been hoping for a relaxing day at the beach, hunting for treasure and getting to know Sam.

Though the kiss had been pretty epic. Maybe they would have a chance to revisit it after lunch.

She sneaked a look at Sam. He tapped his hand on the steering wheel, his focus on the road. A slight frown creased his forehead and his mouth was set in a straight line. Probably thinking about the weapons cache. She hated that he had to go through this sort of thing again, especially somewhere he considered safe.

She stayed silent for the rest of the trip into town, content to let him process what had happened. When he pulled in at Ningaloo Cafe, the car park was about half full.

"Can you get us a table and order me a coffee?" Sam

asked. "I just have to call someone."

"All right." She kissed him and headed inside.

***

Sam waited until Penelope disappeared inside before he rang Sherlock. He had to know whether his friend had found anything about her before things progressed further. He'd wanted to stay at the Ridge and help, but he couldn't without confirming Penelope wasn't involved with Stonefish.

No answer.

He swore. This wasn't the game he wanted to play. *Need a status update on your mission.* He sent the text, urging Sherlock to respond.

Come on. He couldn't leave Penelope waiting for too long or she'd get suspicious.

SOS, Sherlock.

His phone rang and Sam breathed out a sigh of relief. "Have you found anything?"

"She's thirty-two, lived with a guy, Gerard, for eight years and worked doing research on sea snakes before moving to Retribution Bay." Sherlock's voice was dull, listing off facts with no emotion. "A colleague died in a diving accident twelve months ago. Only Penelope was a witness."

"Emelia, right?"

"She told you?"

"Yeah. She tried to go diving with me but couldn't. Had a panic attack."

The sound Sherlock made might have been sympathy, but then he continued. "Sounds like Gerard broke it off after the accident."

"What about family, loved ones? Anyone who could be under threat and make her vulnerable to Stonefish?"

"Not that I could find. Her family seems normal and the guy who checked into their finances said nothing was out of the ordinary, though her mother appears to have an obsession with shoes."

Great. That was one less issue. "Thanks, mate. I really appreciate it." Sam smiled. "We could do with your help up here." He told Sherlock about the weapons cache.

"I'm useless," Sherlock said. "I'd only get in the way."

"No, you're—"

Sherlock hung up.

Sam swore. He couldn't help his friend from this far away and Sherlock needed help, both mentally and physically.

Sam tucked his phone into his pocket and waved to Gretchen, who was across the car park with her son, Jordan.

"We're back on Monday, right?" she called.

"Yep." He gave her the thumbs up and entered the cafe, searching for Penelope's red hair. She sat facing him, but her head was bowed as she read the menu. Beautiful and fascinating. He wanted to get her opinion on all sorts of subjects, and she would be an asset in the search for treasure.

She looked up as he sat. "Everything all right?"

"Yeah, it's great. Just remembered I was going to check in with a mate."

"Is this the one who lost his leg?"

Sam jolted. "Yeah. Did I tell you about him?"

She nodded. "Yes, when you gave me a lift back from the Ridge the other day. How's he holding up?"

"He doesn't want to face the world—thinks he's useless and no help to anyone."

"Is there a task you can give him to show how valuable he is?" She passed him the menu.

"I tried, but it didn't help and he refuses to visit."

"Maybe having you and Brandon here reminds him

too much of what he's lost," Penelope suggested.

"Maybe." He needed to change the subject. "What are you ordering?"

"I'm getting the lemon meringue pancakes."

He raised his eyebrows. "Sweet tooth?"

"They sound interesting," she said. "I like to try something different when I can, otherwise I'll always get the same thing."

"And what would that be?"

"Bircher muesli and a large cappuccino, if I'm being good."

"I'm more of the big breakfast kind of guy. What do you have if you're being bad?" He liked the idea.

"Bacon and hash browns."

Both excellent choices.

The wait person came over and they ordered. After the girl had left, Sam asked, "What are your other go-to orders?"

"There used to be a Vietnamese deli down the road from where I worked. I lived on banh mi and Vietnamese iced coffee."

"How is Vietnamese iced coffee different from normal iced coffee?"

"It's made with condensed milk and the coffee is stronger, has a different flavour to it."

She definitely had a sweet tooth. He'd have to remember that. "Chocolate or cake?"

"Cake."

"Ice cream or pudding?"

"Both together—or custard and pudding, depending on the season."

The coffees arrived and she sipped hers, closing her eyes to savour the taste.

Sam shifted and smiled. "Pizza or chips?"

"Depends on the quality," she replied. "Thick, crispy beer-battered chips with gravy are amazing, but so is a good thin crust Italian pizza with the right toppings." She placed her cup on the table. "What about you?"

"Cake, ice cream—but the good Italian gelato—and definitely pizza, but I'm not fussy as long as the balance of cheese, sauce and toppings is right."

She grinned with such joy that he smiled back. "Have you tried the pizza at the brewery?"

"Yeah. It was another plus in the move to Retribution Bay."

The food arrived and he had to admit, the lemon meringue pancakes looked amazing. The meringue was whipped into a spiral, and the lemon curd was generously drizzled over the pancakes. Penelope cut off a section, making sure she had both the lemon and the meringue on her piece and then bit into it. Her eyes closed and she moaned softly.

He wanted her badly.

"You've got to taste this." Penelope held out a portion on the end of her fork.

He wanted to try something all right. Keeping his eyes on hers, he leaned forward and let her feed him. Her eyes widened as his mouth closed over the fork and he slid the pancake into his mouth. Sharp lemon clashed with sweet meringue in a celebration. He swallowed. "That is damned good."

She nodded. "I'll share if you like."

"Tempting," he replied. "But I'll never finish my big breakfast if I have half of your pancakes."

She glanced at his plate. "Well, you could share your bacon and hash brown and you'd have more room."

He chuckled. "I'm on to you." He passed her a hash brown and a piece of bacon. "The best of both worlds."

"Only if you don't mind. Gerard never liked to share."

"He sounds like a douche."

She screwed up her nose, but smiled. "I wasn't the best person to be around after the accident."

"Doesn't mean you should be given up on." He thought about Sherlock. "My friend was the only reason I didn't want to leave Perth." He sipped his coffee. "I visited him daily at the hospital even though he stopped talking and some days he refused to look at me. He got out on Friday." Sam sighed. "I have to believe I'll get through to him, but I don't know how. The army was his life."

"Then he needs another goal, something else to focus on." She shifted in her seat. "After Emelia's death, I was focused on doing things right. If I had followed the rules, done all the proper checks, she'd be alive now."

Sam shook his head. "No way her death was your fault," he said. "You said so yourself. She went in after the sea snake without doing the checks. *She* broke the rules, not you."

"But I was the one who prepared the equipment."

"Still her job to check it. You said you hadn't finished."

Her eyes widened as if surprised.

"You can't take responsibility for others' actions," he said. "You just have to do the best with what you've got."

"The same goes for your friend," Penelope said. "You can't help him if he doesn't want to be helped."

Sam's smile was sad. "I know. It's hard."

Penelope squeezed his hand. "You'll work something out, I'm sure of it."

Her confidence was nice, if a little misplaced. "Do you want to try diving again?"

Her fingers tightened on his. "At some stage."

Sam wouldn't push it. He didn't want to scare her off. He ate the last of his brunch, saving the pancake to the end. "I can't believe it's not even midday."

"I know. It feels as if we've been through enough for several days."

"Want to head back to my place? We can chill there for the afternoon." He wasn't ready to say goodbye, and he wanted somewhere more private.

Penelope smiled, but before she could answer, her phone rang. She frowned. "Sorry, it's work." She answered. After a pause, she said, "What do you need me to do?" She nodded. "All right. I'll head out in half an hour."

She hung up. "I'm sorry. I've been called in. Can I take a rain check on the chilling?"

Disappointment filled him, but he smiled. "Where do you need me to drop you?"

"Home. I'll have to get a few things."

Sam insisted on paying and then drove her back to her place. Before she jumped out of the car, he placed a hand on her arm. "Will you call me when you're done?"

Her smile was sweet. "All right." She kissed him far too briefly and then hurried inside.

Sam waited until the door closed behind her before he backed out of her drive. He really hoped Sherlock had done a thorough job on his investigation, because Sam had it bad for the prickly redhead, who was all sweetness underneath.

Chapter 14

Penelope couldn't decide whether Karen had the worst or the best timing. She'd been on the verge of going to Sam's place for the afternoon, which might have been an amazing decision, or a foolish one. Now she'd never know.

She hurried into her bedroom and changed into her uniform, then filled her backpack with a couple of water bottles and a snack.

Dead fish had washed up on South Muiron Island. Whatever had caused this couldn't be good, and her instincts said it had something to do with the poachers.

She drove to the marina and took the PAWS boat out through the markers. It was a long journey to the island, which gave her far too much thinking time.

What should she do about Sam?

There was mutual attraction there, but was it a conflict of interest? She had to monitor his tour licence.

But the way he understood her reaction to Emelia's death, and how he empathised with her, was comforting. He made her consider the accident in a new light, one she hadn't considered before.

She wanted to help him with his team mate. Maybe

Amy could give her some insight into what Brandon was like when he got out of the army. They might come up with a solution.

Then there was Penelope's terrified reaction to him being in danger with the weapons cache. Was it over the top for someone she'd only just met?

It wasn't something she wanted to consider.

Still Ceiveon's words stuck in her head. *Go for it.*

What did that actually look like?

She hadn't felt this relaxed, this alive since before the accident. She wanted to be the person she was before, the happy, adventurous person, not this person who was too scared of making a mistake to live a full life.

Old Penelope, the person she was when she was single, would have jumped at the chance to spend time with Sam, would have been the one to jump his bones.

She smiled.

Maybe she'd call him when she got back in and invite him to the brewery for pizza.

The idea made butterflies flutter in her stomach, but for the first time in a long time they were nice butterflies.

By the time she reached the islands, the sun had passed its zenith and was heading back to the horizon. She followed the coordinates Karen had sent her and found the fish washed up on the shore of South Muiron Island. The stench turned her stomach and she breathed shallowly through her mouth. Far too many fish for the cause to be natural. She estimated the tides, anchored the boat and then grabbed her things and headed for a closer look.

She took photos and samples of the different species so she could get them tested to find out what killed them. Then she bagged the rest to dispose of back on the mainland. She didn't want any birds getting sick from eating them.

Penelope checked the time. She'd have to head back soon, but first she wanted to search further along the shore in case there were other areas where dead fish had washed up.

No one had booked to camp on the island this week, so there shouldn't be anyone she needed to question about the fish, but she'd check the designated camping area while she was here.

She sipped from her bottle and got out the binoculars before lifting her backpack. She'd give herself an hour before she returned to the mainland.

The wind had picked up, blowing a strong westerly which pushed her sideways as she headed north.

Up ahead was a slight rise, which would give her a better view across the island. She reached it, raised and focused the binoculars, and slowly scanned the shoreline. No mass of birds to indicate a feeding frenzy, not much at all in fact. She scanned south of her and still nothing. Good. It might be an anomaly. She'd assess the currents and tides to figure out from where they would have washed up and then investigate when the results came back and she knew what she was looking for.

She rubbed the goosebumps on her arms and then turned inland, scanning the land for any sign something was off.

Smoke.

Just a wisp, almost unnoticeable with the heavy breeze. Camp fire or scrub fire? Either way, it shouldn't be there. Hopefully she'd have enough water in her bottles to put it out.

She jogged towards it and the smoke increased, the fire probably rekindled by the wind. She ran harder, her backpack bouncing against her back. The islands were a haven for birds and it was nesting season. If the fire got out of control, it would threaten nests.

Breath coming in gasps, she reached the small grass fire. She emptied her water bottle over it, but it did little to douse the flames. She dumped her backpack on the ground and threw sand on the fire to smother it, and then stomped on the smouldering ground, careful not to melt the soles of her shoes.

Finally, she got the blaze under control and a few minutes later it was out.

She wiped the sweat off her forehead and examined the area.

Definitely used for camping. The ground had been cleared and close to the fire, the disturbance was more pronounced, as if something had been buried.

She took a couple of quick steps back, the memory of today's weapons cache far too clear. Whoever camped here might have buried their waste, but she wouldn't bet on it. She took some photos and recorded the GPS coordinates. This wasn't near the usual camp site for the island.

She'd call the police as soon as she got back.

With a last look around, and with her skin prickling, she hurried back to the boat. She was done for the day.

***

Sam sat on his balcony, which gave him a view down the canal to the marina. From here he could see all the boats entering. He would deny to anyone who suggested it that he was waiting for Penelope to return, but that was exactly what he was doing. He didn't like the idea of her going out alone. The sun was already low in the sky and she should be back by now, even with the water rougher than it was when she'd left.

He scanned the ocean through his binoculars. A boat was heading in, but it was too far away to recognise the person behind the wheel. He sipped his beer and waited for it to get closer.

He'd tried Sherlock again, wanting to let his friend know he was still valued, but there'd been no response. Sam sent him a long text message instead. Still no reply.

He'd try again tomorrow and if he couldn't get through, he'd call Sherlock's occupational therapist and get her to pass on the message when she visited him during the week.

Next, Sam called Brandon.

"Didn't think I'd hear from you so soon," Brandon said as he answered.

Sam smirked. "Penelope got called into work. I heard from my guy today, and she's in the clear. He couldn't find any link to Stonefish."

"I'm glad. No news from Dot yet, but the bomb squad has to have arrived. No boom either."

It would be interesting to find out what was in the bag if Dot relented and told them. "Tell me when you know." Sam finished his beer and took the empty bottle inside to the recycling. By the time he returned, the boat was close enough to make out the PAWS logo on the side. One passenger and though the hat was pulled low, he was fairly sure it was Penelope.

"I'll call you tomorrow." Sam hung up and smiled. He'd walk down to the marina and bump into Penelope there. Then perhaps he could convince her to have dinner with him.

On the way out, he grabbed his hat and sunglasses, and tucked his phone and wallet into his pocket. He took his time walking down, not wanting to beat her there, and his timing was rewarded when she motored into the marina as he arrived. He used his pass to get through the gate and grabbed the rope she threw to him when she entered her pen.

She smiled. "I'm beginning to think you're stalking

me."

He grinned. "The other night was coincidental. This was completely planned. I saw you come into the marina and thought I'd come down and ask how you went."

Her smile faded and as he moved to help her off the boat, the smell of dead fish filled his nose. "Smells like you found what you were looking for."

She nodded and handed him a heavy, stinky bag. "I need to get these sent to the lab, and I need to speak to Dot."

He jerked, focusing on her. "What did you find?"

She pressed her lips together and seemed to fight with herself. That sense of playing by the rules. Finally she said, "I saw smoke which led me to an illegal camping spot. Looks like something might have been buried there recently."

His body went cold. "You didn't dig it up?"

She shook her head. "After this morning, I didn't dare. Do you think Dot is still out at the Ridge?"

"Brandon hasn't seen her yet, but she usually drops by to give an update before she heads back to town."

"I need to deal with the fish first," Penelope said.

She finished tying up the boat and carried her backpack and a second bag of fish with her as they walked back to her car.

"How about I call Brandon? Do you need a hand with this?"

She hesitated. "Yeah, that would be great."

A sense of satisfaction filled him as he helped her get the things into the car and then they drove to the PAWS office.

"Do you want to go to the brewery when I'm done?" Penelope asked.

"Love to," he answered. "I'll call Brandon about the island." At Penelope's nod, he called Brandon and explained the situation.

"We left one of the Ridge's radios with her. I'll radio her and call you back."

Sam hadn't been out the back of the PAWS building, but Penelope led him through to where there was a small laboratory. She divided the larger bag into two, placing the smaller division on the bench and the larger one in a big chest freezer. The waft of dead fish turned his stomach.

"I need to run a few tests to see if I can identify what killed them." She opened the smaller bag.

"Any thoughts?"

"Normally something like this is associated with coral spawning, but it's the wrong time of year."

Sam's phone rang. "What did Dot say?"

"She'll call Penelope when she gets back to town," Brandon said. "Depending on the time they finish here, they might go out to the islands in the morning."

"Thanks, mate." Sam hung up.

Penelope was on the phone reporting what she had found to someone. When she hung up, she said, "I need to send some samples to the Department of Fisheries. What did Brandon say?"

"Dot will call you when she gets back."

Penelope nodded as she prepared samples of fish and water. Sam leaned against a bench to watch.

She was focused, muttering things under her breath as she worked, talking through what she needed to do. Did she even realise she was doing it?

He waited until she looked up and blinked at him. "Are you staring?"

"Admiring," he replied. "Did you know you talk to yourself when you work?"

She blushed and ducked her head. "It's a bad habit of mine. It used to really annoy Emelia."

"I think it's cute, and the way you handle those

samples is very sexy. Intelligent women turn me on."

Her cheeks grew redder, but she smiled. "I find heroic men really attractive."

"Then we're a perfect match." He shifted away from the bench and moved towards her. She took a half step towards him and then glanced at her gloved hands.

"Hold that thought. I need to finish this."

Damn.

He went back to the bench and watched her work as she cut samples and labelled things. Efficient and competent. Would she go with it if he lifted her onto one of the clean benches over there and kissed her senseless, or would propriety get the best of her?

She would have an office somewhere, so maybe that was a better location, more private. He checked for security cameras. Clear.

"What are you looking for?"

He jumped at Penelope's voice and grinned. "Security cameras."

"Why?"

"I figured you wouldn't want it recorded when I kiss you."

"You're incorrigible." She shook her head with a smile.

"I know what I want."

"There are cameras at the doors." She placed the final sample in a bag and sealed it. "I'm done."

Sam moved fast, crossing the room in a flash and pushing her against the empty bench. She only had time for a quick gasp before his mouth was on hers.

Finally.

She opened for him, their tongues tangling in a desperate desire which had been building for hours, if not days. He lifted her up on the bench and her legs wrapped around him. More. He had to feel her. He slipped his hand under her shirt and with little finesse, cupped her breast, using his thumb to tease her nipple to a point.

She gasped and leaned into him, dragging at his top.

He was going to combust.

Vaguely somewhere behind him he heard a door slam. His instincts kicked in and he shifted away, moving towards the sound.

"Penelope!"

Sam sighed as he recognised Declan's voice.

Penelope swore, a word he hadn't thought she would use, and it made him smile. She leapt off the bench and tucked in her shirt as Sam did the same to his own.

"Will you get into trouble having me here?" he murmured, searching for somewhere to hide.

"Penel—" Declan's voice petered off as he entered the room.

Too late.

Sam smiled as Penelope shifted past him. "I was just about to call you, Declan."

Declan glanced at Sam and raised his eyebrows.

"Sam was kind enough to help me with the bags when he noticed me at the marina," Penelope continued. "I've contacted Fisheries, prepared all the samples. Preliminary water tests show nothing abnormal."

Sam had to hand it to her, she handled the interruption with style. It wasn't what he would have expected from the Penelope he'd first met, but something in the past day had changed, and he liked it.

Declan nodded as if pleased. "You could have called me if you needed a hand."

"I was in the area," Sam replied.

Declan ignored him. "Have you arranged the shipment?"

"Just about to," Penelope replied. "There should be

a flight out tonight that can take them."

"Anything else?" Declan asked.

Penelope glanced at Sam and he took it as a hint to leave. "I'll get out of your hair if you don't need me for anything else."

"We can take it from here." Declan gestured to the door.

Yeah, he was taking the hint, but Sam didn't like the way Declan looked at Penelope as if sizing her up. He hoped he hadn't caused her any trouble. At the door, he glanced over his shoulder. Declan was watching him and behind him Penelope made the sign for a phone call and mouthed *I'll call you.*

He couldn't wait.

Outside he debated whether to wait for Penelope there, but in the end he walked home. He took his time, enjoying the cooler temperature now the sun had gone down.

The buried item on the island was a worry. Best case scenario it was someone illegally camping and not bothering to take away their rubbish, but after this morning, he wouldn't discount anything. The poachers might have been there on other business. They'd have ready access to weapons if they were smuggling them.

It was tempting to check it out himself, but he didn't want to miss Penelope's call. They needed more men on the ground. He tried Sherlock again, but there was no answer.

He should hop on a plane and drag Sherlock's sorry arse up here. At least then his friend would be forced to face the issue, and it might get some life back into him. If there was a flight tonight, he could be back by tomorrow.

Car lights illuminated the street, and he shifted further to the side of the road. The car pulled up next to him. "Need a lift?"

Penelope.

He grinned and got into the passenger side. "I thought you would be longer."

"Declan decided there was no point doing the tests ourselves when the lab in Perth has better equipment. He offered to take the samples to the airport."

"That was nice of him."

"Yeah. Still I might go in and run the tests in the morning on the ones I put aside. There was something odd about the fish kill and I can't figure out what it is."

"I'm sure you'll work it out."

Penelope pulled into her driveway and parked. "I'll get changed before we go for pizza."

He smiled and followed her inside. "Or we could get delivery."

The door had barely closed behind them when she had her shirt off and it was closely followed by her bra.

Women's empowerment was a wonderful thing.

He pulled her close and kissed her, his hand cupping her breast, and she moaned.

Music to his ears.

He ran his hand up to her hair and encountered her braid. That would have to go, but right now he tugged gently on it and she arched her head back so he had access to her luscious neck. She tasted salty, and he nibbled his way up to her earlobe and her sound of appreciation set him even harder than he already was.

Sam stripped off his T-shirt, prying his sneakers off with his toes, and then made quick work of the button on her shorts, his lips constantly on her. He wanted her horizontal so he could touch her everywhere. "Bedroom."

She tugged his hand and he followed her down the hallway, admiring the way her butt jiggled in her pink lacy underwear. The image would make him hard every time he saw her from now on, wondering what type of underwear she was wearing underneath her plain uniform.

Penelope stopped at the edge of the bed and reached for her underwear band. Sam stopped her. "Not yet."

As badly as he wanted her, he also wanted to savour the moment. He got rid of his shorts and socks, so they both only wore underwear. "I need to touch all of you, but first, I need to untie your hair." He pulled her close again, enjoying the heat of her breasts against his chest. He slowed their kisses, long, languorous as his hands found the elastic band in her hair and unravelled it. Then he used his fingers to loosen the braid.

Damn thing was harder to do than it appeared.

He spun her so her back was facing him and untwisted the rest of her hair, running his fingers through it and massaging her scalp. All her glorious red curls fell past her shoulders in a waterfall of colour. Yes.

This time when he spun her, he lowered her onto the bed and her hair cascaded around her face. "Beautiful."

Her eyes widened as if surprised by the compliment.

"You are absolutely stunning, Penny. You take my breath away." He kissed her again, pouring all of his passion into the kiss, and then slowly made his way down her body, tasting, kissing, licking, worshipping her skin. He sucked on her breasts until she arched from the bed.

"Sam!"

He loved the breathless way she said his name.

Finally, he reached the last scrap of clothing. She was so hot, and the lace wet. She lifted her hips as he licked her core, tasting her through the scrap of fabric.

"Sam, more."

He grinned, happy to oblige. He slid the lace down her body and feasted on the core of her desire, listening to her sounds of pleasure, feeling the tension in her muscles increase as she neared her peak. Then he slid his fingers slowly inside her and she screamed in triumph, exploding around him.

Penelope overwhelmed him. Her skin flushed pink, her body trembling, her head thrown back, her eyelids heavy.

He wanted to see it again, but this time he wanted to be inside her when she came.

Sam stripped off his underwear and grabbed a condom from his shorts, sliding it on before he rejoined her on the bed. He kissed her deeply, and she sighed into his mouth. "I don't know if I can do that again."

"Are you willing to try?"

She opened her eyes a little wider and grinned. "Absolutely, but I may not be coherent at the end."

"I'll take that as a challenge," he murmured in her ear and then caught her laugh with his lips. She moaned and he took his time exploring her décolletage, teasing her nipples again until they were tight with desire, tasting and savouring every millimetre of her delectable breasts until she was again quivering underneath him. So responsive. So sensual.

He pressed his mouth to her core and she arched into him again.

"Please, Sam. I need you inside me."

He pressed against her and as he slid inside, they both moaned. Tight, hot, and so very slick. He gritted his teeth to keep his thrusts slow, teasing them both by almost withdrawing before thrusting deep again. She clenched around him.

"More. Faster."

He had to obey. He gave in to his urges and thrust into her again and again, feeling his own climax build as she arched up and orgasmed. Her breasts thrust forward, head thrown back, her glorious red hair a sunburst around her and he was lost.

He groaned, every muscle in his body celebrating.

When he finally collapsed next to her, she threw her arm over his and murmured something unintelligible. He grinned. "Mission successful."

She laughed.

Chapter 15

Penelope woke to the smell of coffee. She frowned and stretched, the dishevelled sheets reminding her of exactly what had happened the night before.

Repeatedly.

She smiled at the sound of cupboard doors opening and closing. Sam must be looking for mugs. Then the sound stopped, so she figured he'd found them.

What a night.

Penelope had never laughed after being so thoroughly satisfied, but Sam had a way about him.

What a way.

Every muscle and bone in her body was limp and satisfied and she could barely think coherently. She lay there basking in the memories. They'd ordered pizza, which they'd eaten in the kitchen, and then she'd taken the opportunity to explore Sam's hard, muscled body as thoroughly as he'd explored hers.

He'd been equally incoherent when she was done.

She grinned as Sam walked in naked, carrying two mugs of coffee.

"Your smile makes me think you're up to no good." He handed her a mug and kissed her. "Good morning."

"Isn't it just?" She sipped the perfectly brewed coffee. "I was remembering last night."

"That's definitely something to smile about." He sat next to her. "Have you got plans today?"

There were the fish samples to test, but if the Perth lab received the other samples yesterday, maybe there was no point. She glanced at the sheets. Would it be completely indulgent to spend the whole day in bed with this sexy man?

"I'm in." Sam grinned.

She glanced at him. "What?"

"You were contemplating something to do with this bed, and if it's what I'm also contemplating, then I'm totally on board."

She laughed. "Good to know." She placed her coffee on the bedside table and stretched. "Though a shower might be in order first to warm my muscles."

"I know another way to warm them." He winked, but was then serious as he asked, "Are you feeling all right?"

"I feel amazing."

He ran a hand up her leg, to her stomach, and then her breast. "I'll say you do." His chuckle sent a thrill through her, as did his kiss on her shoulder.

"How about you?"

"Better than amazing," he replied. "I can't seem to get enough of you." He caressed her breast and her body responded, shifting closer to him.

Oh my.

She moaned, part protest, part desire. "You're going to kill me."

Another chuckle, low and satisfied. "That wouldn't do." He took his hand away and sipped his coffee.

Damn. She should have kept her mouth shut.

Her phone rang somewhere in the distance. She had no idea where it ended up last night.

"I'll get it." Sam moved with a speed and grace, not even placing his mug down as he left the room.

His butt was delicious. She hadn't touched it nearly enough. Something to fix later.

The phone stopped ringing and she heard his voice. Had he answered it, or had it stopped ringing?

He laughed as he returned, phone to his ear. "Has anyone told you you're very nosey, Ceiveon?"

Penelope grinned. Her best friend would have a field day about Sam answering her phone, particularly at this time of morning.

"I'll let Penelope answer that." He handed her the phone.

"Morning, Five."

"Oh my God," Ceiveon shrieked. "You slept with that sexy hunk, didn't you?"

Sam's answering grin made it clear he could still hear her.

"That's none of your business."

"Tell me everything. Was he as good as he looks?"

Sam raised an eyebrow, so she went with it.

"Better. Much, much better."

His answering grin was worth it and he kissed her once before leaving the room to give her some privacy. She sighed.

"I want all the details."

"All I'll say is—" She checked to make certain he was gone and then lowered her voice. "The best sex of my life."

Ceiveon shrieked again and Penelope held the phone away from her ear. "This is brilliant. I'm so happy for you. What are you going to do now?"

"Well, I wasn't planning on moving from my bed until I go to work tomorrow."

"Yes! I remember those days." She sighed. "OK. I'm going to go, but the minute you surface I want a call with all the details."

"All right. Love you."

"Right back at you."

She hung up and went to find Sam. He was in the kitchen looking through her fridge. "You were quick," he said. "I thought you'd chat for a while."

"I told her I'd call her later."

"I was going to make pancakes, but you don't appear to have any decent toppings."

"It's so I can resist making them all the time."

"Then we'll have to have museli," he said.

She wasn't hungry right now. Seeing the handsome naked man in her kitchen made her ravenous for something else.

"How about we shower first?" she suggested.

Water, soap, and close confines seemed like the perfect remedy.

He grinned. "Lead the way."

***

Much later, they finally sat at her kitchen bench to have breakfast. It was a lovely day outside and she wished she'd bought some outdoor furniture so they could sit in her backyard while they ate.

Her phone rang. It was Dot. "How did it go?" Penelope asked, putting the call on speaker.

"Both issues have been dealt with."

Penelope pulled a face. "Was it another weapons cache on the island?"

"I can't tell you."

Not helpful. "Dot, I need to know how much danger I'm in. What should I do if I discover any more?"

"Call the police."

So it can't have been someone burying their rubbish. What else had Dot found? "Do you think they'll be back?"

"Possibly. You see anything odd, you call us. *Do not* investigate on your own. I'll tell the Stokes and Sam the same."

"Already know," Sam said.

Silence for a moment. "Right," Dot sounded resigned. "Try to keep each other out of trouble."

"We'll be careful, Dot," Sam promised.

"That's not a promise to stay out of trouble."

Sam smiled. "Trouble seems to be attracted to us."

"I'll say." She sighed. "Penelope, I'm having a small get together for my birthday tomorrow night. Nothing special, just dinner at the brewery if you want to come."

Penelope grinned. "Thanks. I'd love to. What time?"

"Six-thirty. Sam, I'd invite you, but it's a girls' night."

"I look good in a dress," Sam joked.

Dot laughed. "I'd like to see that someday."

It was good to hear Dot's laugh. She'd had a rough couple of months. "I'll see you then," Penelope said and hung up.

Sam was frowning when she turned back to him. "You're worried about whatever was buried."

He hesitated only a moment before he nodded. She appreciated he wasn't trying to keep her in the dark in order to protect her. "More weapons?"

"Possibly. Dot didn't mention whether the cache out at the Ridge was booby trapped. Maybe I overreacted."

"She said we shouldn't uncover anything we found."

"That might be to do with contaminating evidence," Sam replied.

"Should I call her back and ask?"

"She won't answer. If we know it's not booby trapped, she'll think we'll open anything we find and mess with the evidence."

"And would you?"

He grinned. "Yeah."

Penelope shook her head. She wanted to forget about all this for a day. "So, did you have plans today?"

Sam sighed. "I should get a few things ready on the boat for tomorrow," he said. "Assuming my suspension has been lifted." He raised his eyebrows, but smiled as he did so.

"It has." She paused. "I'm sorry about that. I didn't know you then."

"You did what you thought was right," he answered. "I get that, especially after what you've been through." He kissed her. "Besides, I had been planning to get between the calf and the orca before Rob stopped me. No hard feelings."

"I hated to disappoint all those people who booked."

"We got most people on other charters, and those we couldn't, we either refunded or gave them a voucher so they could re-book the next time they were up here. Some come up every year."

"How about comments on social media?"

Sam grimaced. "We posted a statement to explain the situation. Not everyone will believe it, but there's nothing we can do about that."

"Do you need a hand with the boat?" She wasn't ready to say goodbye yet.

"There's not a lot to do. Rob and I have been going over things the past few days and I wanted to see if I can remember by myself."

Well then, she could get to those fish after all. She wouldn't deny the disappointment, but she could also continue working on the baby blanket now Amy had given her a few pointers.

"I should be done by midday if you want to get lunch," Sam said.

"Sounds great. Call me when you're done."

Sam washed their dishes and then kissed her in a

way that made her want to drag him back to bed. When they broke apart, she said, "I'll give you a lift."

She put her knitting in her backpack and drove Sam to the marina. When she arrived at work, she called the twenty-four-hour lab number to confirm they received the samples.

"We haven't received anything from Retribution Bay," the person she spoke to said.

"Are you certain? It should have been couriered straight there when it arrived last night."

"I've been through last night's work, and there's nothing from your area."

Penelope hung up. She didn't want to disturb Declan on his day off. Luckily she'd kept some of the fish aside in case the samples she'd prepared got lost. She spent an hour preparing samples for the lab and running the few tests she could run up here. The results were odd. High levels of a chemical she didn't recognise. She printed the report, packed up and called Declan on her way to the airport to get her new samples on the next flight.

"The lab didn't receive the samples," she told him. "I've packed a new batch and I'm taking it to the airport now."

"Using fish from the freezer may change the results," he replied.

"I kept some in the fridge just in case," she said. "I've had labs lose my samples in the past."

"Good work. I look forward to receiving the results." He hung up.

After Penelope returned from the airport, she decided to get a coffee in town and spend time on her knitting project. She didn't want to be alone. Not after spending so much time with the Stokes and Sam.

Penelope arrived at Coral Connections in the small shopping complex, to find it bustling with people enjoying Sunday brunch. She inhaled deeply, enjoying the strong aroma of coffee and bacon, and the constant whirr of the coffee grinder. A quick glance didn't reveal a spare table. Damn it. She scanned again. Declan was with his wife and kids in the corner, and Mitchell was by the window with his family. Some teenaged girls were at a table in the middle and from the gifts on top it appeared as if it was someone's birthday. And there, over by the wall, was Gretchen sitting by herself.

Penelope didn't know her well, but this was a good opportunity.

Nerves fluttering in her chest, she approached. Gretchen looked up from her phone as Penelope reached the table and smiled. "Hey, Penelope."

"Hi. I hope I'm not interrupting."

Gretchen laughed. "No, some company would be nice. I came in with Jordan, but he's found better a better option." She gestured to where her son was sitting with a friend and what Penelope assumed was his family. "Please, have a seat."

"Thanks." Penelope slid into the chair opposite her.

"I have to thank you," Gretchen said, after Penelope had ordered a coffee from the passing wait person.

"What for?"

"For suspending our licence," Gretchen replied. "I've spent the week catching up on assignments and even got ahead." She sighed in happiness. "It's the first time I haven't been completely stressed about studying."

"What are you studying?"

"Occupational therapy. Now I've finished those assignments, I've just got a final exam and a practicum before I can graduate." Her face fell.

"You're not looking forward to the practicum?"

"I am, but I have to go to Geraldton or Karratha for a placement, but I don't have anyone to look after

Jordan."

That would be difficult. "How long would it be for?"

"Three weeks."

"Can I ask about his father?"

Gretchen's eyes shuttered. "Not an option. My family took his side during the separation, so it's just Jordan and me."

How horrid. Penelope wanted to help her, but her job had varying hours. "Maybe we could work something out," she suggested. "I could have him some days and I'm sure Georgie, Amy, and Faith would help too."

Gretchen sighed. "I hate to ask, and I also hate to leave him. We haven't been apart since he was born."

"I'll talk to Georgie. She knows everyone in town."

"He's in the same class as Lara," Gretchen said. "He'd probably enjoy spending a week at the Ridge. I'll call Amy."

Penelope's coffee arrived and she sipped it. "I'm glad there were some positives from suspending Sam's licence."

"I hear you've been spending a bit of time with him."

Penelope blinked in surprise. "How did you know?"

"Georgie," Gretchen said. "She was gloating about setting you up the other day."

Penelope chuckled. "Remind me to thank her the next time I see her."

Gretchen raised her eyebrows. "That good, huh?"

"Better," she confirmed.

"I thought Sam would be." Gretchen leaned forward. "He came on a tour a couple of months ago when Brandon got married. He was with some of his army buddies and they were all hot."

"Anyone catch your eye?"

She shrugged as if she didn't care, but her shoulders hunched. "I don't have time for men at the moment."

Definitely some bad experiences there.

"To completely change the subject, can I tell you how much I love your hair?" Gretchen leaned forward. "I tried going red a couple of months back, but it really didn't suit me."

Penelope touched her hair. "Thanks. I tried going blonde at university and it made me look washed out."

Gretchen smiled. "We should be happy with what we've got." She sipped her coffee. "What have you got in the bag?" Gretchen gestured to Penelope's backpack.

"My knitting," she replied, her cheeks heating. "I taught myself to knit, and Amy gave me some pointers. I thought I'd come down here and get a coffee and knit some rows." She shrugged, self-conscious. "It probably seems so old-fashioned, but my best friend just had a baby and I wanted to make her something."

"It's a wonderful idea. I have a few handmade things from when Jordan was a baby, and I've saved them for keepsakes. Your friend will appreciate it."

"If I ever get it finished." She withdrew the knitting and showed Gretchen the few rows she'd done.

"It's more than I could do." Gretchen leaned over and touched the yarn. "It's so soft. The baby will love it."

Penelope smiled, glad for the encouragement. She started on the next row as she asked, "Do you work weekends?"

Gretchen shook her head. "Not usually. Rob knows it's hard for me with Jordan, so I only work one weekend a month and then Jordan stays with one of his friends and has a sleepover."

"He must love it. Sleepovers were always the best when I was a kid."

Gretchen nodded.

"Mum, can I go play at Dylan's place?" Jordan stood at the table, his friend next to him.

"Is it all right with Mrs Knudsen?"

"Yeah, Mum's fine with it," Dylan said.

Penelope glanced up and saw Dylan's mother nod and smile.

"All right, but call me if you need anything, and be home by five."

"Thanks, Mum." Jordan ran off with his friend.

"It's starting already," Gretchen said.

"What is?"

"Jordan wanting to play with his friends rather than his mum." Gretchen's smile was sad. "It's great he's so confident, but it's a tear to the heartstrings as well."

"I can only imagine," Penelope said. She'd always assumed she'd have children one day, but had never had the urge with Gerard.

They spoke about Retribution Bay and swapped stories about the ocean until Gretchen checked her watch and stretched. "I should get going. I've been neglecting the housework this week, and I need to get it back under control before I go back to work."

Penelope packed up her knitting, pleased at the dozen rows she'd managed. "I should go too. I've enjoyed talking to you."

"Likewise."

They paid and then walked to the door. "I'll see you later."

Penelope waved to Gretchen and got out her phone. Sam would almost be finished. As if he'd heard her thought, her phone dinged with a message.

All finished. Are you at home?

In town at Coral Connections. Heading home now.

I'll meet you.

She grinned and glanced up to make sure she wouldn't walk into anyone. Across the way, a man caught her eye. She froze as recognition hit her.

Murray, the poacher.

Heart pounding and hands trembling, she watched him lift a black crate onto the back of his ute. He hadn't seen her. She ducked behind a tree and dialled triple zero. The woman who answered wasn't someone she knew.

"I'm in Retribution Bay. I've spotted a man who evaded police after he drew a gun on me last week." Penelope exhaled. "He was caught poaching at the Muiron Islands."

"Exactly where are you, ma'am?" the dispatch asked.

"Outside Coral Connections." Or near enough. She'd walked towards the street as she'd texted Sam. She scanned the area for a street sign and caught Grant walking towards her from the carpark, expression fierce.

Shit.

She backed away. "The other man is here as well—Grant. He's coming towards me."

"Go into the cafe," the dispatch said. "Surround yourself with people."

Penelope backed away, eyes still on the man making determined steps towards her. He was between her and the cafe. Across the road was the skate park where a bunch of children were hanging out, but she couldn't go there and risk them. All she had was the street.

Over by the ute, Murray had spotted her and was backing the ute out.

She was in real trouble. "There's no one here," she gasped. Yelling would attract the attention of the people in the car park, but if Grant still had his gun, she could put them in danger.

"Are you still there?" The dispatcher's voice was far away, and Penelope realised she'd lowered the phone.

"Yes." She called to Grant, "The police are on their

way."

He didn't hesitate, just kept coming towards her.

"How far away are the police?"

"I'm still getting in touch with them," dispatch said.

She was so screwed. Her nerve left her and she turned to run as a car pulled up beside her. Grant's eyes widened and his steps faltered.

Sam stormed past her. Grant spun, sprinting for the ute Murray was driving. He leapt into the passenger side and the car roared out of the car park.

Penelope's gaze went back to Sam who had stopped chasing them and turned. Relief made her knees weak and she stumbled towards him. "Good timing."

He swept her into his arms. "Are you all right?"

She clung to him for a minute, secure, and nodded. "I called the police." She stepped back and held her phone to her ear. "They drove off in a black ute." She gave the woman the number plate.

"Impressive observation," Sam said, keeping his hand in hers.

"I'll contact the local police," dispatch said. "Are you safe?"

"Yes, my friend scared them away."

"The local police will be in touch."

Penelope hung up and hugged Sam again. "Thank you."

"He's lucky he got away. What happened?"

They walked back to Sam's car, and he drove them into the car park. "I spotted Murray at his car and called the police, but Grant saw me. I didn't want to endanger anyone."

"You should have yelled," Sam said. "They wouldn't want that kind of attention." He parked. "How about we grab some rolls from the bakery and go back to my place?"

Penelope nodded. She'd had enough of being in

public. What had they been planning to do?
What had they wanted?

Chapter 16

Sam kept his voice light, but his hands clenched around the steering wheel as he followed Penelope back to his place. When he'd seen Grant going for Penelope, he'd felt equal parts rage and fear. The thought of something happening to her was not worth contemplating. It had taken all of his willpower to stop, make sure Penelope was safe, and not go after them.

They shouldn't have come back to town. They shouldn't have gone after Penelope.

Why had they?

Penelope had the same question as she leaned against his kitchen bench, finally safe. "Why would Grant come after me?"

"I don't know, but I don't like it." Sam scowled. "Maybe because you can identify them."

"So can you."

"But I wasn't there, and I'm a lot more intimidating." He puffed out his chest and waggled his eyebrows. Her laugh was like a balm to his soul.

"You look like a gorilla."

"Exactly," Sam said. "They won't mess with me unless they've got the upper hand." He got a couple of plates out of the cupboard and placed the rolls on them.

She frowned. "We both need to be careful if they've come back to town."

He nodded. "It means they've got unfinished business, otherwise why risk it? Retribution Bay isn't that big."

"I'll inform the other marine rangers to be on the lookout."

He poured them both a glass of water and then they carried their lunch to the outside table. "You shouldn't go out alone."

Penelope raised her eyebrows. "It's my job. I won't let them scare me away. Besides, out there I should have plenty of warning. A boat can't sneak up."

He still didn't like it. He'd keep an eye out for her when he went out tomorrow. Maybe he could ask Declan which area she was covering and ask Jasmine to search for humpbacks around there.

Brandon would be busy at the Ridge. What he needed was Sherlock up here to help him keep an eye on her, but he wasn't certain of his friend's mental state.

Penelope's phone rang. "It's Dot." She put the call on speaker and explained the situation.

"We've got people looking for them," Dot said. "I don't think they've left town, or else we would have seen them."

Not a comforting thought. Someone must be hiding them. "What are they up to?"

"I wish I knew," Dot answered.

She sounded almost defeated. Stonefish had been a thorn in her side for months now and as far as Sam was aware, they were no closer to catching who was behind it all.

"Keep aware," Dot continued. "Avoid going anywhere alone if you can. Penelope, I'll speak to

Declan."

"All right." Penelope hung up and turned to Sam. "This can't be related to the buried treasure," she said. "It must be another part of their business. If the man responsible for the animal smuggling was killed, could Grant or Murray be his replacement? Maybe they were smuggling ocean animals too."

"They wouldn't have killed them if that was the case," Sam pointed out. "But maybe they were killing time while waiting for something else." He wanted to hunt them down himself, but he wasn't ready for Penelope to go yet. "Did you get the results from the lab?"

Penelope shook her head. "The samples were lost in transit. I sent another batch this morning and ran a few tests of my own, but didn't recognise the chemical composition."

"Don't you have a chain of custody?"

She nodded. "Declan has the receipt and I'll chase it down on Monday."

He didn't like that it had gone missing. It spoke of Stonefish's involvement. He'd ask her about it again tomorrow. In the meantime, they had to figure out what Stonefish were smuggling this time. "If what you saw at the camp site on Muiron was more buried weapons, that could be what they're up to."

Penelope shivered. "Those guns were terrifying."

Sam nodded. No individual needed weapons that powerful. It spoke to organised crime and weapon smuggling.

So maybe he'd have to investigate it tomorrow night. Penelope would be at Dot's birthday celebration. He could invite Brandon into town for dinner and they could take a look.

He smiled. No one needed to know.

***

The next day after work, Penelope shut the door behind her, dropped her keys on the kitchen bench and sighed. She'd been on edge all day, expecting to see the poachers at any minute. Having four familiar walls around her was safety and comfort.

She had an hour before she was due at dinner for Dot's birthday. She debated calling Sam, but she almost wanted a break from him as well. Things had moved rapidly between them, and while she'd really enjoyed her weekend, the intensity was scary.

She'd found herself thinking of him throughout the day, wondering what he would do in certain circumstances, wishing she could share things with him.

She'd rarely thought of Gerard while she worked.

Penelope headed for the shower, taking her time under the spray to wash away the rest of her tension, and then getting ready to go out. With still half an hour before she had to be at the restaurant, she picked up her knitting. She'd done more rows after arriving home last night and it was resembling a blanket and not a random bit of knitting. She might even have it finished by the end of the month. Ceiveon would be so surprised.

It was dark by the time she left her house to make the short drive to the brewery. She brushed her hand over her belly, the movement and the silky fabric of her black dress helping to calm the small bundle of nerves dancing in her stomach. These women were welcoming and friendly. There was nothing to be worried about.

As she got out of the car, she glanced around the car park, but saw no one lurking. Maybe that's what the nerves were about.

Dot sat at a table made from a large, recycled cable spool, her emerald green top drawing Penelope's gaze as she crossed the yard strewn with blue metal. It was such a contrast to the blue uniform Dot normally wore, and Penelope smiled. With her were Nhiari, wearing a subdued brown, and Gretchen, her floral maxi dress typical of the style a few years ago.

"Any problems today?" Dot asked as Penelope sat.

"None," Penelope answered. "And I'm sure you want a break from police work tonight."

"There's not much chance of a break when you live in a small town," Nhiari answered.

"What's been going on?" Gretchen asked.

Dot widened her eyes in a stare. Gretchen mustn't know about Stonefish. "Just a few people not doing the right thing."

Luckily, Amy arrived with Faith, and Georgie was right behind them. By the time the greetings were over, conversation had shifted to what everyone had been up to.

"Seen Sam lately?" Georgie asked Penelope.

Penelope smiled. "Yesterday."

"I knew you too would be amazing together," Georgie continued.

"Brandon's on his way there now," Amy said. "They're going to catch up." She pursed her lips together.

Penelope frowned. Sam hadn't mentioned that. She glanced at Gretchen, but didn't ask the question she wanted to know. What were the men planning? She caught Amy's eye and Amy gave a tiny nod. Yes, they were planning something.

Good to know she wasn't being paranoid. She'd get the details later and try not to worry now. Both men were highly trained and knew what they were doing.

"Presents!" Georgie called and handed Dot a brightly wrapped box.

Dot held up a hand. "I don't need presents."

"Too bad." Georgie raised her palms so she couldn't take it back. "You can't refuse."

Dot tried her glare, but Georgie laughed. With a large sigh, the sergeant unwrapped the package and opened the box. Dot shook her head, but her lips curved in a smile. "Georgie!"

"It was Amy's idea," Georgie said.

Nhiari took the box and picked up what was inside. A stress ball shaped like a stonefish and a hammer. Penelope grinned, but Gretchen looked confused.

"What's the significance?"

"An annoying case," Dot said.

Penelope handed over the envelope she'd brought with her. "Mine next." She hadn't known what to get her so had bought her a voucher for the beauty salon in town. Dot could do with some relaxation time.

"Thanks, Pen," Dot replied.

After the presents were unwrapped, Penelope asked Gretchen, "Were you out on the boat today?"

"Yeah, it was a fantastic day. Sam's taken to it really well, for his second time out."

Penelope winced, but no one seemed to notice.

They ordered and the conversation turned to Faith's pony club. "Jordan's enjoying his lessons," Gretchen said.

"He's doing really well," Faith said. "He's my best student, after Lara."

"I think Lara might be part of the reason he's putting in so much effort." Gretchen smiled.

"Oh, he likes her?" Georgie asked. "Lara likes him too."

Gretchen sighed. "He's growing up so fast."

"Why don't the two of you come out to the Ridge on the weekend?" Amy invited. "You can go riding, or you can stay with me while Faith takes them out."

"Jordan would love it. We're free on Sunday."

"It's a date," Amy said.

"Are you working on Saturday?" Georgie asked.

"No, I promised to take him and Dylan snorkelling," Gretchen said. "I'm working the weekend after and he's asking if he can stay home alone rather than going to his friend's place."

"He's welcome at the Ridge at any time," Faith said. "Call me if you need a backup."

"Thank you. That would be great." The relief on her face made Penelope wonder how hard it had been for Gretchen being a single mother with no family support.

Why had she chosen to move up here in the first place?

Maybe she was like Penelope, trying to get as far away from memories as she could.

Their meals arrived, and the conversation flowed to books and movies, and then gossip in town. Penelope excused herself to go to the bathroom. On her way back to the table, she noticed Gretchen arguing with a man close to the kitchen door. Gretchen shook her head and backed away, anger and fear on her face.

Penelope's heart leapt, and she headed towards them, taking in the man; mid-thirties, dark, close cropped hair, broad build, but short, with a tattoo of a rose on his upper shoulder and a name scrawled underneath. Penelope couldn't quite make out the name from the distance. Before she could reach them, Gretchen strode away.

Penelope intercepted her. "Are you all right?"

Gretchen jumped and huffed, breathing heavily, her eyes damp, muscles tense. "Shit, I didn't see you there, Penelope." She exhaled and then smiled. "I'm fine."

Penelope nodded back towards the kitchen, but the man was gone. "Was he giving you trouble?"

Gretchen paled but shrugged. "Just a guy who wouldn't take no for an answer. It's fine. Let's get back to the others." She walked away.

Penelope scanned the restaurant, but she couldn't see the man anywhere. She frowned. She'd keep an eye on Gretchen, make sure she had a lift home.

*****

Sam had all the gear packed and ready to go on the rubber tender by the time Brandon arrived. He took Brandon straight through the house and out the back door to where the tender was tied up to his jetty.

"What did you tell Amy?" Sam asked.

"I told them I was staying the night here and helping you on the boat tomorrow."

Sam raised his eyebrows. "Amy wasn't suspicious?"

Brandon winced. "She told me to be careful."

So no, they hadn't fooled her. At least she hadn't tried to stop them.

He motored out through the canals into the gulf. They'd jagged a still night, so he accelerated across the water, the purr of the engine too loud for conversation.

When they eventually arrived at the island, the wind was causing the moon's light to ripple across the water and in the distance, clouds were incoming. Sam bumped his way around the reef, doing a wide lap of the island with all lights onboard turned off. On the northern side, they hit the jackpot. The large luxury boat Penelope had stopped was anchored close to the shore and there was a small dinghy on the beach.

Brandon brought the night vision goggles to his eyes while Sam cut the engine.

"No movement," Brandon reported.

Someone might still be on board, but all the lights were out. "Boat or island?" Sam asked.

"Island's going to give us the best chance of catching them in the act," Brandon said.

Sam turned the tender around and returned to the

location he'd gone to with Penelope the other day after their initial run in with the men.

Brandon anchored them while Sam grabbed his backpack. They'd passed only a couple of boats on the trip and no other lights shone on the water or land to signal people were around. He put on the night vision goggles and scanned the area, checking for something they might have missed in the dark.

"Anything?" Brandon asked.

"Not yet."

They moved together, years of practice making each of their roles second nature. The island was long but not overly wide and it didn't take them long to reach the centre. From there, they turned north, looking for traces of whoever was on the boat.

After only a few minutes, they spotted the torches. Three lights, all pointing towards whatever it was they were doing. Sam scanned the surrounding area to ensure no one else was around. Light wind tickled the grasses, but no heat signatures showed.

Brandon got out his camera and they moved closer, coming from downwind. The incoming clouds had obscured the moon, making it dark and whoever was there wouldn't have great night vision because of the lights, so they moved as close as they dared, before crawling the remaining distance. Murray and Grant were digging a hole and nearby the grass was burnt. Must be where Penelope had found the disturbed earth. Either they didn't know the police had found it, or they were burying something else.

Sam guessed the former, which gave him hope there wasn't a spy in the local police force.

Neither man worried about keeping his voice low.

Murray stopped digging and leaned against his shovel. "This is a stupid idea. What if the police come back for more evidence?"

"Boss doesn't think they will. They got everything the other day." Grant wiped sweat off his brow and then continued to dig.

So they knew the police had found it. That was interesting.

"Still, it's risky. What if we get caught?"

"I told you, we're dispensable. Boss didn't care his own son was killed, he doesn't care about us."

Murray looked at Grant, a flash of uncertainty followed by anger. "We've got a sweet deal here. Do you want out?"

"No, I'm just saying the boss has lost his focus." Grant adjusted the hand gun stuck in the back of his pants.

Brandon stiffened and Sam scanned for other weapons. They had brought the Ridge's rifle, but if Murray was armed as well, they'd be in trouble.

"He's curious," Murray defended. "It's not as if he needs the money."

"He's obsessed." Grant leaned on his shovel. "He's got half a dozen people working on some translation which is all he cares about."

It had to be the Dutch captain's journal they were talking about.

"It's gotta be important."

Grant ignored the comment and continued his rant. "He's forgetting about the big picture. We've spent years off anyone's radar, and now everything is falling apart."

"Clark got us into this mess, not the boss." Murray started digging again.

Grant swore. "Let's get this thing buried and get out of here." He continued digging.

Sam tapped Brandon and made the sign to fall back. They'd heard and seen enough.

When they were a safe distance away, he checked his

phone. No reception.

"Best bet is the radio on the boat," Brandon said. "But Stonefish monitor those communications. These guys will be long gone by the time Dot gets here."

"So we just leave?"

"I got some photos. We'll phone it in when we've got reception and she can get someone out here."

"Those guys went after Penelope," Sam stated. He didn't want to let them get away. He'd been having nightmares about what they might have done to her if he hadn't got there in time. "We can take them."

"There's no cover," Brandon pointed out. "One of them will see us coming and they both have guns. If I shoot first, Dot will have to arrest me, and I'm not doing that to Amy."

"Give me the gun then."

Brandon stared at him. "No. I get your frustration, but it's smarter this way."

Sam jolted. "You sound like Sherlock."

Brandon chuckled. "He must have rubbed off on me."

They fell back and jogged to the tender. They moved quickly to launch and soon they were heading back to the mainland. It would be useful to have Sherlock in town, someone who wasn't known to Stonefish, someone who could watch them rather than the other way around.

Sam would call Sherlock tomorrow and if that didn't work, he'd tell Brandon. Sherlock couldn't refuse the both of them.

Chapter 17

Penelope scanned the streets as she drove to the marina the next day. Grant and Murray should be long gone, but she couldn't help taking a second look at every dark car. She parked in an area with plenty of free bays so she couldn't be boxed in and then hurried across the bitumen to the gate into the marina. When the gate clanged shut behind her, she let out a sigh.

What had they been planning to do if they'd caught her?

She had done nothing to them, she hadn't even fined them.

The PAWS boat was in one of the first pens, but she scanned the luxury boats in the marina to ensure the *Joy Ridin'* wasn't there. Quickly she ran through her checks and then motored into the gulf. Her muscles relaxed when water surrounded her with no boats nearby.

Today she was doing spot checks on the tour boats, which operated on the east coast of the peninsula, so she would see Sam.

He'd sent her a good morning message, and she'd asked if he'd had a good night. All he responded was it had been enlightening, but then hadn't responded to further questions.

What had he and Brandon been up to?

She'd debated calling Amy, but decided she wanted Sam to be the one to tell her.

The way he'd rescued her on the weekend had been nothing short of heroic, and if she was honest with herself, she was a little bit in love with him for that alone.

But she didn't know how he felt about her.

Would he call her now he had his licence back? She shut the thought down.

Sam wasn't like that.

But she hadn't spoken to him since Sunday and it felt odd after seeing him every day for five days.

Jimmy was the closest operator to her, so she radioed him and arranged to come on board. Everything was as it should be, with no extra passengers, and she watched from afar to ensure they were keeping the correct distance between the boat and the whales.

Then she contacted Sam's boat, *Oceanid*. "This is Victor Sierra Foxtrot. Requesting permission to come aboard."

"Permission granted," Sam replied. "You're welcome anytime, Penny."

She smiled and ran through her checks. Sam joined her. "I guess it would be unprofessional to kiss you in front of everyone," he murmured.

"Very," she replied, but couldn't stop her smile.

She finished her checks and before she climbed back onto her boat, she kissed his cheek. "Call me tonight."

"Absolutely." Sam saluted and blew her a kiss.

Her heart was light as she motored away. She was beginning to feel more like the person she'd been before Emelia died. The recent Penelope would have been mortified kissing Sam, even if it had been on the cheek.

She continued north to monitor the bird life on the islands in the gulf. The data would be valuable in ascertaining whether anything was changing.

When she was done, she checked in with the office. It was mid-afternoon and many of the tour boats were already heading back to the boat ramp after a successful day out.

"We've had a report of a dead whale floating off the north-east coast." Declan gave her the coordinates. "Can you check it out? Assess whether it's likely to end up on the beach?"

How sad. "Copy that," she answered and turned the boat north. She should have enough time to get out there and back before the sun set.

She passed a few small fishing boats, tourists who came up to trawl and catch big Spanish mackerel and other such game fish, but most were heading back to the harbour as well.

It didn't take long to spot the dead whale calf. Birds hovered over the area, diving into the water to either feed on the whale carcass or the fish feeding on it. She looked up the prevailing currents and calculated where the carcass would end up if it was left where it was.

Right on a popular swimming beach.

A dead whale would attract sharks. Better she tow it a few nautical miles north so it would drift past the peninsula and further out to sea.

Quite a lot of the body was intact and Penelope scanned the area for an orca who had yet to finish its meal. Nothing, but a large boat heading back to the coast and the water was heaving with bull and tiger sharks. A feast for them, but they made it difficult to get a rope around the dead whale's tail in order to tow it.

She studied the logistics as the sea breeze whistled

around her and the waves jostled the boat. Would her boat be large enough to tow it the required distance even if she could get a rope around it? She circled the carcass, looking for somewhere to attach a rope. There were some strange markings around its head, holes of some kind. They almost looked like large bullet holes.

She took a couple of photos, shifting the boat around to get a better angle.

Odd and disturbing. She took a few more photos for reference.

No one would shoot a whale and then leave it here. What would be the point?

Unless Grant and Murray were having fun.

The boat she'd spotted.

Her skin prickled, and she turned to check her surroundings.

Joy Ridin' was heading straight towards her, Murray behind the wheel.

Shit. Penelope's heart jumped, and she grabbed the radio, her other hand shoving the throttle into forward. "Mayday, this is Victor Sierra Foxtrot." She frantically turned the wheel one handed as she continued, "I have a vessel approaching with known fugitives on board." The boat turned slowly and she increased speed, frantically trying to steer in the right direction. "I'm at the whale carcass." The boat bumped against its side as she gave the coordinates, and then gunned the engine, but she was too late. The vessel cut in front of her, blocking her escape route.

Grant stood on the deck holding a military grade gun like someone out of the movies. Her legs wobbled. At least the boat was in front of her. She had the bow and screen between her and the weapon.

"Sending help," Karen responded. "What's your situation?"

"They're here." She shifted into neutral to avoid

damage to the boat.

Reversing wouldn't get her far, and the whale carcass blocked one side. One hand clenched the radio and the other the wheel. How was she going to escape?

There was a tiny cabin under the bow, which was her best shelter, but it wouldn't help if they boarded.

And the bullets would rip through the fibreglass like it was butter.

She stared at Grant.

"The boss wants the Stokes to stop messing in his business," Grant called. "You're the warning."

Penelope reacted on instinct, diving onto the floor as the shots exploded, smashing the windscreen and peppering the deck with bullet holes. She hissed as something hit her forehead, and covered her head to protect herself from the shrapnel flinging around.

The noise was deafening and she squeezed her eyes closed, shifting closer to the cabin, but then the shots came crashing through the bow and she curled into a ball, her heart pounding.

The shots cut off and the silence was pulsed in her ears. Then the radio squawked. "Penelope, report, damn you."

Karen sounded frantic.

She opened her eyes as another round exploded, but this time lower, around the waterline of the boat. Something warm ran down her face and she swiped at it, finding her fingers covered in blood. She applied pressure to the cut.

Then something cold touched her ankle. Sea water. Water was flowing in through a hole in the side.

They were sinking her boat.

Normally it wouldn't worry Penelope. She had a life jacket, she was a strong swimmer, and she'd sent her coordinates to Karen, but she was right next to a dead whale and a feeding frenzy of sharks.

The final shots of the round were directed at the motor, which died and immediately began to smoke. When it was over, Grant shouted, "Good luck with the sharks."

Then the luxury boat sped away.

Penelope moved fast, grabbing the radio, but keeping her head low. "Mayday, mayday. Parks and Wildlife boat Victor Sierra Foxtrot. My boat is sinking. Request immediate assistance from any nearby vessel." She gave her coordinates again. Then she crawled over to the edge of the boat and stuffed a spare life jacket in the hole.

"We're sending a boat," Declan replied.

But would it get here in time?

With little hope, she turned the key for the engine. No response.

She peeked over the side, saw the luxury boat heading out to sea. They shouldn't be able to hit her from there.

Chest tight, she stood and took stock of the situation. The boat was much lower in the water than it had been. There must be more holes under the deck.

She needed rescue. There'd been multiple fishing boats in the area when she'd come this way, but now she scanned the horizon, it was empty.

The tour boats she'd audited were much further to the south and by this time might even be back at their moorings.

All around, the sharks splashed as they competed to bite off as much of the whale as possible.

There had to be at least a dozen tiger sharks, maybe six bull sharks and another handful of black tip reef sharks around. Fins broke the surface more than ten metres away as they moved towards and away from their floating meal.

No need to be scared. They were far more interested

in the whale than they would be in her. That meal wouldn't fight back.

The sun was low now. Another hour and it would be on the horizon and she would be harder to spot.

She sloshed through the ankle-deep water and collected all the life jackets, inflating them and then using rope from her survival kit to tie them together into a makeshift raft. They might keep her above the surface.

The water was up to her knees and it was just a matter of time before the boat would go down, and go down fast. She had to get away from it, and the whale carcass before it did. She activated her personal EPIRB and grabbed the radio. "Abandoning ship. Will make my way south from the whale carcass and try heading for shore."

Problem was, the currents would push her and the carcass in the same direction. She scanned the water in the fading light and snatched the waterproof torch from the cubby hole next to the wheel.

Though it was probably foolish, she slipped her backpack on. If no one found her quickly, she had enough in there to survive a couple of days.

The sea breeze blew strongly from the west and as she picked up her handmade raft, the wind snatched it from her grasp and blew it away from the whale, sending it about ten metres away before it landed in the water. Clear of most of the sharks. She just had to reach it.

The sharks should be too busy feasting to be interested in her.

Taking one last scan to check for a rescue boat, she slid over the edge of the boat and into the cold water. The water was dark, the angle of the sun making it difficult to see below the surface. She fought her urge to race to her raft, instead using breaststroke to move fast through the water without splashing.

Nearby, a fin broke the water followed by a tail flick. She kept moving, confident strokes despite her heart trying to burst through her chest.

The sharks she could see, she could deal with. It was the ones she couldn't that she was worried about. The ones that might attack from below.

A fin broke the surface in front of her, heading straight for her. Her calm shattered.

***

Sam grinned as he headed back to the marina. It had been a pretty awesome day. He'd seen Penelope, the passengers had been terrific, the whales inquisitive, and the fact he'd had to go a little further north than usual wasn't enough to bother him.

This was what he'd been hoping for when he'd bought the business.

The whales had approached the swimmers, and he didn't know who was more curious and thrilled. He'd even handed over the wheel to Rob and swum with the whales.

Magical, majestic, mind-blowing.

Nothing could spoil his day now. His crew were downstairs chatting with most of the passengers, though a couple were enjoying the cool breeze on the top deck next to him.

It was then his radio squawked.

"Mayday, this is Victor Sierra Foxtrot. I have a vessel approaching with known fugitives on board. I am at the whale carcass."

Penelope.

His blood froze as he turned the boat west, already calculating how far she was from him from the coordinates.

Gretchen stuck her head up the ladder. "Where are

you going?"

"Penelope's in trouble," he barked. "Get the passengers seated and get Rob up here."

Gretchen called to the couple who were on the top deck. "Please come to the lower deck. It's going to get bumpy."

It sure as hell was. He slowed only long enough for them to get safely to the lower deck as Gretchen announced they were answering a distress call.

Then he opened the throttle as Rob clambered up the ladder to join him.

"What gives?" Rob asked.

"Penelope's in trouble. I need you to show me the fastest way there. Are there any reefs I've got to watch out for?"

"Just here." He pointed to the map. "Follow this channel and you'll be fine."

Sam had never pushed his boat so hard. The engines roared and his passengers held on as he crashed over the waves.

He had to get to Penelope. If those bastards hurt her, nothing would stop him from hunting them down. He should have gone after them yesterday.

The boat crashed over another wave and the radio squawked again. "Mayday, mayday. Parks and Wildlife boat Victor Sierra Foxtrot. My boat is sinking. Request immediate assistance from any vessel nearby."

She was alive.

Good. She could swim, and she'd have a life vest on. The bastards must have just damaged her boat.

Then the words from her first mayday sank in.

Whale carcass.

There'd be dozens of sharks around the body, and she'd be in the water with them when her boat went under.

He accelerated as fast as he dared.

Murray and Grant. He'd kill them.

He scanned the water, searching for the boat, and spotted the birds circling about a kilometre away.

Sam grabbed the binoculars and handed the wheel over to Rob. There had to be more boats out here, closer than he was.

Nothing.

If the police had launched into action, they would still be getting to the marina. They couldn't help her.

But maybe Jasmine could give him eyes.

He snatched the radio and called, "Jasmine, are you still flying?"

"Just doing the last sunset flight of the day," she replied.

"I need your help. PAWS called in a mayday. I'm heading there now, but still some distance away. Can you fly north and report on the situation? You should be able to see the birds flying over a whale carcass."

"Roger that. I've been avoiding the birds, but I'm nearby."

Sam clutched the radio, waiting for her report.

"Boat is going under. One person is in the water. Looks like they've made a raft of life jackets. A couple of sharks are circling."

Nothing he could do except pray. "Roger."

"I'll stay overhead until they make it to the raft."

He jolted. "She's not on the raft?"

"No, she's swimming to it."

And the sharks were circling her. Fuck.

"I'll have to slow when I get to her," Rob said. "If there's space, I'll go between her and the whale. It should be enough to scare the sharks away while we get her on board."

Sam hoped so.

He stayed on the top deck as they neared the area, binoculars glued to his eyes. The waves were a decent size and he couldn't see Penelope in the water, though occasionally he glimpsed the yellow life raft she'd made. She wasn't on it.

Come on, Penelope.

The tightness in his chest made it difficult to breathe.

Where was she?

***

Penelope shrieked and thrust her arms and legs in front of her, more instinctual than with any actual plan. The fin swerved and went under.

Maybe she'd scared it off, maybe it was coming around for another try. In the distance she thought she heard the rumble of an engine, but the sea was too rough to see anything. She glimpsed her raft only a few metres away and she powered towards it, using every bit of energy she had to get there fast, not caring about splashing any more.

Her fingers brushed the plastic before a wave carried it out of reach. She stretched again, thinking at any moment sharp teeth would seize her leg and drag her away from safety.

This time her fingers grabbed a strap, and she gripped it, hauling the raft towards her. With adrenaline born from fear, she lifted herself onto the raft and brought her knees to her chest so nothing dangled over the side.

The raft sank, the jackets she was on bobbing below the surface, but those making up the sides above it. Maybe the plastic would be enough to hide her from beady eyes and sharp senses.

She lay there breathing heavily, curled into a ball while she got her breath back. The danger wasn't over yet. She had to get to land, and all she had to paddle with were her arms.

The sun was on the horizon now.

Penelope opened her eyes, staring up at the sky, and spotted a glider in the distance above her. She waved her arms, and the raft dipped alarmingly.

The glider circled twice above her.

They'd seen her. If the sharks didn't get her, someone knew where she was. They could lead the rescue team to her.

The wind blew over her skin and she shivered, but no matter how cold she got, she wasn't getting into the water again.

The glider moved east, away from her, and she watched it go and then circle again.

Penelope lifted her head and spotted the top of a boat heading straight for her. It was coming from the wrong direction to be Grant and Murray coming back.

Rescue.

Someone had answered her mayday call.

She shifted and lifted an arm to wave, but the movement forced her raft further underwater.

The engines slowed, and the boat circled around to come between her and the carcass. A tour boat with a large marlin board on the back, and standing on the marlin board, arm outstretched was Sam.

Her hero.

She stayed where she was as the boat reversed and cut its engines. Sam threw a rope to her, and she caught it, holding tight as he pulled her in.

The raft bumped against the marlin board as the boat rocked with the waves. Before she had a chance to shift, Sam hauled her into his arms. Warm, strong, safe.

"You're safe," he murmured, carrying her onto the deck. She wrapped her legs around his waist, not caring she was soaking him as relief made her weak.

Vaguely she heard cheering as he carried her into the cabin and the door shut behind them. He sat with her on the seating which ran around the edge.

"Jesus, Penny. What happened?" He pried the torch she still clutched from her hand and tucked it into his pocket, and then slipped the backpack off her shoulder and placed it on the ground next to them.

She couldn't bring herself to move, to let go of him. "Give me a minute." She clung to him, inhaling his scent, running her hands over his back. She was out of the water.

He stroked her hair. "You're safe now. Everything's all right."

She nodded as her heartbeat slowed. Finally she drew her head away and shifted off his lap. "Thank you."

His lips crushed hers and she was swept away with his passion.

When they finally came up for air, Sam's hands trembled as they stroked her arms and then brushed the cut on her head. "Tell me."

"Declan asked me to check a reported whale carcass. I went out, decided it needed to be towed a little further north so the currents would take it away from the beaches and was going to head back to get the equipment when I spotted the luxury boat."

His frown deepened. "They've got to have a mooring and access to fuel somewhere."

"What about Coral Bay?" she suggested.

"Dot sent the description to all the towns along the coast. They should have reported the *Joy Ridin'*."

"Unless they have people helping them," Penelope pointed out. "Stonefish have a way of influencing people."

"Yeah. What happened next?"

She shivered. "Grant had a gun, some kind of semi-automatic thing like you see in the movies. He shot the boat until it sank. Then they left me to the sharks."

"They didn't shoot you?"

"They said this was a warning to the Stokes to stay out of their business."

Sam growled. "They completely misunderstand the Stokes. This will make them even more determined. They don't want anyone else hurt."

Penelope rested her head against Sam's shoulder. Outside the cabin, curious passengers were glancing their way. "They have to be stopped. I haven't done anything to them and they've targeted me."

"I know. I'm sorry." His arms tightened around her again.

"It's not your fault. I'm glad you heard my mayday call."

"Scared the shit out of me when I heard they were after you. I've got to apologise to my customers for the rough ride."

She hugged him. "I'm fine now. I appreciate the fast rescue." She wanted to cling to him and not let go, but it was better if he spoke with his customers. She didn't want them to leave bad reviews. "Go talk to your passengers. I need to contact Declan."

"There's a radio down here." He pointed to it and then kissed her again. "Be right back."

She waited until he left the cabin before she moved, being cautious to make sure her legs would hold her. The adrenaline was wearing off and exhaustion and fatigue were taking its place. She had the ridiculous urge to burst into tears. She was fine, safe, no reason to cry now.

Penelope made her way to the radio and changed the dial to the right station. "Declan, are you there?"

"Penelope. Thank God. Where are you?"

"Rescued by one of the tour boats. I'm on my way in now. Can you get the police to meet the boat at the marina?"

"Sure. Do we need to send another boat to tow yours in?"

She shook her head. "No, it's gone. I'm not sure it will be salvageable even if you can refloat it."

"What happened?"

"I'll explain when I get back." The less information she gave Stonefish, the better. Sam had mentioned they listened to the radio chatter.

She replaced the radio and as she turned, Gretchen came in. "Oh my God, I'm so glad you're all right." She smashed Penelope in a hug. "What happened?"

Penelope debated whether she should tell her friend the whole truth, but decided it was safer to keep her in the dark. She didn't want Stonefish to target her too.

"A couple of guys disagreed with something I did," she said. "They sank my boat right next to a dead whale."

"I would have been terrified," Gretchen said. "Let me get you a drink. Rob has a hidden stash of whiskey here somewhere." She opened cupboards and drawers until she found it and then poured Penelope a healthy dose. "Knock that back."

Penelope did as asked, enjoying the burn as the whiskey slid down her throat. It warmed her insides and strengthened her muscles.

"Sam was a sight," Gretchen continued. "Barking orders, getting people to react quickly. I think half the women on board are in love with him. He only let go of the wheel when we got close to you, to pluck you out of the water."

Penelope smiled at Gretchen's enthusiasm. "He was definitely a knight in shining armour." She glanced outside. "I should go outside and thank Rob and apologise to the passengers for the delay."

"I didn't hear any complaints," Gretchen said, but followed Penelope out to the deck.

Chapter 18

Sam shook his head as Penelope apologised to the passengers for their delay. Trust her to think it was the least bit required. He stood back and listened as she was peppered with questions about the dead whale and the incident, and then stepped in when she was looking tired.

"I think that's enough," he said. "We'll be back to the marina shortly, so make sure you have all your things."

He took Penelope by the arm and steered her back into the cabin. "You look exhausted." Her pale skin accentuated the dark rings under her eyes. "Sit and rest." He pressed her into a chair and kissed her forehead. The cut there wasn't bleeding any longer but it still looked like it might need a stitch.

"I'm fine, really."

"Those dark rings say otherwise," he said. "Let me take care of you. You terrified me." He couldn't stop himself from squeezing her hand, brushing her hair, touching her to convince himself she was here and safe.

He needed some quiet time to process the whole situation. Something about it didn't sit right with him and it wasn't just the fact her boat had been shot to bits.

How had Grant and Murray known she was there?

They might have been monitoring the radio, but for them to get there so fast meant they hadn't been far away, and boats in the area were being monitored. That big a coincidence screamed at him to pay more attention.

Declan had sent Penelope there.

Maybe it was time he paid the man a visit.

He stayed with Penelope until it was time to dock and then he left her in the cabin while he said goodbye to the passengers and apologised for the delay again. Their enthusiasm told him there would be multiple videos of the rescue on the internet before the day was over.

Gretchen took them to the bus and when the crowd had cleared, Dot, Nhiari and Declan were standing on the docks. He waved them forward as Rob came down the ladder.

"Thanks for your help, mate." Sam shook Rob's hand.

"That was some pretty good driving you did," Rob replied. "You barely needed me."

Dot climbed on board. "I should have guessed it was you." It was resignation more than anything.

"I was in the right place at the right time," he responded.

"Where's Penelope?" Declan asked, his eyes darting around. Was it concern or guilt in his expression? Sam couldn't quite tell.

"In the cabin." As he spoke, she walked out, still pale.

Declan hurried over. "You're OK? What happened?" He glanced at Dot and then back at Penelope.

Definite guilt.

Sam narrowed his eyes. They would be having a little chat soon.

Around him the rest of his crew were washing stinger suits and equipment, and cleaning the deck. "Why don't you take Penelope to the hospital?" he suggested to Dot. "Get her checked out and then she can answer your questions. I'll finish packing up here and join you." He didn't want to leave Penelope, but better he get the answers he needed from Declan before the trail grew cold. "Declan, I'll give you the coordinates for where the boat sank."

Declan looked between Penelope and him, undecided.

"I don't need a doctor. I wasn't injured."

"Except for that nasty cut on your forehead," Sam said, brushing it with his thumb.

Nhiari stepped forward. "No need for you to come with us, Declan. We'll call you. Why don't you chat with Sam and then head home?"

Declan hesitated and then nodded. "Of course. I'll need a full doctor's report for my records and a copy of the police report."

"I'll call you later," Penelope promised. "The dead whale still needs to be towed before it hits the beaches."

"I'll arrange it," Sam said. It would give him an opportunity to find those bastards. "Declan can tell me what I need to do."

Penelope frowned. "No, they might still be out there."

"They'll be long gone," Sam said. "You don't want to shut the beaches because of the carcass."

She glanced at Declan and Rob and pressed her lips together. There was something she hadn't told him.

"Rob, you can go," Sam said.

He reluctantly left, and Penelope hugged Sam. "The whale was shot multiple times," she whispered. "Don't go out there, please."

Son of a bitch. Penelope had been set up. Her plea pulled on his heart, but he wouldn't promise. Not when he had an opportunity to stop them. "I won't go out alone."

It was the best he could do.

She nodded, relief on her face. He was certain she thought he would take Brandon, but it would take too long to get him into town. No, Declan wasn't going anywhere.

While Penelope left with the police officers, he called to his crew, "You can all go home. I'm going out again to deal with the whale."

He waved them goodbye and then gestured Declan into the cabin. After they were both inside, he shut the door with a click.

"You want to tell me who reported the whale carcass?" Sam asked, his tone mild.

Declan blinked and took a couple of steps back. Smart man. "It came through our reporting line."

"The police can track that," Sam said. "How about you tell me the truth before I tell them to check?"

Declan flinched but frowned. "What are you talking about? I am telling the truth."

"The whale was shot. Who do you suppose would shoot a calf in the head?"

Rage flashed over his face. "They said it was already dead."

Bingo. "Who said?"

Declan's eyes widened, and he swore under his breath. "They'll hurt my family if I tell you."

"Stonefish have hurt a lot of families already. The only way to keep your family safe is to tell me what you know."

The man shook his head. "You don't understand. They'll take my children from me."

Crap. Someone else in the wrong place at the wrong time. "Nod if I'm right. They told you about the dead whale and told you to send Penelope."

Declan nodded.

"This isn't the first time they've contacted you."

He nodded.

Last month it was animal smuggling. "You're told where to send rangers and when."

Declan deflated like a balloon and sat hard on the couch. "It didn't seem like a big deal. My mother needed to go into a nursing home and I couldn't afford the care. They offered me money as long as I did what they said." He looked up. "I put a limit on it. I said I'd only do it a few times."

Idiot. "It didn't stop after that?"

"They threatened to tip off the police. Said they had recordings of our conversations. I told them no when they told me about the whale and then they threatened my family. Knew exactly where my kids were going to be this week."

Shit. "How about when Penelope caught them?"

"She wasn't supposed to go to the Muiron Islands that day, but she was being her usual efficient self."

That made sense.

"Have you got contact details for them?"

"No."

Damn it. He wanted to end this. "The next time they contact you, I want to know."

"What will you do?"

"I'll stop them. But if you put Penelope in danger again, it will be me coming for you, got it?"

Declan swallowed hard. "Got it."

Good. "What do we need to tow the whale?"

"We've got equipment we can use back at the

office."

"I'll drive you there." He couldn't trust Declan.

It didn't take long to get the equipment, but it was dark by the time they reached the area where the whale had been. He put his spotlights on and scanned the water. The wind had died and so had the waves, leaving a much calmer environment, but it still took a few sweeps and some back and forth before Declan yelled, "It's over there."

Sam followed Declan's directions and backed up to the carcass. The thunk of the harpoon hitting the body made him cringe and the smell made his eyes water. Declan tied off the ropes and gave him the thumbs up. Sam motored north, keeping the speed low. Declan joined him.

"Head east," he said. "It'll be quicker to catch the currents."

Sam adjusted his course, and it was about half an hour before Declan called, "This will do."

He cut the engine. In the distance, the islands in the gulf were shadowed. "Are you sure we're far enough away?"

"We're in the perfect location." The satisfaction in Declan's voice seemed a bit off and as Sam turned, something hard hit his skull and everything went black.

*****

Penelope gave in to the prodding and poking by the doctor, too happy to be alive and on land to care about how unnecessary it was. Next to her, someone had found a towel to wrap her wet backpack. She'd have to go through it and dry everything, but most of the stuff was waterproof. Dot and Nhiari stayed with her, and when she was cleared to go, they took her down to the police station to get her statement.

She'd had far too many dealings with the police

lately, but she didn't begrudge their questions. The only thing that worried her was Sam out there. Who had gone with him?

"He'll be fine," Dot said as she led them into an interview room.

Penelope jumped. "Who will?"

"Sam. You've got worry all over your face."

"Stonefish are still out there. They might go after him as well."

Nhiari came in with her laptop. "He's taken his boat. Does it have a tracker on it?"

She grinned. "It does. Can I see where he is?" He should have started towing the whale by now.

Nhiari pushed over the laptop. "Go for it."

Penelope typed in the website, which allowed people to track marine traffic and scanned the area to find Sam's boat. She frowned. "It shouldn't be there."

Nhiari stood behind her. "Where should it be?"

Penelope pointed. "Further north. If they drop it there, it will be pushed back to shore."

"Declan went with him," Dot said. "Maybe he chose there for a reason."

"Only if he wants a bigger headache to deal with tomorrow. He knows better."

Her stomach swirled as Dot and Nhiari exchanged glances. "Give us the short version of what happened this afternoon," Dot demanded.

"The office radioed to tell me about the whale. I went to assess the situation. Grant and Murray found me and shot up the boat, sinking it."

"Who at the office?" Dot asked.

"Declan." As their faces became grim, she realised what they were thinking. "Declan's involved."

"Possibly. We need a boat."

Penelope glanced at the screen to get the coordinates. Another boat popped up on the screen, just next to Sam's. She recognised the name.

Joy Ridin'.

Her heart lurched. "They've got Sam."

***

Sam came back to consciousness, but his instinct told him not to move. He struggled through the dark fog and took stock of his body. Arms stretched uncomfortably behind him, feet tied together.

Dark. Water lapped against the sides of the boat and quiet voices were nearby, but not in the same room as him.

Cautiously he opened an eye and took a moment for his vision to adjust. He definitely wasn't on his boat any more. The carpet he lay on was plush, not the hardy marine carpet on the floor of his cabin.

Declan had hit him, knocked him out and if he was a betting man, he'd bet he was now on board *Joy Ridin'.* He lifted his head and spotted a digital display glowing nearby. He must have only been unconscious for a few minutes. The luxury boat had to have been hiding nearby, lights out, ready to pounce.

How had Declan told them he would be out here? Maybe it had been them he'd messaged rather than his wife to tell her he would be late home.

Sam never should have trusted him.

No point worrying about that now. He had to get free.

The clock was part of some other equipment, maybe a radio. He rolled towards it, and something hard in his pocket dug into him making him wince. What the hell was it? He rolled onto it again. Something cylindrical.

Penelope's torch.

Not quite the knife he had hoped for, but it might help blind them temporarily.

Refocusing on his goal, he crunched up and got to

221

his knees.

He would never complain about ab day again.

The box next to the radio was a tracker, a similar model to the one he had on his boat. The one which showed where you were on the ocean.

Quickly he leaned forward and used the momentum of his arms smacking against his butt to snap the ties around his wrists. Amateurs always thought cable ties were unbreakable.

With a grin, he shifted and switched the tracker on.

Footsteps sounded outside the door.

He kicked out his legs, but the first attempt didn't snap the ties. Quickly he fell back to the ground, pretending to still be unconscious. Light flashed on, making his eyelids a pale pink.

"He's still out," Grant said. "How hard did you hit him?"

"Hard enough so he couldn't fight back," Declan responded.

"We need answers from him," Grant continued. "Get some water and splash it in his face."

Sam prepared for the shock of water. When it came he jerked, and opened his eyes, blinking a couple of times as if confused and then used his feet to push himself into a seated position, his back and hands to the wall to hide the fact he was no longer restrained.

He pinpointed Declan, who didn't look nervous or upset. "You lied." He kept his voice low and full of venom. "You're not an innocent bystander. You're working for Stonefish."

Declan smirked but said nothing and gestured for Grant to speak.

"The boss wants answers, and you'd better hope you've got some he likes."

The urge to attack was strong, but maybe he'd get some answers of his own before he taught them a lesson. Sam grinned. "I've always been good at trivia."

Grant scowled, but asked, "How did you find the weapons cache?"

"What weapons cache?"

"The one at the Ridge."

"Luck," Sam said. "Or misfortune, depending on how you view it. We were having a beach day and decided to build some monuments for those who died on the Retribution. We were digging near the plaque, and there they were."

"Bullshit," Grant said.

Sam ignored him and addressed Declan instead. "You know what Lara's like. She gets an idea in her head and soon everyone's helping her."

He gave a small nod and gestured for Grant to continue. Outside the boat engine purred to life and moved. Murray must be driving.

"Where's my boat?" Sam asked. "Tell me you at least put the anchor out so it won't crash on an island."

"You're not in any position to ask questions," Grant said.

Sam stared at Declan, waiting for an answer. "It's anchored."

"Thank you." Did Declan actually care about the environment, or was he avoiding more work for himself tomorrow?

"Who told Penelope about the cache on Muiron Island?" Grant asked.

The soundproofing in the cabin was pretty good. The engines weren't loud enough to prevent easy conversation.

He almost told them to ask her, but he didn't want to give them any ideas. "She stumbled on them in her work."

Grant glanced at Declan and then back to Sam. "How close are the police to uncovering what's going on?"

"You'll need to ask them. Dot is annoyingly tight lipped about that kind of stuff. I wish she'd tell me." He let his annoyance show then asked, "Where have you guys been harbouring? They haven't found a trace of you."

"None of your business."

"How much do you know about Stonefish's operations?" It was Declan who spoke this time.

"Not enough. If I did, it wouldn't exist anymore." Sam saw the hit coming and prepared for it. He shifted, letting the punch slide past his head and grabbed Declan's hand with his freed one and tugged him off balance, grabbing him in a choke hold. "Don't move."

Declan froze, and it was quite satisfying to hear the hiss of fear.

Grant swore and reached behind his back.

"Move and he's dead." Sam kept his voice low in case Murray could hear outside.

"You won't kill him."

"Are you willing to bet on that?" Both men had put Penelope in danger, and Sam wasn't feeling very forgiving right now.

"Don't, Grant," Declan said.

Good. At least one person realised how serious he was. He shifted and kicked out his feet to snap the ties. "Get up."

He didn't loosen his hold on Declan as they both climbed to their feet.

"Slowly place the gun on the table and step back," he told Grant.

Three against one weren't the worst odds he'd ever had.

Grant did as he asked, placing the gun on the table and stepping back towards the door.

Sam patted down Declan, hoping to find a gun, but

he had nothing. There were cable ties across the room though. "Grab the cable ties and tie your feet, then your hands together."

Grant moved slowly, taking the cable ties and bending.

The boat slowed, the sudden change in speed enough to make Sam stumble. Declan reacted, grabbing Sam's hands and forcing them down, twisting his neck so Sam no longer had access to his throat.

The man had training.

Sam swept Declan's legs out from under him and lunged for the gun on the table, but he was too slow.

Grant raised it and pointed it at him. "Don't move."

Fuck. He clenched his hands as Declan climbed to his feet.

"We need to dispose of him," Declan said. "He's going to cause us too much trouble alive."

Not words he wanted to hear, but as long as they didn't shoot him in the head, he had a chance. A lamp over by the door looked heavy. If it wasn't bolted to the table, it would make a good weapon.

Declan backed up, so he was next to Grant. "Keep the gun on him. Let's get him out on deck."

Grant nodded. "You heard the man. Move."

"So Declan's in charge, is he?" Sam asked as he calculated the distance between him and Grant. How quickly could he cross it and how fast could Grant shoot?

Grant's finger was on the trigger, so Sam didn't like his odds.

Grant grunted and waved his gun. Declan had already left the cabin.

Sam moved closer, but Grant gave him a wide berth, stepping away from the door so Sam wouldn't come anywhere near him.

Sam inhaled the salty air, assessing everything he

went past. Round orange life preserver attached to the wall, but aside from that, the walls were bare and so was most of the deck.

But there was a potential escape if he could get to it.

Two BCDs attached to oxygen tanks leaned up against the stern of the boat. Murray and Grant must have been scuba diving before Declan had called them.

Beyond the light of the boat, all was dark. He stepped further away, towards the scuba gear, to let his eyes adjust. If those specks of light in the distance were the mainland, then he had to be about a kilometre offshore. The gulf wasn't too deep, only twenty metres or so and a short swim to shore. If he could get to the tank, he could lose them while he swam underwater.

Declan and Murray were conversing on the other side of the boat.

This was his chance.

Sam leapt to the edge of the boat. A shot exploded and so did pain in his right calf, the one he'd just put all his weight on. He stumbled, lunging for the side so he could slip over, but Grant hauled him back. "None of that." He pointed the gun at his head.

Fuck.

Sam ignored him and the excruciating pain, and stripped off his shirt, ripping it to form a tourniquet and then applied pressure to the wound. The bullet had just grazed his calf, but still hurt like a mother-fucker.

"Don't waste your time," Grant said, holding the gun to Sam's head. "You're going over soon enough."

Murray carried an anchor and chain towards them.

Shit. This was not ending well for him.

Behind Murray a light bobbed in the water, coming towards them. Boat. That would delay them.

He nodded in the direction. "You might want to wait until there are no witnesses."

Declan swore. "I'll turn off the main light."

Murray crouched, wrapping the chain around Sam's ankles and locking it in place with a padlock. A practised move, but his hands shook.

Grant held the gun low, but still hard against Sam's head and Sam knew he was a dead man if he moved.

"You really want to be an accessary to murder, Declan?" Sam called.

Declan flinched but continued over to the control panel and flicked off the main light. Now the only light came from the cabin.

"You don't need to do this," Sam continued, seeing his options rapidly dwindling. "The police will figure out what happened. These two might get away, but you've got family. What will they think?"

"Shut up." Grant pistol-whipped him and his head cracked against the fibreglass of the boat. Stars blurred his vision and he fought for clarity as they hefted him up and pushed his upper body over.

He clung to the edge, desperately kicking out, pulling himself towards the stern. He got free long enough to lunge for the BCD with the scuba tank. Then Murray and Grant lifted his feet and his hands brushed the BCD. He clutched a clasp and hauled it close, getting a better grip as Grant noticed what he was doing.

"Hey!" Grant stretched for the tank, but he was too late. The weight of the anchor pulled Sam overboard and Sam flung himself away with it.

As his head sank underwater, he prayed the tank had air.

Chapter 19

The moment Penelope pointed at the new boat on the screen, Dot and Nhiari leapt into action. Dot barked orders at Colin and the other officers still in the station, and Nhiari left the room only to return moments later with a couple of bags and some keys.

"Stay here," Dot barked as she and Nhiari headed out the door.

Like hell she would.

Penelope grabbed her damp backpack and ran after them. "I'm going with you."

"No, you're not," Dot stated.

"Either you take me with you, or I follow in the other PAWS boat. Your choice."

"Get in," Nhiari said as they reached the police car.

Penelope jumped in the backseat and they sped to the marina. When they stopped, Penelope tried to open the door. Locked. "Let me out."

Nhiari grimaced. "Sorry. I'll send Colin to let you out when we're gone."

Shit. She tugged on the door handle while they got their bags out of the boot and then strode towards the boat.

Her phone. It might have gone swimming with her, but it was supposed to be waterproof. She dialled Georgie, tapping her palm against the door while she waited for her to pick up.

"Hey, Penelope."

"Georgie, please tell me you're still in town."

"Yeah, I'm just finishing work. What's up?"

"Stonefish have Sam. Nhiari's locked me in the back of the police car at the marina while they go after him, but I need to know he's all right."

"I'll be right there."

Penelope sighed and hung up. Nhiari and Dot were already motoring out of the marina.

By the time Georgie arrived, they'd cleared the rocks. Not too much of a head start. Georgie opened the back door and Penelope clambered out.

"I've got the PAWS keys," Georgie said. "Let's go."

Penelope snatched them from her. "You're not coming. I don't want you to get hurt."

"Sam's my friend. Besides, someone's going to need to drive the boat home while you two cuddle." She grinned as they ran to the PAWS boat.

Penelope didn't have time to argue.

Georgie drove while Penelope checked the boat tracker to see where they were. They hadn't moved from the original position. She made note of the coordinates and then searched the cabin to see if there was anything useful. Empty except for a first aid kit and spare life jackets.

The water had stilled, so they sped smoothly over the surface. They followed the police boat, which was far faster, and further in the distance were the lights of another vessel. The main lights switched off as she watched.

She checked the tracker. Definitely Stonefish's boat. Maybe they saw the police boat approaching.

Not far away, Sam's boat was anchored, the outside lights still on illuminating the logo. "Go there first," Penelope called over the engine noise. Further away drifted the carcass of the whale. A problem for another day.

There was a possibility Stonefish might have tied Sam up and left him and Declan on board.

Not a high possibility, but worth checking while Dot and Nhiari arrested the others.

Georgie pulled up next to the tour boat. The lights were on, but no one stood at the captain's seat and no one was on deck. Georgie put the boat into neutral as Penelope yelled, "Sam! Are you on board?"

Nothing, but if they'd gagged him, he wouldn't be able to reply.

She glanced over at the other boat some distance away as gunshots popped. She flinched, whirling around, but in the dark and from the distance she couldn't see what was happening.

Gunshots there meant it was unlikely the bad guys were still here. "Pull up to the marlin board. I'm going to check."

Georgie did as she asked and Penelope leapt off, moving quickly to check the cabin and then to climb down the steps to the engine room.

Empty.

"Sam!" She listened for a muffled answer and checked the bathrooms as well. She went back to Georgie. "Anywhere I might have missed?"

Georgie shook her head. "Get on."

The radio crackled. "Penelope, is Sam over there?" Nhiari asked.

Georgie answered. "No one is."

Penelope climbed back on board. If they were asking where Sam was, it meant he wasn't on *Joy Ridin'* either.

Possibilities, all of them horrific, flooded her mind

and she stumbled to the chair.

"Can we approach?" Georgie asked.

Lights illuminated both boats and Nhiari and Dot were on board *Joy Ridin'*.

"Can either of you scuba dive?" Nhiari replied.

"Yeah," Georgie answered. "Why?"

"Murray says they threw him overboard attached to an anchor."

Though her head spun, Penelope moved to her backpack and emptied it onto the deck while Georgie sped towards the luxury boat. The gear Penelope had put in her BCD pockets was still in there from her failed dive attempt with Sam—dive torch, waterproof notebook and pen, safety marker buoy. She gathered it all up as they reached *Joy Ridin'*.

Dot and Nhiari stood on the deck. Grant was dead, Murray bandaged and handcuffed, and Declan knelt on the deck handcuffed as well.

She'd process that later. "Where?" she yelled as Georgie pulled alongside.

Dot pointed to the scuba gear at the back of the boat. Penelope vaulted over and shoved her gear into the pockets of the BCD. She attached the regulator and turned on the air as Georgie demanded, "Where did you dump him?"

Murray spoke. "We've been drifting. It was about five minutes ago."

Penelope checked the gauges. Sixty bar. Not a lot. She had to find him fast. As she slipped on the BCD, she said, "Declan, where is he?"

Declan didn't look at her.

Georgie was still on the PAWS boat and Penelope called out the last coordinates she had for *Joy Ridin'*.

"Get on," Georgie yelled.

Penelope climbed back, hating the slow movement because of the weight of the tank. Nhiari passed her a mask and fins and Georgie motored to a spot nearby while Penelope finished getting ready.

Georgie reached the coordinates.

Penelope hadn't done her checks.

Fear tightened her throat, making her gasp for breath.

"Go, Penelope," Georgie called.

"Checks," she gasped, trying to shake away her fear. Sam was drowning. She had to get to him.

Georgie strode over, tested the regulator and air. "Go!"

Penelope splashed backwards into the water and gasped as the cold water hit her. She breathed through her regulator, trying to stop the panic.

She checked her coordinates.

This was where *Joy Ridin'* had been five minutes ago.

Sam could be right below her, desperate for air.

That image was enough for her to start her descent despite the panic in her chest. She switched on her torch, impressed by its wide beam. She rotated, shining the light in each direction, looking for signs of life.

A few fish darted out of the beam, but no Sam.

She sucked in another breath and equalised her ears as she sank. He could be just out of beam range and if she went in the wrong direction, she would never find him.

The thought brought a different type of panic that eclipsed her fear of diving.

Methodical. That's what she needed to be. A grid pattern, searching the floor around where he should be.

She could do this.

***

Darkness surrounded Sam as he sank below the water. It wasn't more than twenty metres in the gulf, so he didn't have to worry about sinking too deep that no one would find him. No, the dark would be more of an issue for that.

He fumbled for the regulator on the BCD, shoving it in his mouth and sucked.

Nothing.

Fuck.

His lungs squeezed as he sank, his hand scrabbling to find the top of the scuba bottle. There. He twisted it open before taking another breath.

Air. Sweet, sweet air.

Quickly he slipped the BCD on and clipped it up. He was still descending and his ears hurt. He equalised and was debating whether to use some of the air to inflate his BCD to slow the descent when he hit the bottom.

Sam breathed slowly, knowing it wasn't good to hold his breath, but not wanting to use up his precious supply. If only he knew how much he had.

In the pitch black he felt around for the gauges and found a couple. Now if he had a light, he might see something.

Penelope's torch. He grinned and reached for his pocket.

Sam flicked it on and then opened his eyes, bringing the gauges as close as he could. Everything was blurry, and the salt water stung his eyes, but a button on the gauge illuminated it, which helped him pick out the numbers as they cycled. Twenty bar, twenty-two metres.

Maybe twenty minutes if he was very lucky before he ran out of air.

He switched off the light, not sure whether they would see it from the surface, and closed his eyes again. No point keeping them open when he could barely see in front of him.

He just needed to move far enough away from the

boat that they wouldn't see him surface.

Sam hauled on the anchor, but it didn't budge.

Shit. Bending down he felt around, found the smooth cold anchor and the sharp coral reef. He tugged and it shifted, but not much. It must be lodged under a ledge.

A push of water against his skin like something large swimming by him.

Don't think about it. There was almost nothing he could do if a shark wanted to take a bite out of him. The blood from his bullet wound had probably attracted them.

He slowed his breathing and focused on what he could control.

Getting the anchor free.

It was stuck tight, jammed underneath an outcropping.

Another wave of water and this time Sam felt the brush of something swimming past. He switched on the torch, waving it around in an arch, hoping to scare off whatever was there. Then he tugged on the anchor again.

Part of the reef broke off.

He'd apologise to Penelope when he saw her next.

The thought of her gave him strength, and he yanked again. He sucked in a breath.

His air was gone.

***

At the bottom Penelope rotated again, sweeping the torch beam around looking for debris which would come from an anchor or body hitting the reef.

A bit of haze in that direction, but it was enough to make her choose. She swam forward, arching the beam in each direction as she went.

Over there, was that a light? She marked her place

on her dive compass and swam a little further, where a light flickered on and moved frantically.

Penelope kicked, propelling herself forward and her torch picked up a body.

Sam.

His eyes were closed and he was floating there, BCD on, but no mask or fins and a chain wrapped around his legs held in place with a padlock. Still.

No. He can't be dead. She had just seen a light. She propelled herself towards him and he moved, eyes opening.

Alive.

Her relief was short-lived as Sam did the out of air symbol.

Shit.

She grabbed her spare regulator and stuck it in his mouth, stroking his cheek. He inhaled deeply, once, twice, three times.

Anger filled her as she examined the lock. It needed a key and she couldn't leave Sam to get it, because he'd be out of air before she returned.

So they needed to carry the anchor to the surface.

The anchor had caught underneath a rocky outcrop, one of its spikes inserted in a hole. She checked Sam.

He floated, waiting, trusting she was going to help him. He wouldn't even know who was with him.

The regulator hose was long enough for her to bend closer to the anchor without pulling it from Sam's mouth, but he bent down with her, as if he knew what she was trying to do.

She clipped her torch to her vest, then placed his hands on the anchor and showed him the direction he needed to push. Then she tapped once, twice, three times on the back of his hand. At the same time as he pushed, she tugged on the anchor and it came free.

And immediately dropped back onto the rock.

Damn, it was heavy.

She checked her air. Usually she'd start her ascent at this level.

It wasn't an option.

She checked the chain, but it was padlocked tight around his ankle, with no room to slip a foot out.

She tried lifting it again, and Sam helped. They held it between the two of them, but when she pushed off and kicked, they didn't go more than a metre before sinking down again. It was just too heavy and Sam couldn't kick with his ankles chained.

She detached the connection which inflated her BCD and plugged it into Sam's. She inflated his BCD as far as it would go, and he floated like a balloon being held down. This better work, otherwise she'd wasted precious air.

Then she unplugged the connection from his jacket and plugged it back into hers. She undid one of her buckles and clipped herself to his BCD so she wouldn't float away when she inflated her BCD.

Together they lifted the anchor again and there was a slight lift. She inflated her jacket a little at a time until it was fully inflated.

They had to push off together and swim for the surface. She pointed her torch upwards and swept it around, hoping someone would see it and have a rope ready.

A shadow crossed the torch.

Shark.

A tiger shark by the size of it. Hopefully it was satiated by the whale earlier that day.

She tapped on Sam's chest three times and then jerked his shirt upwards, hoping he would understand she wanted him to push off on three.

Then she tapped three times and together they pushed. She kicked hard, and it was impossible to know if they were getting anywhere in the dark.

Her lungs burned. Using too much of her precious air. If this didn't work, they were going to be very low.

Her fins hit something. The bottom.

They still weren't buoyant enough to surpass the weight of the anchor with the two of them.

Shit.

Despair filled her, and she tugged on the lock again, trying to break it, looking around the reef for a sharp rock, but she couldn't get enough momentum to hit it hard.

Down to thirty bar. They had maybe one last try.

Sam grabbed her hand and pointed to the surface, shooing her away.

No way she was leaving him behind.

She slowed her breath. Think. She was always prepared for the worst. She patted the pockets and found her notebook and pen, then her inflatable safety marker buoy. Elated, she scribbled a note. *Found Sam. Low on air. Need key to lock. Anchor too heavy.*

She tied the notebook to the marker buoy, ensuring it was secure, and then used some of their remaining air to inflate the buoy, ensuring she had a firm grasp on the end of the rope. It shot straight up and disappeared from the glow of the torch.

A moment later, the rope tugged and her hope raised. They'd found the message. Would Murray turn over the key?

She checked her air. Twenty bar. Not long at all with both of them using the same tank.

A minute later, the rope jiggled in her hand as if they were strapping their own note to the buoy. When it stopped, Penelope pulled it in.

Her heart leapt.

Taped to the buoy was a key.

Carefully she pried the key loose, conscious if she

dropped it she would effectively kill Sam. With shaking fingers she bent and stuck the key into the lock. It turned.

Saved.

She closed her eyes for a moment, dizzy with relief.

Then before she unhitched it, she released most of the air from their BCDs so they didn't shoot to the surface. No point getting there alive and getting the bends.

Sam waited patiently, as if trusting she knew what she was doing. She unhooked the lock and unwrapped the chain from his ankles. Not enough air for a safety stop.

She had to risk it. Had to hope they hadn't been down long enough for the bends to set in. Had to hope somewhere around town there was a decompression chamber if they had been.

Otherwise she might lose Sam anyway.

Her chest cramped as she wrapped her arms around him and slowly kicked towards the surface.

By the time their heads hit the air, they were on their last few bars.

Sam spat out his regulator, opened his eyes, ran a hand over his face to clear the water, and grinned at her. "I love you."

Chapter 20

Penelope had saved him. Sam had a jolt of hope and fear when he'd first seen the light slide past his eyelids. He'd wondered whether Murray was coming after him, then he'd considered he was dying and this was the light coming to claim him, but the moment he'd felt the light touch on his cheek and the regulator at his mouth, he'd known it was Penelope.

He didn't question how she'd found him, he didn't much care as he'd sucked in the life-giving air.

She'd faced her fears of diving to come for him. In that moment, all his fear and anxiety when he'd gone to her rescue earlier made sense. He loved her. Every quirk, every laugh, every bit of her being.

He'd followed her instructions knowing what she was doing, because it was what he would have done in her position.

But when they'd landed back on the ground, weighed down by the anchor, the real fear had returned. She'd ignored his attempts to get her to surface and when he'd opened his eyes to see what she was doing, he'd seen a bright orange safety marker buoy in front of him.

Genius.

And so like Penelope to have one on her.

He had to tell her how he felt.

"I love you," he said again as he took stock of the surroundings. The luxury boat was lit up with Nhiari and Dot in the spotlight. Next to it was the empty police patrol boat and floating just nearby was a PAWS boat with Georgie in it.

He turned back to Penelope and dragged her close, kissing her. "Thank you."

She squeezed him back, but there was a slight wariness in her tone. "How long were you down there? You might have the bends."

He grinned, not offended that she was questioning his sanity. "Not long. I'm fine."

"Let's get you out of there," Georgie called.

He gestured for Penelope to go first and helped her aboard the PAWS boat before he climbed up and shed his scuba gear. Then he swept her into a hug and kissed her. "You're my hero."

She clung to him, her body shaking. "You need to go to the hospital. We didn't do the safety stop."

"It's fine. We weren't down long enough." He squeezed her. "We're all right. You were so brave."

She shook her head. "I almost couldn't go down."

"Almost doesn't count. You went down."

He kissed her again and then kept his arm around her as he assessed the situation. Grant lying dead on the floor of the luxury boat and both Murray and Declan handcuffed on the deck.

Murray called, "I told them where you were, and gave them the key."

"That might count if you hadn't been the one to chain my feet in the first place," Sam called back.

Declan stared at the deck, not moving, not saying anything.

"Declan isn't an innocent bystander," Sam told them. "He's as involved as those two were, maybe more so."

Dot glared at Declan. "Right. We'll take them into the station. You two are going to the hospital before you come in and give your statement. It's going to be a long night." She glanced at Grant and grimaced.

There would be a lot of paperwork for her to fill out.

Sam saluted and Georgie started the engine, heading back to town. He moved over to her. "Drop us at my boat." It was anchored not far away.

"Are you both well enough?" Georgie asked.

He waggled his eyebrows. "More than well enough."

She rolled her eyes, then gave him a quick hug. "I'm glad you're all right. You had me scared for a while."

"They make 'em tough in the army." He smiled but couldn't hide the involuntary shiver at the memory of being underwater with no air.

She squeezed his arm and drove towards his boat.

Penelope was correctly storing the scuba tanks so they wouldn't roll around. "How are you?"

She nodded. "Fine. I'm glad you're alive."

"Me too." He skimmed a finger down her arm, not able to stop touching her. "It was genius to send the buoy up, but how did they know to send the key?"

"I wrote a note explaining what we needed."

He would never, ever tease her about being prepared. They reached his boat. "Come with me," he said to Penelope.

A slight hesitation which worried him. Why was she concerned about being alone with him?

"All right."

He held the two boats together while she climbed aboard and then he joined her, pushing the PAWS boat away. "See you back at shore."

Georgie waved and motored away.

Penelope was heading for the bow. "Wait." He jogged over to her. "What's wrong?"

"Nothing." She shifted away. "I'm getting the anchor."

He pulled her back. "Tell me."

She stared at him, eyes wide and glistening. "You nearly died. I can't understand how you can be so blasé about it, how you can act as if nothing happened."

He pulled her close. "Training," he replied. "If I can't escape and keep moving, I'm a dead man." He stroked her back. "I can't dwell on what happened, not until I'm safe at home."

"You were floating there, eyes closed, and I thought I was too late."

He imagined their positions reversed and could feel her pain. "But you weren't. I knew it was you the moment you touched me. I knew we'd work it out somehow."

She shook her head. "You can't have known. I didn't know how to save you when the anchor was too heavy."

"But you used your wonderful brain and figured it out."

She burrowed deeper into his arms and his heart expanded. He exhaled. "I really do love every part of you, Penelope."

She stilled and then stepped away. "I bet you say that to all the women who save your life."

"No," he said, grabbing her hand so she couldn't walk away. "Only you. Everything from the way you laugh, to your attention to detail, to the way you stick to your guns. You are an amazing woman, Penelope, and I love all of you."

She stared at him, uncertainty on her face. She shook her head. "I'm scared. Love is too soon, too much.”

That practicality again. He wouldn’t dismiss it or be frustrated by it. It was part of why he loved her. “Love is what it is.” He grinned. “What would Ceiveon say?”

She laughed then, and his grin widened. “I can’t win if the two of you gang up on me.” She sighed. “I love you too.”

He whooped and dragged her close, kissing her until he was almost dizzy. He stepped back and turned her towards the bow. “Now go haul the anchor, my hearty wench, so we can go home.” He patted her bottom.

Her laugh echoed through the night as she obeyed his command.

***

When Penelope returned from pulling in the anchor, she spotted the torn shirt tied to Sam’s calf. “What happened?”

“It’s a flesh wound,” Sam replied.

“Who hurt you?” She bent down to examine it.

“Grant shot me.”

Penelope gasped. “You were shot?” Her fingers trembled as she tried to undo the knot holding the bandage in place so she could get a better look.

Sam stopped her. “It’s a graze. Don’t worry, I’ve had worse.”

So calm all the time. She couldn’t imagine what he must have gone through in the army. “You’re going to the hospital as soon as we get back. Should I call an ambulance?” The thought of him having the bends also lingered in her mind.

“No need. Trust me, Penny, I’m fine.” He tucked her under his arm and she stayed next to him as they motored back to the marina.

Georgie drove them to the hospital and between the doctor examining him, and Brandon calling for the story, they didn't have time to talk, but Penelope was happy to be with him. They were both alive, and the future seemed so much brighter. It was more than a couple of hours later before Dot led them into the interview room. She looked as if she'd aged ten years.

"Where are Murray and Declan?" Sam asked.

"Already on their way to Carnarvon gaol." Dot gestured to a seat. "Tell me what happened."

Penelope sat next to Sam as he explained about suspecting Declan and then being knocked unconscious. "When I woke, I was in the cabin of the luxury boat. I turned on the tracker and tried to free myself, but they got the upper hand." He sounded disgusted with himself.

Penelope squeezed his thigh. She'd heard the story when he'd spoken with Brandon, but it didn't make it any easier.

"Grant shot me, Murray attached the chain to my legs and pushed me over. I grabbed the scuba tank on my way off, but it didn't have much air in it."

"Enough to save your life," Dot pointed out.

Thankfully. Penelope could still close her eyes and see him floating there. Hopefully both men would be locked away for a very long time. "Did Murray or Declan tell you anything useful?"

Dot pressed her lips together.

"Come on, Dot, give us something," Sam said.

"Murray is talking. Declan hasn't said a word. Nhiari has gone to tell his family what's happened."

That couldn't be easy. Penelope couldn't believe Declan had been so involved. She'd trusted him. But now that she reviewed the past few weeks, so much made sense. "Declan called you in when Sam had the licence breach," she said. "Do you think he knew about Sam's relationship with the Stokes and was punishing them?"

"It's possible," Dot said. "Did he do anything else that seems strange to you now?"

Penelope thought about it. "Declan was very insistent about checking in with the office each day, in particular if we changed our plans. I always thought it was a safety measure."

"I bet it was so he could make sure you didn't run into any of the smugglers," Sam said.

Penelope nodded. "The dead fish samples went missing as well. Declan probably never put them on the plane."

"That might be why Murray and Grant went after you in town and then again at the whale," Sam said. "Declan wanted to stop you from getting too close."

"Have you got the results for the fish?" Dot asked.

"I wasn't in the office this morning," Penelope said. "But the official results should be there."

Sam ran a hand through his hair. "Unless Declan destroyed them."

"He can't have. The results will be in the system, both the lab system and on email. Perth will have a backup even if Declan deleted it." They'd be able to identify the chemical she couldn't.

"I want a copy of them," Dot stated.

"I'll make sure you get it. There must be more than gun smuggling out there."

Sam groaned. "Did Brandon call you about the cache on Muiron Island?"

Dot gave him a laser glare. "Which cache?"

"We saw Grant and Murray burying something else out there last night."

"No, he didn't." She made a note. "What were you doing out there?"

"Night dive." Sam even looked innocent as he lied.

Dot shook her head. "You two…" She didn't bother finishing her sentence.

Penelope wholly agreed. She smiled sweetly at him. "You want to tell us both what happened?"

Sam winced and explained how he and Brandon had gone out to the island while they'd been at Dot's birthday dinner. "They figured the police were finished with their investigation and wouldn't go back and check it again."

Dot sighed. "We wouldn't have. We don't have the time."

"Haven't major crimes got involved yet?" Sam asked.

"I can't answer," Dot replied. "Is there anything else you want to add to your statements?"

Penelope shook her head. It was getting late, and all she wanted was a long soak in a shower with Sam.

"I'm done," Sam replied, getting to his feet. "Thank you for getting there so fast."

"You can thank Penelope. She was the one who was worried and noticed you were in the wrong place."

Sam pulled her up and kissed her. "Thank you for saving me twice."

"You're welcome." She smiled, though her cheeks heated at his affection in front of Dot.

"Go home," Dot said. "Call me if you think of anything else." She walked them out of the station.

"Are you going home now?" Penelope asked her.

"Not yet. There's more paperwork to do." She ran a hand through her short black hair.

On a whim, Penelope hugged her. "Thank you for everything."

Dot hugged her back briefly and shifted away. "Just doing my job." She waved. "Stay out of trouble for a while." Then she headed back inside.

"She's an interesting woman," Sam said as they walked over to his car.

Penelope nodded. One she wanted to get to know

better.

It didn't take long to get back to Sam's place. Penelope followed him inside and placed her still damp backpack on the kitchen bench. She sighed. "I need to unpack everything and dry it properly.

Sam shook his head, placing himself between the bench and her. "What you need is a shower."

The idea was tempting, but, "If I don't dry it, some things will rust."

"Fine, then I'll dry it while you shower."

"That's ridiculous. You almost died. You need to relax."

He just smirked at her. "I love the way you reason. You conquered your fear rescuing me. That takes strength and guts. *You* need to relax."

She pulled a face, though couldn't ignore the thrill at him using the 'l' word. "Fine. How about we both shower and then I'll dry everything?"

He herded her out of the kitchen. "Now we're on the same path, except I'll help you when we're done. That backpack helped on multiple occasions. It deserves to be treated with respect."

She laughed then she slapped him on the bottom. "All right. Now hurry up and run me my shower."

His bellowed laugh made her grin.

Was it any wonder she loved him?

Epilogue

Life was pretty damned good as far as Sam was concerned. Penelope loved him and the bad guys were behind bars. They might not have stopped Stonefish for good, but they were closer than ever. He placed plastic wrap over the salad he'd made and made space in the fridge for the bowl to fit.

"There's definitely enough food," Penelope said.

"Yeah, I won't start the barbecue before everyone arrives." He was holding an impromptu house-warming party, part welcome for moving here, and part celebration of life. He'd invited his crew, plus all the Stokes and Dot and Nhiari. The only one missing was Sherlock.

"What's wrong?" Penelope asked. "Have you forgotten something?"

She read him so well. "I was thinking about Sherlock. I wish he was here."

"He's your friend who was injured, right?" Penelope asked. "Have you asked Brandon for help convincing him to visit?"

Sam turned to her. "That's the problem. I promised Sherlock I wouldn't tell Brandon. He's actually Amy's brother, and he doesn't want them to know."

Penelope's eyes widened. "Oh. Why not?"

"He and Amy are estranged and then he went on a mission where he was injured instead of going to her wedding."

"That's complicated. He must regret it. Do you think seeing her would be salt into the wound? If he'd gone to the wedding, he wouldn't be in the situation he's in."

Sam nodded. He'd never really seen it from that perspective. "Yeah, you could be right, but I think it's time I told them. Brandon's been asking about him."

Penelope slipped her arms around his waist. "I understand your loyalty to both of them. I think Brandon and Amy will understand."

Her words comforted him and his decision solidified. "I'll tell them tomorrow. Tonight should be a celebration."

He kissed her and then someone pounded on the front door and walked in.

"You decent?" Brandon called.

"Depends on your definition," Sam responded and went to greet his guests.

Later Sam tossed the sausages down on the sizzling barbecue as Penelope switched on the music, and Brandon helped himself to another beer. The party was in full swing and Lara was giving Gretchen's son, Jordan, a tour of the place like she owned it.

Life was pretty sweet.

The only thing which would make it sweeter would be to get Sherlock to move here, and he'd sort that tomorrow. Telling Penelope had been a relief.

His phone rang, and he recognised the number as that of Sherlock's therapist. Concern flittered over his skin and he passed his tongs to Darcy as he answered.

"Hey, Anne. What can I do for you?"

"Sam, Arthur's in hospital." Her tone was sombre.

"What happened?" He headed inside, away from the music, grabbing his tablet from the bench to check when the next flight out of Retribution Bay was.

"Overdose," she stated. "I found him this morning. I'm not sure when he took the tablets."

Sam froze. "Intentional?"

A pause. "He knew the maximum number of tablets he could take for the pain."

Sam closed his eyes. He should have dragged Sherlock up here kicking and screaming. He never should have left him alone. "What's his status?"

"He's stomach has been pumped and they're waiting for him to wake. Does he have any family I should contact?"

"I'll do it," Sam said. "I'll catch the next flight to Perth."

"Thanks, Sam. I don't need to tell you he's going to need to be watched for a while."

"I'll sort it out," Sam answered. "Thanks for the call."

He hung up and turned to find Brandon behind him. Shit.

"What's going on?"

Sam closed his eyes. "I didn't tell you because I was protecting Sherlock."

His best friend scowled and glanced over his shoulder outside where the others were gathered.

"Get Amy. You both need to hear this."

"You're not making me less worried," Brandon said as he walked out.

Penelope slipped inside. "Is something wrong?" She crossed the room to him and he slid his arm around her, glad for her presence.

"It's Sherlock."

Brandon walked back in with Amy, and Sam wasn't sure where to start.

"What's going on?" Amy crossed her arms across her stomach.

Brandon placed his arm around her. A team. "It's something about Arthur."

"I didn't tell you because Sherlock swore me not to."

"What's changed?" Brandon asked.

"Let me start at the beginning."

Amy nodded.

"His last mission, the one he went on while you got married, ended badly," Sam began. "Land mine took his leg, and he was evacuated home. He was in hospital for months and wasn't coping."

Amy gasped, placing a hand over her mouth. "Why didn't you tell us?"

"I was worried about his mental state. He was discharged from the army and he stopped talking to anyone. He was in a low place and I was worried the extra pressure of seeing you would send him over the edge."

Brandon scowled, but he gave a small nod of acknowledgement.

"I visited him every day and the doctor and nurses kept me up to date with his progress. He wasn't coping with his prosthesis, and had given up. He was discharged just after I moved here, but despite my prompting, he wouldn't join me."

"The army was his life," Brandon said.

"Yeah," Sam agreed. "I just had a call from his therapist. He's back in hospital, this time because of an overdose."

Penelope slipped the tablet from his hand and started looking for flights. She knew exactly what was needed.

"Accidental?" Amy's eyes filled with tears.

Sam glanced at her. "He knew the correct dose."

Brandon tried to pull Amy into his arms, but she pushed him away. "That coward! I'm going to kill him. How dare he do that to me again!"

Penelope spoke. "I can get three tickets on this afternoon's flight, but it leaves in an hour."

"Book it," Amy ordered.

Sam shifted away from the women towards Brandon. "Again?" he murmured.

"Amy's mother died of an overdose when she was fifteen."

Shit. That was low.

Amy turned to her husband. "As soon as he's discharged, we're bringing him up here, whether or not he likes it."

Sam almost felt sorry for his friend.

"We'll help him," Brandon agreed.

"We all will," Penelope said. "He's not alone anymore. Amy, do you want to borrow some clothes for the trip?"

"That would be great."

Sam squeezed her. "Brandon can take some of mine."

Brandon nodded and headed upstairs.

Penelope handed him the tablet. "Tickets are booked, and I've emailed them to you. I'll call Rob. Ask him to stand in for you for the next couple of days."

Always thinking ahead. "Thanks, Penny."

"You're welcome. I'll take Amy home and be back in ten."

She kissed him and the two women hurried out.

Was it any wonder he loved her?

Sam jogged upstairs to pack.

Thank you for reading!

Do you want to find out what happened between Gretchen and the man she argued with at the brewery? If so, simply sign up to my reader group for a free story.

Sign up at
https://www.claireboston.com/reader-group/

Acknowledgements

Jimmy Small deserves a huge thank you for this book. He owns Ocean Eco Adventures in Exmouth and was kind enough to show me around his boat and talk to me about running whale shark and humpback whale tours. He also answered my follow-up questions and gave me the idea for how Sam would get suspended.

I also must thank Joe Morgan at Parks and Wildlife for again answering questions about park rangers and what they can and can't do. Both of these men were instrumental in making this story more authentic.

As always I want to thank my team, Ann Harth, Teena Raffa-Mulligan, Michelle Diener and Mayhem Cover Creations for their feedback and work in making this book come together.

Adrift in Retribution Bay

Aussie Heroes: Retribution Bay #5

Arthur and Gretchen's story is coming in 2023.